DRAGONS' TEETH

SONG OF THE ICE LORD BOOK 1

J. A. CLEMENT

Copyright © J A Clement 2014 as Song of the Ice Lord

Second edition: June 2020

Cover design by GermanCreative

Western Emerald photo - Copyright Joseph C. Boone - This file is licensed under the Creative Commons Attribution-Share Alike 3.0 Unported license.

JAC2020-05-31-0010

ISBN- 978-1-908212-47-4

Second edition: May 2020

❀ Created with Vellum

This book is dedicated to the memory of
David "Rusty" Steel,
at whose funeral I first heard the moving text
which ultimately inspired the shipspirits,

and

to my good friend and fellow mischief-maker
Dr. Tamsyn Mahoney-Steel –
opera singer, mediaevalist, and general genius.

I can still ace you with a laggy band though.

JAC

A TIME OF DARKNESS

Nearly three thousand years ago...

"Ah, there you are!" An older man dressed in flamboyant clothes lolled in a chair in Lodin's workshop, drinking wine. A glossy cloak lay on the workbench, carelessly slung in a pile of wood shavings and dust.

Lodin smiled and picked up the awl that had been knocked onto the floor, setting it carefully back in its place. "Kuhrin! I might have known you'd arrive. I just had a delivery from the Royal Vineyards at Laerzinan, which I see you've discovered already." He picked up the cloak, brushed it off and slung it over the back of the chair. His oldest friend and sometime lover had a talent for making himself comfortable anywhere, and treated Lodin's house as a second home in any case. "I can't stay long. I have to be at the Aviary at three bells." He pulled his battered work stool over to the low table by the window and poured himself wine from the skin his friend had already half-drained.

Kuhrin raised his goblet in salute. "So, what wisdom does our esteemed Council of the great and good have to impart? Is the Ice Lord coming our way?"

"Almost certainly, I'm afraid. And it seems he has only one end in mind: which is to say, ours." Lodin sipped his drink and stared out at the maze of terracotta roofs and tall, slender towers that jutted irregularly below him. The tiny city to which the Court retired in summer huddled against an outcropping of mountains at the end of a long peninsula. At the landward end it was guarded by the much larger city of Laerzinan and always before that had been the focus of any attack. Unless they were particularly targeting the King, this made little sense. He drank again, more deeply. The rich scent of the basil in its pot on the windowsill mingled pleasantly with the cool sharp taste of the wine.

Kuhrin refilled his goblet, slopping a little onto the stone flags of the floor. "Why must it be war? The Gods know we have no interest in fighting. Who is this Ice Lord and why is he so set on destroying us?"

"Not just us. It's as if he wants to destroy everything, but I don't understand what benefit there is in that. I can't work it out. It's senseless. No-one even knows who he is, just that the usual skirmishes between the tribes on the plains did not end at Sorrow-tide last year as they always do. The tribes all joined together under his leadership, and one after another every country they have entered since, has been burnt down to the soil. The people have been forced into the army and the land left so desolate that it will be a long time before anyone can live there again."

"But what does that get him?"

"Who knows? I suppose it hinders all the other countries; we've lost trade and nearer the borders we've been flooded with refugees, fleeing either the devastation or the press-gangs."

"The press-gangs?" Kuhrin's goblet paused in mid-air.

"How do you think they keep their numbers so high? They round up stragglers to join the Ice Lord's army, and are vicious in keeping them there."

"The soldiers aren't fanatics then? By reputation they are quite rabid."

Lodin scratched his chin. "Fanatics? Maybe some of the officers. It does sound almost religious, but there is no talk of what the religion involves. Rumour has much to say about the Ice Lord himself though: they speak of him as a leader of chilling ruthlessness, with many faces, who cannot be killed."

"Many faces? In the sense that he is deceitful?"

"That isn't how the terms the plainsmen use translate, but we're not really sure what they mean by it. By all accounts he strikes fear into the most hardened fighters. Nobody even knows why they call him the Ice Lord. Perhaps it's a mistranslation... but of what? It's a term the plainsmen don't really use, so it can't have started with them, even if that's where we became aware of it."

Kuhrin frowned. "Sounds a bit poetic for them. The plainsmen don't tend to use figurative language. And now he's heading for the Court we're all to be sent packing...?"

Lodin shook his head. "Honestly, Antor needs to be more careful or one day he'll wake up and find you're Chief of Intelligence, not him. I swear if there's news, you seem to have it before he does!"

Kuhrin was not to be put off so lightly, and simply waited, one eyebrow cocked.

Lodin traced a pattern on his goblet with one finger, thoughtful. "Yes, you're right of course. It just seems so unreal. It's hard to believe that the Ice Lord has finally set his sights on Lyria. Why would he do that? We're not particularly rich in anything but culture and knowledge, and that he could have for the asking. There's so much risk and cost to him and so little to be gained. It doesn't make sense."

"I cannot disagree, but if he is coming, it really is time to leave. War is such a dirty pastime. This city will go downhill drastically when it's flooded with a ragtag of warriors from whichever countries their leader has decided to add to his empire today." Kuhrin flicked a sly glance at his companion. "The level of conversation has already been polluted, you know, even in the literary salons where one might hope to discuss higher things. Palfit has just brought out a new thesis on the effect of love on the complexion. He claims it is the natural equivalent of rouge, which I was sure should ruffle feathers all over the city, and I can't get a soul here to give me their opinion of it! I suggested that ladies went in pursuit of love not to reach an exaltation of emotion but to improve their fading looks and—well, you have never seen anything like it."

"Really? What happened?"

"*Nothing*. A tremendous lack of reaction."

Lodin laughed out loud at his friend's outraged face.

"Three professors, a philosopher and my Lady Literature, and all of them looked at me for three heartbeats, and then went on discussing the war." Kuhrin shook his head, disgusted. "And Palfit an old lover of hers, as well. I was sure it would get her."

"Poor Kuhrin! How will you cope when there are more incendiary things than you in the social sphere?" Lodin teased, getting up.

"Ach! Life will be a bore! There is nothing for it but to go elsewhere in search of more interesting conversation."

"Talking of which, I need to be going. One does not keep the King waiting!" Lodin drained his goblet and walked over to set it on the table by the window.

Kuhrin joined him, leaning on the sill to look out over the graceful spires and domes of the city below them. "So where will you head for?"

"I don't know. How can I leave this?" Lodin gestured across the wide, shady square and sparkling fountains. "I've worked long and hard to make our city beautiful. These towers might be slender but they will stand through any storm. We're guarded on one side by cliffs with dashing waves below, and on the other by the precipitous slopes of the mountains. It's very late in the year to climb so high, and the weather will make the mountains almost impassable. I have made plans of escape, but I find it hard to think we truly need to do so. It's illogical, I know, but I just don't see how all this can disappear."

"It *is* illogical, my dear, and I am absolutely with you on that score." Kuhrin sipped at his wine meditatively. "But on the other hand, look at the wreck old age has made of me. Once upon a time I was the most dashing young fellow in four counties. The lovers I had when I first got here! Men and women swooned over me, vying for my favours—not that any of them had to work that hard, mind you."

"None of us had to work very hard at all." Lodin teased in agreement, taking his jerkin from its hook by the door. "In fact, as I recall you found it difficult to decide whether we should get in line, or just all turn up in your bed at the same time."

"Yes, and then you threw me over for that long-haired girl."

"She was lovely, and it was a youthful fling. As were you for that matter."

"Lovely? And am I not still?" Kuhrin struck a dramatic pose.

Lodin dashed him a sideways look. "A fling, I meant. Though youthful too, in those days, more or less."

"Ooof! Don't spare my sensibilities!" Kuhrin toasted him with the goblet. "We had fun though."

"We had a lot of fun. I thought for a while that we would be together for always."

"I thought perhaps we might, at one point: but I suspect that would have been a mistake."

Lodin nodded. "Yes. You may be the best friend I have, but you're no soul-twin."

Kuhrin snorted with laughter. "Skies above us, no! I am a better entertainment than I am a commitment, and that suits me very well."

"Yes, well I was still working out what appealed to me in those days."

"And to what conclusion did your scholarly undertakings bring you?"

Lodin considered this. "Gentleness. I am attracted to a gentle heart."

"Ha, well I don't think I've ever been in that category! And now, in my dotage, I am reduced to making mischief in the literary salons to amuse myself." Kuhrin adopted a despairing look though the twinkle did not fade from his eye. "What a fall from grace! Highly mortifying. The corollary to this little plaint is that nothing lasts forever. Me, I have my exit planned, and I'm heading off as soon as the rockets go up."

"I suppose you're right, but it will be such a wrench. Anyway..." Lodin paused by the door.

"Yes, yes, one does not keep the King waiting if one is high and mighty enough to be meeting with him!" Kuhrin returned to the table and filled his goblet again. "Go! Go! Don't worry about me, I have the wineskin to keep me company, and I'm sure your excellent housekeeper will oblige if I need a refill." Kuhrin made shooing motions. "It would never do to be late for His Majesty!"

Laughing, Lodin bowed with an exaggerated flourish and went on his way.

"GREAT MAKER," the guard acknowledged.

"Casim. How's that daughter of yours?" Lodin smiled as he mounted the marble stairs into the Palace.

"Aliya? Pretty as the dawn and mischievous as a monkey." The guard shook his head. "Still not sleeping through the night yet, though. See these bags under my eyes? The last time I had a full night's sleep was midwinter, and that was only because I was drunk!"

Lodin laughed. "Come to me when it's her birthday and I'll make her a toy."

"That would be a great honour! Thank you, Maker!"

The guard saluted smartly and Lodin went on through the cool of the high arched walkways. He admired the beautiful gardens on either side. The Palace Gardener was a man of no small talent, and Lodin was proud to have worked with him on the irrigation system that kept the gardens lush even under the blazing Lyrian sun. As always, he was bewitched by the fragrances that wafted through the walkways on breaths of warm air from the garden.

Nearer the Aviary courtyard, he had to pass through several more sets of guards and eventually was ushered through finely-wrought gates, almost filigree in the complexity of their design. These were the work of the fourteenth Maker, and a great treasure, depicting the wedding of the beautiful Queen Laerzi to her co-ruler, Haradian. The doorman let him through and then opened the inner gates, these of glass and simple gilded mesh, and he walked into the Aviary Courtyard itself.

Lodin took a seat on the bench under the great date palm that shaded the corner and admired his surroundings. High above him arched a graceful glass dome with linen shades which could be pulled across when the sun was too fierce. Nearby, an artfully constructed stream trickled from a hillock and chattered its way over multi-coloured pebbles down to a pool. The laughter of the stream was overlaid by birdsong, melodious and serene. In the wooded area nearby, colours flashed as birds swooped between branches, alighted, called, and flew again. Down by the pool, tall water plants raised spears to the sky, amongst which flowers flared like bright butterflies. A cloud of tiny hummingbirds darted and weaved in and out of them. Reflected in the silver water, the flickering dance of colour was incredible. Lodin stored the image in his mind. *If I could make a device to replicate that, what a gift it would be!*

The gates slid open again, and Lodin stood respectfully to

greet his King. "Sire." He laid one hand on his heart and bowed deeply.

"Maker." It was a sign of the King's respect for the craftsman that he merited an inclination of the head in return. "Walk with me."

The King was still a young man, though the worries of these last few years had streaked the black hair at his temples with early grey. He had a gentle, intelligent face and as the two of them paced the beautiful walk that threaded its way through the court-yard, he paused among the trees, and whistled. At first nothing happened, but he did it again and the third time, a dainty little bird swooped out of the trees and landed on his outstretched finger. It was a tiny little thing with delicate shades of emerald on its feathers, and black eyes that glinted as it cocked its head at them one way and another.

"This is Tiris. I raised him from an egg, you know. Many are the hours of delight he has given me, with his quaint antics and the sweetness of his song." The King ran a gentle finger over its head. "As you have heard in council, the Ice Lord has finally turned his attention to us. He will attack the city, and soon. I do not know what can survive. All the beauty and learning we have worked for so long to build about us will be destroyed, but I am determined to save what I can. I have sent our greatest treasures on ahead to the city of Laerzinan for safety, the scrolls from the Royal collection, works of art and craft, and some of the finest dogs and horses from my stables. My people are readying them-selves to follow on shortly. I would have them all in the safety of the fortress before the Ice Lord arrives. Once they are safe we will have a better idea of whether it is best to stay and risk a siege, or to go down into the caves and flee through the darkness under the mountains." The little bird chirped, and pecked lightly at the King's hand, where the sparkling jewel on his ring had caught its attention. "Anything that we leave here will be lost, including my little friend here and his brethren. I have asked you to come here today because we must leave all this behind, and I need your help to free my birds."

Tiris swooped off the King's hand and circled to land on his shoulder.

It was a moment before Lodin could reply. "But Sire–all your work..."

"Counts for naught now." The King walked on a few steps to look over the pool. "We are running out of time, Lodin. If the Ice Lord's army comes, who will have time to think of birds when the fate of my people hangs in the balance? I have coaxed them all from egg to adulthood, and have taken great joy in rearing them. I would not have them die shut in here when we are gone, or leave them as food for the enemy. They deserve their chance too. It is time to free them." Tiris crooned quietly in the King's ear, which made him smile briefly. He turned back to Lodin. "Now is a time for sad farewells. Later we, too, will attempt to fly. We are not warriors, Maker. We are lovers, philosophers, and poets. We watch the stars and study the earth. We have amassed a library of knowledge that is unequalled anywhere in the world, but we are not an army, and this is not a fortress. It was built to be beautiful, not defensible." He gestured to Lodin to walk with him, the movement earning him a scolding chirp from Tiris. "We cannot fight the fury of the Ice Lord. We can only flee, but it is my hope that with the talents of my courtiers and the time we have left, it may not be a terrified scramble but an organised departure. The people pack their bags now, and those on the outer wards of the city have already been called to set off along the coast. I have not heard that the Ice Lord has yet reached Gai Ren, so perhaps the Potentate will give us sanctuary. But to get the people there safely, we must start now. And so, the birds."

"Yes, Sire. What do you wish?"

"Open the skylights," the King replied softly. "Not a little, but as far as they go. Then we will take down the trees and the bushes, and make sure there is not one of the little souls left in this trap when death comes to the city."

"Yes Sire." Lodin bowed again and then, greatly daring, suggested, "Would it please you to help?"

The King raised an eyebrow, almost affronted, but then his face softened. "Yes, it is well thought of." He followed the craftsman to the centre of the courtyard.

Lodin set his hands to a great wheel. At first it would not move, but with some difficulty he started to turn it, and as it screwed shut the fountain slowed to a trickle and stopped, while the water in the bowl flowed away. When the bowl was dry, Lodin climbed up the little hillock at its centre. At the top was a structure of metal, overgrown with the winding tendrils of a vine dotted with tiny white flowers.

Lodin pulled it aside, exposing the parabola of slender metal rods. "First the pins." He gestured at an ornate tracery of metal halfway up, where knots of metal flowers graced the rods. Beside him, the King took hold of the cluster of flowers. With a sweet metallic sound, the silver pin drew from its home. Lodin extracted pins from the ones nearer to him, and the King took the rest.

"Now we can open the skylights." Lodin took one of the rods and raised it carefully. There was a grating sound, and one of the glass panes of the roof raised itself. When it was fully perpendicular, he put the pin back in and the rod stayed upright. The King followed suit. After a few moments nearly all of the windows were open. The last rod refused to move. Even when both men took hold, the rod was stubborn and when they yanked at it, it snapped.

"Shoddy workmanship, that." Lodin tucked the broken end of the pole under his arm. "I never could abide the twelfth Maker's work."

The King looked up at the wide windows above them in the rapidly cooling square. "I don't suppose it matters. All the others are open." He put the silver pin in his robes, jumped down and clapped his hands. A body of men marched in. "You know what to do," the King told them. "Raze it to the ground, and get rid of the detritus–but do it carefully. I want every last bird to fly out of here unharmed. And now, Lodin, come with me. I have a further task which will demand your skills ere the end."

LODIN LEFT THE PALACE, saddened. *So much ingenuity, all brought to nothing! But at least it was done with care.* He had mapped out every part of the Aviary thoroughly in his mind, and he hurried home to record it.

Looking out over the city from his workshop, the idea of the impending waste and destruction sickened him. He sketched his map quickly--at least enough for a reminder--and then laid his papers aside.

He wandered down to the centre of the city, picking his way through the market. It was lively with people jostling and joking, and rich with colour: fruits and vegetables of all shapes and hues, vivid cloths, the bright gleam of copper pans and kettles with the sun glancing off them.

Children ran and squabbled between the stalls, squealing with laughter as they splashed and played in the fountain. By the tavern, an old man snored in a sunny corner, the wrinkles on his dark skin a map of a lifetime's work and laughter. The innkeeper's cat delicately clawed one of the tiny fried fish from his plate and made a hasty—but dignified—retreat. There was a restless, anxious tone to the chatter, but people were still carrying on their daily lives with some semblance of normality.

For the last time, Lodin thought with a pang of sadness. *Tomorrow, everything will change.*

The long, gracious arcade along which he walked was one of the spokes radiating from the amphitheatre which lay at the heart of the city. Others led to the river, the gates, the merchants' quarter, but for Lodin the amphitheatre stood for everything that was best about Lyria. Tall trees shaded the streets, and in their whispering shade clusters of young artists congregated to hone their trade and vie for the attention of wealthy patrons.

At one end stood a statue, now featureless with age, but known as "Old Haruz" after the scathing playwright every Lyrian had to study as a child. Lodin stopped to leaf through the litter of papers pinned to the plinth, each one a scurrilous rhyme about some person of note in the city, written in the style of Haruz. Some of the more clumsy ones were obviously by students, new to the art, but several showed the polish of the lifelong prankster, and at least four were written in the elegant script he recognised as Kuhrin's.

"Maker! Are you joining us tonight?" A woman approached Lodin, her rich, dark hair held back by gold chains from which hung little jewelled ornaments that chimed as she moved.

"A gentle day to you, Bellara." Lodin detached one of the notes and folded it carefully, chuckling to himself. "Have you seen the latest about Kuhrin?"

Bellara grinned. "They have him to a whisker." She assumed an affected pose and quoted in a voice uncannily like their friend, *"How I despair for the youth of today. They swing all directions but never my way!"* Their depiction is pin-perfect, if not strictly accurate."

"He'll love the attention it casts on him. Though obviously he won't admit it until he's expressed suitable outrage." He placed the paper in his wallet and set it away carefully. "What are you playing tonight?"

Bellara fell into step beside him, linking an arm through his companionably. "Ildis has a new monologue to recite." She laughed as Lodin rolled his eyes. "I know, I know, but he'll never get his confidence up if he doesn't get used to reciting. It's a phase we all go through. The temple dancers are putting on the *Tears of Ysalia* again, at the request of my Lord Virtue."

Lodin smirked. "Arral?"

"Who else? He's taken a shine to the girl who dances Ysalia, but hasn't stopped to ask around or he might have some idea that she's been seeing his sister for nearly a season now."

"Ooof. That's going to sting."

"The man has no manners. I'll not have him making things awkward for her in my theatre." Bellara's eyes glinted dangerously. "So. *Tears of Ysalia?*"

"I don't know. I'm in the wrong mood for sad stories. I was hoping you'd be playing something a bit lighter." Oddly dissatisfied, Lodin kicked a pebble and watched it ricochet across the smoothed stones that lined the road. "I might just go find Kuhrin and let him talk nonsense at me for a while."

"Are you all right?" She stopped and turned to him.

"I just wanted one last night of... I don't know. Real life. It sounds as if they'll be making the next set of announcements tomorrow, and when news gets out that the Ice Lord has finally noticed us... all this" he paused and gestured around, "will change. And I think not for the better."

"I know." Bellara squeezed his arm. Then mischief crossed her face. "Though that's always assuming Kuhrin hasn't got news out ahead of the Council. You know what he's like."

"Well?" Kuhrin demanded, later that evening, as he poured another goblet of wine for the pair of them. "What do they have in mind for you? Is the Great Maker too good to be sent down the sewers like the rest of us, shepherding peasants along with all the other turds?"

"Kuhrin, you know that that is not the way of it!" Lodin could not help rising to the bait.

"Is it not, my dear?" the other teased. "So what is it that you're doing, anyhow?"

"After we had let the birds out, the King took me to the Dowager Palace and introduced me to his mother."

"That old boot!"

"Don't be discourteous! She wasn't gracious, I grant you, but the King explained that I was to help her escape. Then when she discovered that it was I who had invented that clockwork palanquin of hers, she abruptly became a lot less querulous."

"If just as rude, I suspect."

"She is a crotchety, demanding old lady in poor health. What do you expect?"

"I expect she asked why you and not a legion of soldiers."

"Well, there was something of the sort. The King took it very seriously, but I got the feeling she was making him work for it more out of mischief than anything else. We are to have a guard of four men, though."

"Four?" Kuhrin snorted. "What use is that? So they can carry her chamber pot?"

"Four is enough to defend us from small groups, but not enough to make anyone think we are important."

"Enough to delay the enemy while you run, you mean."

Lodin looked a bit sheepish. "There is the Dowager Queen to think about. She is old and unwell."

Kuhrin drained the last of his wine and held the goblet out for more. "Yes, and there is that palanquin of hers to look after. They need you to keep it moving. When she gets to Laerzinan, she's not going to want to go into the city on a litter as if she was already dead. She needs to ride in in triumph on her clockwork cart. That sort of thing makes an enormous difference to the way people think about things. They're no fools, the Royal Family–they know how to play the cards they're dealt."

"Ah." Lodin sat back on his chair, considering. "Yes, that does make sense. I wondered why me, but that would explain it."

"Happy to help, m'boy. Now, how about another skin of wine for an old man?"

"You are not old!"

"Not as old as I intend to get, certainly." Kuhrin's mobile face was sad for a moment. "But listening to the reports coming back from the war, I find myself thinking that perhaps I have already lived too long."

THE FOLLOWING MORNING, the Council met to go through arrangements for the evacuation one last time before the heralds were sent out into the city. When Lodin entered the Council Chamber, the others were sitting at the long table with the detailed model of the city at the far end. He took a seat and waited as the chatter died down.

"Maker."

"Bellara." Lodin raised his eyebrows as she took her place next to him, drawing her silken robes about her. "You're looking very ornate today."

There was sadness in the smile that crinkled her eyes. "Making the most of my opportunities, my dear. There is not much room for the theatre in a world at war. My troupe are like family, but we may be scattered to the four winds. We hope to join the theatre at Laerzinan, but even so..."

Lodin nodded. "It had not occurred to me. But your actors are the best in the country. Surely there cannot be much risk?"

Bellara cocked her head, with a jingle of jewels. "How long does it take to recover from war? How long before people have the heart or the money to pay for entertainment? For that matter, how long before we have the heart to entertain them? We cannot assume that there will be time for anything other than rebuilding and healing for a long while."

"Perhaps not, but..." Lodin looked away. "If we lose all the things that make life worth living, we will end up just fighting and eating and sleeping. What are we, barbarians? Can we afford to descend back into that sort of misery?"

Bellara looked to the little model of the city at the far end of the room. "We may not have a choice, Lodin. Many of the plays in our repertoire deal with war. No-one chooses to lose the good things from their life, but many have, over the years. In Lyria we have been fortunate for a long time. We are too little and too remote to have come to the notice of most, and with Laerzinan to protect us we have not been caught up in the odd skirmishes that have come near us. This time... I think this time might be different." She nodded at the rich array of rings and bracelets she wore. "You might want to keep anything of value to hand or put it somewhere a marauding army won't find it."

"You're really serious?"

"I have packed up my library and sent it ahead to Laerzinan to be stored in the caves, and those of my belongings that have personal value are hidden in the ice room under the house. I've had them build a wall across in front of the door so it's not obvious." She smiled at his expression. "When the call comes, I don't think there will be time to start packing. You'd be wise to think about it now."

From the front of the room, there was a cough. A small, nondescript looking man stood. "Councillors all, Antor has been delayed so in his absence, 1 will start the meeting. Our planning has been timely but we cannot delay one moment more than we must. Our spies report that the Ice Lord's armies have reached the other side of the mountains. We have brought the schedule forward. Today we do not just warn the people, we tell them to pack immediately with a view to starting to evacuate in two days' time."

The Council erupted into a storm of questions.

"Are you sure?"

"They were supposed to be heading for Magareyn."

"How can we do all that we have to in two days?"

He held up a hand and waited until they fell silent. "Antor has just received another dispatch and has delayed to decipher it, so he will be able to update you when he arrives. You may be better served keeping your questions 'til then. In the meantime, we have scouts on the peaks with rockets ready to be set off when the Ice Lord's army reaches the pass, but it should take him at least another week. We have a little time to prepare, and it is important that we organise our departure in some detail. Our priority is to get the people to safety with the minimum of panic. We must make sure that everyone knows what they should do, where they should go and how best to get out of the city when the time comes." He walked along the room to the model of the city. "This is how it will work..."

Halfway through the explanation, the door slammed open.

"My Lord Antor, Chief of Intelligence," the doorman intoned.

"Apologies for my lateness." Antor strode to the head of the table and paused. He ran a hand through his hair, disordering it still further. "We have had terrible news from Laerzinan. The Ice Lord's army attacked them at dawn yesterday and they are in need of help." There was a moment's stunned silence, and he sat down wearily.

"The Ice Lord is at Laerzinan? Not the other side of the mountains?" his second-in command asked.

"The Ice Lord is at the head of the force that menaces us here. However, what we thought of as his army was merely a part of it. While our scouts watched the force approaching us, a secondary force branched out or landed from the sea—we don't have any more than bare details at the moment. All we know is that Laerzinan is under attack."

Lodin exchanged a dismayed glance with Bellara.

"It will take us some days to get men organised and go to their aid." Breyn, the Chief of Staff spoke up. "But can we spare the men? The assault will fall upon our own walls soon enough. If half of my men are between here and Laerzinan, the Court will not survive. The main part of our army is based in Laerzinan. If they cannot hold the force that is attacking them, I fear that we will have difficulty holding our own walls." He buried his head in his hands briefly. "I have family there... I cannot see how to go to their aid. If we abandoned the city it might be possible, but that will take days." He looked up at Antor. "You are sure they asked for help? Their walls are very strong and well-defended."

"Their message was that there were overwhelming numbers of the enemy."

"We need to send men out." The High Priest pulled at the neck of his gown to loosen it. "The refugees fleeing there are journeying towards their own death."

"I will send my swiftest riders. It does not need a large force: a handful of riders can be off within the hour." Breyn shouted down the corridor for his aide, and gave him terse instructions. The aide left at a run, nearly knocking over a scruffy man stumbling down the corridor with a dead pigeon in one hand and a tiny scroll of paper in the other.

Seeing him, Antor called "Is it from Laerzinan? Is there news?"

The man staggered into the room and handed over the tiny scroll, too breathless to speak. The Chief of Intelligence read it and exhaled as if he had been punched in the stomach. "They were breached by fire and treachery. There was little warning. I don't know if they even managed to get many people into the caves before the troops swept in. There is a note at the end." He read it aloud this time. "'The gates have fallen. The walls are breached. Everyone is dead but me and the pigeons. Fire devours the city and the palace below me. I cannot get out. Do not come to Laerzinan, for you will find only the enemy and the dead'. It is signed off by the pigeon boy, the child who cleans the cages. His coding is as tiny and neat as any message I have ever seen."

Shock gripped Lodin so tightly that for a moment it was hard to breathe.

Antor passed a hand over his face then, with a visible effort, pulled himself together. "Counsellors, if this is true, we have no time for despair."

Bellara, ever practical, asked, "What should we do?"

"We start evacuating the city now. Not in two days, but as soon as we can get word out. You know the plans." He got up and walked over to the model of the city, looking down at it for a moment: then he nodded decisively and turned back to them. "With the armies so near, our plans for an orderly exit are in tatters. If we cannot head for Laerzinan, our only choice is to take them to Magareyn instead. Do what you can, and save as many as possible. I must go and advise the King that Laerzinan has fallen." He paused to look round the room, smiling wanly at those he knew best. "My friends, it has been my honour to work with you all, and I bid you a grateful farewell. Those of us who survive will be scattered far and wide, and the chances of our meeting again in this world are small. Fortune go with you and the gods look over you as you travel."

He left the room, and the Council members got to their feet in a hubbub of exclamations.

Lodin held out a hand to Bellara. "You were right."

"Never more unhappily so, believe me." She embraced him. "Take care of yourself, Lodin, and may fortune favour you."

"And you, wherever you go. I pray that we shall meet again this side of the Gardens."

"I hope that we may." *But I do not believe we will,* she did not have to say. She embraced him again, and Lodin watched her numbly as she hurried from the room, hair ornaments a-jangle. Then, gathering his wits, he too went on his way.

THE FALL OF LYRIA

L odin left the Council chambers, deep in thought. There was
not much he could to do but advise the Dowager Queen to
prepare. At her apartments, the door was opened by her lady-in-
waiting, a young girl of one of the great noble families of the city.
She curtsied prettily but did not let him in.

"Isthil, I need to speak to the Dowager Queen. It's urgent."

"I'm sorry, Maker, but you will have to come back later. She
has not been well today. She is asleep and not to be disturbed, on
the orders of her personal physician."

Lodin looked up and down the corridor. It was empty apart
from the guards at either end, and they were out of earshot. "You
know the evacuation is imminent?"

"Yes. We have started packing her trunks."

Lodin leaned close and dropped his voice. "The plans have
changed. We must be ready to leave first thing in the morning.
You see why I need to speak with her?"

Isthil frowned. "Maker, I do not wish to be disobliging, but the
physician has charged me with allowing no-one to disturb her
unless it is the King himself. She is an old lady, and her health is
suffering under the stress of this war. Let me offer you a compro-

mise. I shall pack her things so that she will be ready in time, and you may pen her a letter explaining what you wish her to do. In two hours' time, when she wakes, it shall be the first thing she sees, I swear it. But by then at the very least her travel bag will be packed, and I will send on anything else she wants in the days to follow."

Lodin wanted to override her, but it was true that the Dowager Queen would not be preparing anything herself, and this might be the last night she had the opportunity to sleep in safety and comfort. She would need to be well-rested for the journey... "I will leave you the message, but I will also return in two hours' time and then we can go through the arrangements for tomorrow morning. Don't expect to stay longer than that yourself, though. They aren't just evacuating the Palace. Everyone is leaving. You'd do well to be sure you know how and where to meet up with your own family."

Lodin scribbled a hasty note from the quill and ink on the Dowager Queen's own desk, gave it to Isthil and left. As he hurried through the palace, there was a frantic tone to the activity around him. It was like an ants' nest, stirred up with a stick. At that moment all was under control but servants were running where they would normally walk, and they paused in corners to exchange words in low voices, glancing around as they did so. One man took off his tabard, laid it neatly on the side and then hurried away.

That will be happening more and more over the next couple of hours. We had better get ready quickly or there won't be anyone left to help us. Reaching the Court gates, Lodin walked out onto the avenue. He hesitated and rather than turning towards his own workrooms, he hurried to the tavern where Kuhrin was usually to be found. *The more notice people have, the more might be saved. The time for secrecy is past.*

.   .   .

"My boy, what are you doing here at this time of day?" Kuhrin toasted him drunkenly. "This is out of your usual habits. Has gadget-building finally driven you to drink?" Lodin's lack of reaction drew Kuhrin's attention at once, and he gestured away the comely young man who was leaning on him. "Rasal, my dear, may we have a moment?"

The young man glared, but Lodin held up a hand. "No, this affects all of us. You should hear what I have to say." The tavern fell quiet, people crowding round to hear the news, and Lodin explained as best he could. "Start packing now. Tell your neighbours and friends, and if you were going to Laerzinan, do not head in that direction. We do not know how near the army is, and there will already be hundreds fleeing back. Do not head for the mountains, either, for the rest of the army will be coming that way."

"Where does that leave?" the boy demanded. "The coast? And when they follow us there, do we throw ourselves into the sea?"

"There is Magareyn, but plans are still being revised. Listen for the heralds. You will be advised by whoever is guiding your neighbourhood, but we need to make sure that everyone knows not to go to Laerzinan."

"Thank you, Lodin." Kuhrin rose. "People, you have heard what he has to say. Now go and make your preparations." With much worried chatter the tavern emptied.

"Where will you go, Kuhrin?" Lodin asked. "Your family were from Laerzinan, weren't they?"

Kuhrin sat down again. "Yes. My home will be gone by now, ashes lost to the four winds. Fortunately, there were not many of my family left last time I visited; an elderly aunt, and a second cousin." He sighed. "At least it sounds to have been quick. I should hate to think of them being thrown to the mercies of the Ice Guards. Still, with not much left to take, I shall be travelling light, at the very least." He smiled crookedly. "But you should be off. You have your duties, remember?" He embraced his friend and kissed him on both cheeks. "It is time for me to go, too. Be well, Lodin. Journey safely. I do not think we shall meet again this side of the veil, but when you get to the Gardens of Paradise, look for me–I shall be waiting at a shady table with a skin of wine."

"Be well, my friend." He embraced Kuhrin. "And make sure it's the good stuff, not that vinegar you drink here!" Suddenly there was a bang, and another. More followed.

"The Ice Lord—they must have seen him on the mountains." Exchanging a look, the friends went outside to investigate.

"Gods!" Lodin gasped. The warning fireworks were not those high on the mountainside, but the secondary warning, set at the river crossing. Behind them the mountainside was black with the Ice Lord's army, swarming down the mountain like a poisonous flood. They were nearly upon the city.

Kuhrin gripped his friend's arm as if for support. "The scouts on the mountains must have been taken."

"We were supposed to have plenty of warning!"

For a moment neither of them could speak. Then Kuhrin reached into the pockets of his gown and took out a small phial. He unstopped it, but instead of the acrid smelling salts he sometimes carried, it smelt bitter, oddly like almonds. "Time for me to go, I think." He swallowed the liquid in one gulp.

Almonds? Too late, Lodin realised what that meant. "No!"

Kuhrin's face contorted in pain, and his legs went weak. "Apologies, my dear. I decided not to wait."

"Kuhrin..." Lodin supported Kuhrin, guiding him back into the now-deserted tavern.

"I'm going on ahead," the older man gasped, clutching at his stomach as Lodin lowered him back onto the seating cushions on the floor. "Cowardly, perhaps, but I never was one to love the warmongers. Now go. You have a job to do, remember?"

Lodin shook his head. He could not speak. He knelt, helpless on the floor, holding his friend's hand.

Kuhrin's breaths were sharp and he gripped Lodin's hand so

hard it hurt, biting his lip in an evident attempt not to cry out. It was only for a few moments, and then his eyes rolled up in his head, he arched his back and went rigid. His heels drummed on the floor, and his head thrashed on the cushions, disordering the immaculately combed hair so that a receding hairline could be seen. Then, slowly, the arched back relaxed.

"No!"

Kuhrin's grip loosed. His breath escaped in a long sigh, and he was still.

Lodin knelt, hardly able to breathe, holding on to Kuhrin's hand as if he could hold him back, anchor him to life. He knew it was impossible, but he could not let go. He could only kneel, and hold Kuhrin's hand, and stare at that face that he knew so well. But slowly Kuhrin's face, normally so expressive, went slack. Lodin wept as it lost all its character, until a stranger lay there who looked old and somehow like a wax doll.

"...Kuhrin?" he whispered; but his friend had gone.

Lodin smoothed back Kuhrin's hair, and moved his friend's body comfortably onto the cushions which had been scattered during the convulsions.

As he sat and drew breath, he became aware of the sounds of chaos outside. *There is nothing I can do for him now. There isn't even time to mourn him.*

"I have a job to do, yes." *Kuhrin's last words.*

Lodin took another deep breath, though grief gripped his chest like a band of steel. He kissed his friend and sometime lover on the brow and left the tavern, shutting the door behind him as gently as if Kuhrin was only sleeping. Then he set off at a run, wiping tears from his eyes as he went.

There's no time to get my pack from the workshop now. I have to get the Dowager Queen to safety—the clockwork palanquin won't get her to the stables in time. Faced with this imminent threat, he did not trust the stable-boys to wait. They would take the horses and flee. He cursed as he ran. *Too soon, too soon!* They had planned to move her cart and horses into the palace the very next morning.

As he ran a bell began to toll, and another and another until the emergency peal was ringing all across the city. Lodin pushed his way through the throng. Chaos surrounded him–people running, children screaming, horses rearing in panic as their owners tried to ride through the crowded streets. At the palace gates he could not reach the entrance for the mob that beat upon the door and begged to be let in. Lodin caught the eye of the guard, Casim again, who nodded him over to a quiet corner of the courtyard. Lodin slipped through the crowd and round behind the ornate column there to a tiny, discreet door which was opened from inside by one of the guards and closed again as quickly behind him.

"Gentlemen." Lodin nodded his acknowledgments and set off again at a jog, holding his side where a stitch gnawed at it.

"Lodin! You are going to the Dowager Queen?" It was Antor, who fell into step with him briefly.

"Yes."

"The Chief of Staff and the King have ridden out with the Guard to delay the main onslaught on the city. It is unlikely that they will return." Antor glanced to the far end of the corridor, where an aide was running towards them. "Do what you can to get her out of here, and as quickly as you can. They cannot delay the enemy for long. They are too few."

Lodin nodded, his throat too tight with grief to speak.

Antor gripped his arm briefly. "Be well." Then he hurried towards the aide, calling instructions as he went.

WHEN LODIN ARRIVED at the Royal apartments, Isthil snatched the door open at his knock. He had to clear his throat before he could speak. "Is she ready to go?"

She virtually dragged him into the room. "She won't leave until she sees what happens to her son."

The Dowager Queen Estrella sat at her window. Her rooms were high in the palace, looking over the plain with a clear view of the army pooling before the city. The enemy were spreading out, wider and wider over the landscape. Between them and the city were the bright strand of the King's Guard.

"Your Majesty." Lodin bowed.

"Maker." She did not look at him.

"Your Majesty, we must leave. The army is so close that we will have difficulty getting away if we delay."

"I am not going."

"Please, your Majesty. I gave my word to your son that I would take you to safety. To betray my King in his direst need would be a vile treason."

"Do you not see him there?" Queen Estrella demanded. "I am his mother! What kind of woman do you think could leave her son in danger, and not want to know his fate?"

"Perhaps one who knows that it will give strength to her son to know that she is safe?"

There was a long silence.

The Dowager Queen gripped the arms of her seat until her knuckles went white. "You cannot ask this of me."

"Then I will beg you, on his behalf." Lodin knelt before her. "Your Majesty, your son told me that he had spent much of his life looking for a Queen, and for the first time he was glad he had not found one. He was consumed by the thought that you might fall into the hands of the Ice Lord. He knows how brutally they treat their prisoners. My Queen, your son is proud to ride out to save his people, even at the cost of his own life. He knows he can only delay the carnage, but if he saves one child by his actions, he will go to the Gardens of Paradise confident that he was the best King that he could have been. He cannot last long but he will fight until he gets the signal that we have left the Palace. He will not retreat until he can be confident that when he falls, he is not leaving you to the tender mercies of the Ice Lord's officers. Please, Queen Estrella, let him do this for you."

The old woman stared at him, torn between grief and anger. "He is my son!"

"Your Highness, he is your King, and he has commanded it."

There was a long pause, and then she sagged in her seat as if she had aged a thousand years in those brief seconds. "Where are your men, Maker? Where are your horses?"

"They are awaiting us, your Highness."

"Then call your men and have them bring the horses to the courtyard down here. When the horses are here, I will come down, and leave my son to die on the field. I am too old and slow to be dragged through stables and armouries. The horses can come to me, and then I shall leave."

Lodin met her gaze uneasily. It was not the plan he had discussed with the King, but the circumstances were not as the King had expected, and it was clear that the Dowager Queen would take no other course.

"Very well, your Highness, but I pray you, in the meantime, put on poorer garb. The army is getting closer with every breath and if they know who you are it will not go well for you. There will be a servant or maid whose garments will fit you, and these will be a better protection than any armour."

"Very well. Isthil, you have heard what the Maker said. Can you find me something of the sort?"

"Yes, your Highness. My own maid is of your height and build. I believe her dresses would fit you."

"Very well, child." The Dowager Queen laid a hand on the girl's cheek. "Change into something similar yourself, and hurry."

"Yes, your Highness."

"Your Highness, I shall be back presently." Lodin left Queen Estrella sitting alone at the gracious arch of the window, watching the black-cloaked troops march against the thin ribbon of her son's men.

LODIN DASHED down through the palace in search of the men who were supposed to accompany him and cursed to find the guardroom empty. Struck by a thought, he ran along to the palace entrance where Casim and his men were barring the gates. The street was mostly empty, scattered with discarded belongings, and further off there was shouting and screaming. A woman hurried past, dragging her squealing child by the hand.

"The crowd is mostly gone to their escape routes, sir," Casim reported. "The way is clear if you need to get through."

"Not this way, Casim. Are you finished here?"

"Yes sir."

"Your family?"

"Safely at my wife's mother's house in the country, thank the Gods!"

"Then I need you–all four of you–to help me get the Dowager Queen to safety. Are you willing to come with me?"

"Us sir? But we're only the doormen! Us, see Queen Estrella and all? It wouldn't be right! You need guards for that, sir, proper armed guards!"

"The guards have run away. I need loyal men who won't desert her. It will be dangerous though."

"Sir, everywhere in this city is dangerous right now. I'm in–are you up for it lads?" Casim glanced at his men, who all stepped forward. "Yours to command, sir."

"Thank you Casim, from the bottom of my heart." Lodin thought for a moment. "The horses will be long gone now. We'll need a cart for the Dowager Queen. Go find something of the sort. Casim and I will get the clockwork palanquin as far as the Aviary Courtyard. Meet us there. Quick as you can, mind!"

They scattered, and Lodin and Casim jogged back along the

arched walk through the gardens to the Royal apartments. The fragrance of the jasmine was piercingly sweet, belying the destruction that waited so close to the walls.

He led the way back up to the Dowager Queen's door. Isthil opened it, now dressed in an ill-fitting black gown.

"Smut your face with a little soot," Lodin told her. "You look far too refined to be a scullery-maid."

"Isthil, is that the Maker?" The Dowager Queen's voice echoed in the marble antechamber.

"Yes, your Highness."

"Very well. Draw the curtains, my dear, and then go to your family while you still can."

Isthil drew back the curtains of the Queen's chamber. "Your Highness, I gave you my word…"

The old woman was now wearing a sack-like garment and a white head-dress similar to those Lodin had seen his housekeeper wear. "And I release you from it. You have been a good girl to stay with me, but you will be better off with your family. Pass on to them my regrets at our parting, and my best wishes for their journey."

Isthil threw her arms round the old lady and kissed her on the cheek.

Queen Estrella was startled but pleased. She took a ring from her finger. "Here, child. This was given to me by my late husband, the King's father. If any of Lyria remains after the Ice Lord, give this to the Royal family and they will help you. If there are none of us left, sell it and use the money with my blessing."

"Thank you, Queen Estrella." The girl curtsied again, wiping tears from her cheeks, and ran to find her family.

LODIN BROUGHT the clockwork palanquin out into the corridor and with Casim's help, the Dowager Queen clambered into it. Lodin waited as she settled herself comfortably in the seat, which was cunningly sprung so that every time it bounced, it wound the clockwork as well as absorbing the lesser bumps and jolts of the journey. She reached forward to take the lever which steered it to left or right, and flicked the catch which held it immobile. There was a clicking, and slowly the palanquin lifted one of its four legs, then another, and after a slightly creaky start it was scuttling along at a slow walking pace, ticking and whirring to itself.

"This was your own invention?" Queen Estrella asked after a moment.

Hoisting her pack upon his back, Lodin nodded. "It was, your Highness."

"There is no point Highnessing me now, Maker. If I am dressed like a housekeeper, you should address me like a house-keeper." Her tone was acerbic.

"Your Highness, I--"

"How would you address your housekeeper?"

"My Lady." Actually, Lodin called his housekeeper by her first name, but he did not suppose that the Dowager Queen would know that.

She glared at him with all the scepticism of a mother. "You call your housekeeper 'My Lady'?"

"Yes, your Highness."

She rolled her eyes. "You should call me Estrella, I suspect, but that will do." They passed along the corridor and she turned the palanquin towards the stairs. "As I was saying, this is a very useful contraption, but it does make one a little seasick on the stairs."

"Does it?" Lodin was immediately interested. "There may be something I could do about that–an adjustment to the gait perhaps..."

"Now is not the time, Maker."

"Oh! And I have left all my tools in the workshop!"

Queen Estrella gave him a look that was half sadness and half amusement. "You are a Maker to the core, Lodin. I suspect that in the middle of a battle you'd be inventing ways to make a shield work better."

Lodin flicked her a sheepish glance. "It is the way my mind works."

"And fortunate for some of us that is the case." The palanquin reached the bottom of the stairs, its roughened wood and leather paws echoing on the marble of the walkways. For perhaps half the length of the corridor, its regular clacking was the only sound. Then, as they neared the open windows of the Aviary Courtyard, the noises of chaos began to filter through. "Have you been outside the Palace? Is it bad out there?"

"The people are afraid, my Lady, and understandably so, but there are plans in place to get them all away."

A rumble of drums; Lodin and Casim paused. Queen Estrella pulled convulsively at the lever of the palanquin, stopping it mid-stride. The drums rumbled on and were answered by the bright brave call of trumpets.

"They are sending forward a champion..." Casim breathed.

"A champion?" The Dowager Queen looked up at him with burgeoning hope. "Our swordsmen are the best in the world. If they put up a foreigner against one of the Guards we might yet win!"

"Yes..."

"You don't sound convinced."

Casim fell silent.

Lodin answered instead. "My Lady, if there is a combat between champions, we will surely win. But what then? I cannot believe that of all the other cities the Ice Lord has attacked, none have called a challenge between champions. If nowhere else, I am certain that they would have tried it at Laerzinan."

She twisted to look at him. "He has taken Laerzinan?"

"Yes, my Lady. I am sorry, I assumed you knew."

"I suspected as much, from the way they were whispering." She sighed. "I grew up in Laerzinan, you know. I have a lot of fond memories of that city. But more pressingly, that was to be our refuge. Have you an alternative destination in mind?"

Lodin shook his head in frustration. "Antor suggested Magareyn but this has all happened so quickly. We must flee the city before it is surrounded. Once free, we can discuss what to do next."

"Ha! You are thinking of giving me choice in the matter then?" she demanded bitterly. "You know what my choice is now and have ignored it."

"I am sorry, my Lady. My King commanded that it be so. We will wait here for the moment though. The others are to meet us with whatever transport they can find."

"They are leaving it rather a long time, don't you think?"

"They were to come back when the drums sounded," Casim said thoughtfully. "It has only been a few minutes. Would you like me to climb up and see what I can see from the top?"

"From the top of where?"

"The top of the Aviary dome. As kids, we all climbed up there at one point or another. We used to have races to see who could get up there first. I think I could still do it."

Lodin stared up at the skeletal frame. "Will it take your weight?"

"The glass won't, but the structure is quite sturdy." Without further discussion, Casim hurried into the Aviary, followed by the other two, and crossed to the far side where handholds were set into the wall. Queen Estrella stopped her palanquin at the open gates and took in the devastation around her. Lodin looked around in dismay. Where the stream and pool had been was only bare earth, the water stopped and the banks levelled. All the trees and shrubs were gone, and the path was lost in the loose earth. Only the skeleton of the fountain remained, stripped of its greenery, its singing stilled.

"And so all beauty passes," Estrella muttered.

The trumpets blared again, triumphantly, and a yell was heard from the battlefield. Edging along the slender path around the rim of the dome, Casim clambered onto the brick wall, holding onto the open skylights for balance.

"What can you see, Casim?" Lodin called. "What were the trumpets?"

"The champion! I think it is the King!" Casim nearly fell in his excitement. "The other man is on the floor. He is not getting up. The King is bowing over him–others are coming to look. The King has stood straight–his arms are in the air!" The trumpets sounded again, a real fanfare this time. "It looks–it looks like they are celebrating! The King has won! The Ice Lord's champion is defeated!"

There was a long, grumbling rumble of drums, and then a few yells sounded clear on the still air, before a dead silence fell.

"No...!" Casim clutched at the wall. Lodin could not bear to ask what had happened. He did not want to look down at the Dowager Queen, whose face was alight with hope and pride.

The drums rumbled again.

"Tell me, Casim," Queen Estrella ordered.

"They killed him. He won, and they killed him." Casim leant back against the wall, high above them. "It must have been an arrow. The Ice Lord's champion was down, not moving. The King turned away, then stumbled and fell. They are lifting him onto their shoulders. They have set him down behind the lines. He is dead. They shot him in the back when he had won." The drums rumbled again. "They have a new champion. They are playing with us like cats with a mouse."

"They have made their intentions clear." Tears were streaming down the Dowager Queen's face and suddenly she looked very old. "There is no reason for us to stay now. There is still less for us to go, except that he wished it."

Lodin looked back up to the guard. "Casim, can you see the others? They should be making their way back to us by now–are they in sight?"

Casim twisted around on his perch and strained to see over the wall. "Gods!" he exclaimed, and with a huge effort scrabbled up to teeter on the top.

"What is it, man?"

He stared the other way. "Time to go, and fast!" Balancing precariously on the wall, he felt around for the first foothold. "They have come behind us. Fires are burning in the city. The wind is blowing from the battlefield, so all the noise and action there is keeping us distracted while the smoke and screams from the western quarter are blowing away behind us!"

"No sign of the others?"

"None."

Queen Estrella knew quite well what he was trying not to say. She wiped the tears from her face and sat straighter in her palanquin. "No matter. We shall see how far my clockwork steed can take me. There will no doubt be some cart or a pony or something of the sort on the way." All of them knew how slender the chances of this were.

"No doubt you are right, my Lady."

Casim jumped down from the steps as the Dowager Queen flicked her palanquin into action and began to steer it round to leave. At that moment there was a flutter of colour above them as something dipped and fell through the open windows. There was a clink, and Lodin lunged forward to catch the flash of green as it dropped towards them.

"What is it?" Casim bent to pick up a silver pin with a knot of flowers, now stained scarlet.

Lodin straightened carefully. "Look–it is Tiris."

Wordlessly Estrella held out her hands to take the little creature as it gasped.

Lodin took the pin from Casim. It was that which the King had kept when they opened the aviary. He wondered if the King had sent it, or whether the bird had an eye for a shiny thing and had just returned to its home, forgetting that it no longer existed. Either way, the pin was suddenly more precious to him than he could say. He clenched his fist around it until it hurt. "Come. They are close."

AT FIRST, they made reasonable speed. The palanquin could keep up a fast walking pace, and on the smooth marble, it clacked along without undue stress.

Casim led the way down from the gardens to a tiny back gate from the palace. He checked to see that the street outside was free of soldiers. "The Ice Lord's men have breached the city gates to south and west, but as far as I could see, the east of the city is relatively untouched."

Lodin glanced behind them as Casim pulled the gate shut. "If we can get to the river there may still be boats. We should avoid the amphitheatre though. They will march through the city unhindered once they have the amphitheatre."

"If we are not too late." There was a chirp from Queen Estrella's lap as the bird sat up. "Ah, little one, my son would be glad to see that you have recovered." It hopped about her lap, and then settled against her, apparently unfazed by the clomping of the palanquin.

They headed off through the maze of backstreets. The palanquin began to labour, and a couple of times Lodin and Casim had to grab the sides as it caught its leathern paws on the uneven stones of the road. They exchanged worried glances, but said nothing.

"This way." Casim peered round the corner.

Lodin leaned near to mutter, "Can you smell the smoke?"

"They must have swept round faster than we anticipated."

"I surmise from your whispering that we are getting near the conflict?" the Dowager Queen snapped.

Abruptly the palanquin caught its foot again and the Dowager

Queen was nearly tipped out. Tiris, flung from her lap, soared up, scolding, and swooped onto a nearby rooftop.

"That was close! Are you all right?" As she nodded, Lodin set the cart straight again, but it would not settle. He looked underneath. One of the feet was broken. "Casim, can you hold it? This might jolt a little, my Lady." He ducked underneath and after a bit of tugging, managed to pull away the broken pad. He pocketed it, just in case there was time to fix it, and wiped his muddy hands on his robe. "Try that."

Queen Estrella let it off the latch, and the palanquin lurched forward. Casim grabbed at it again, and she nodded at him. "It might not be a smooth ride, but if you two will support it on this side as we go, we can manage."

The palanquin marched on, jolting every second step, but they managed to get a few streets further. The smell of smoke was getting stronger, overlaid with the stench of burning flesh. Distant screams and shouting echoed between the buildings, and the two men exchanged glances over the Queen's head, trying to hurry the palanquin as best as they could.

"We're not far now," Casim muttered. "After the end of this street there is a fountain, a tall one. Next to it is the trapdoor that will lead us down into the sewers, where the river will take us to the sea."

The Dowager Queen looked up at him sharply. "How can we get down the trapdoor with the palanquin?"

"I'm sorry, my Lady. We may have to leave it behind." Lodin patted the palanquin a little sadly.

"And then I shall be just another old woman who cannot walk."

"No, my Lady. You will be a Queen who has her Great Maker in attendance to make another palanquin just as good, maybe better, when we get to our destination."

"Always the Maker. You really can't help inventing things, can you, or altering them? Promise me one thing, though."

"What is that, my Lady?" Lodin watched Casim coming back from the end of the street, signalling that it was clear.

"Promise me that you will not make anything that will make this war worse." The Dowager Queen laid a hand on his arm. "War is bad enough when men hit each other with blades. I am afraid of the lethal traps you could add. Promise me that you will not do so."

"As you wish, my Lady. I promise."

Suddenly the palanquin stalled. It froze with one paw upraised, and there was a whirring sound as of something unwinding, faster and faster.

Queen Estrella exhaled slowly. "What was that?"

"The spring has broken," Lodin answered. "And now we *are* in trouble."

"Can it be fixed?"

"No, only replaced. I could make another if I had the use of my workshop and plenty of time, but as it is, we need to leave it and get to the trapdoor."

"We're not far short of it anyway," Casim encouraged. "I will--"

Shouts sounded from the other end of the street. Lodin grabbed at the palanquin as Casim fell to the ground, blood pumping from the dart in his throat.

"They're here!" the Queen hissed. "Go! Save yourself! I am lost in any case!"

"No! I gave my word!"

Ragged figures were advancing down the street, shouting in a hoarse language. Helmets shaped like sharp-jawed reptilians covered their faces, smeared with blood.

"Go, I tell you! My son is dead! You no longer owe him anything."

"I cannot." As he said it the words were true. "They are behind us as well."

"Then help me out of this contraption of yours, onto my own two feet."

Lodin helped the Dowager Queen to the side of the street then darted back to Casim. The guard was dead. Quickly, he closed Casim's eyes. "If the Gardens exist, I shall see you there, my friend."

Lodin straightened. They were nearly upon him and he had to defend the Queen. Turning to the palanquin, he wrenched off its steering bar. The soldiers were shouting and all around him the air was thick with smoke and panic. He backed towards the Dowager Queen. The soldiers laughed among themselves, shouting what were obviously taunts as they neared him. Lodin was no fighter and they knew it from his fumbling lunges with the iron bar.

There are so many of them. He tried to watch all of them at once, react to every flicker of movement as they came forward, now some, now others. They backed him into a corner, and with the wall at his back there was nowhere to go. He waved the bar in front of him, trying to imitate some of the moves he had seen the sword-dancers use.

The soldiers jeered. One drew his weapon. It was long and curved with a wide, mirror-like blade, darkly stained. He jabbed it at Lodin. The blade clanged against his metal bar, jarring his arms, and the soldiers cheered.

The swordsman swung again, slowly, and Lodin tried to parry. The clang nearly knocked the bar out of his grip and the soldiers roared with laughter. They were playing with him, but there was no way of escape and he was all that stood between them and Queen Estrella, so he swung time and again with all the strength of despair. It did no good though.

Eventually the soldiers bored of their game. The swordsman barked an order, and the others closed in. Desperately trying to keep them away, Lodin caught one of them a resounding blow to the helmet. The soldier staggered away, clutching at his head.

The swordsman raised that blade again, sharp as death.

It severed Lodin's arm between wrist and elbow.

For a moment he stared at the obscene stump. Scarlet sprayed from it in great warm spurts.

It was only as he dropped to his knees that he understood that it was his own life-blood, ebbing fast…

Somewhere far away, there were shouts. The ragged figures left him with a kick or two and ran. He lay marvelling at the sculpted perfection of the severed hand that twitched feebly in the mud, but searing pain clutched at him and it obscured everything.

LATER, what brought him round was constriction. There was noise and a feeling of being smothered. His body jerked and convulsed, there was a smell of meat burning and the most excruciating pain. A wiry hand clamped his head in place, rocking him and crooning to him. He could not understand it at all.

Words; they floated over his head like clouds in the sky. Once he had understood words like these but the agony in his arm filled his brain with fire and he could do nothing but weep.

"It was well done to tourniquet his arm, lady. You saved his life."

"He saved mine. He is all that is left to me. My duty is lost to all, save this one weary soul."

"I don't begin to understand what you mean, lady, but he will live. We have cauterised the stump. We will bind it with whatever we can find in this house."

He recognised one of the voices. *I should know who that is. There is something I have to do...*

But it was all so difficult. Much easier to slide back into the darkness, and let the words float away without him.

FLIGHT FROM THE CITY

He did not know how much later it was when he awoke fully. His arm was a burning agony that he did not want to think about. It was bound up in front of him, strapped to the opposite shoulder so that it could not move. Wherever he was, it was dark and cold. There were others around him, he realised slowly, and whatever it was he was lying on, it was uncomfortable. It was moving, too, a slow rocking like a baby's cradle. There was a horrible smell, and sounds were coming from all around him. He was surrounded by a trickle and swish, a constant sibilance coinciding with the swaying of the surface on which he lay. There were sounds which he slowly identified as sobs, gasps, whimpers. At first he thought there were hundreds, but gradually realised some were echoes.

He made as if to sit up, and was restrained. "Where am I?" The words were high and panicky, but Lodin did not care. "The Ice Lord--"

"Is not down here."

He sat still, and the restraining arm eased off him. *I should know that voice.* "My Queen?"

There was a bitter little chuckle. "The very same, though Queen of what is a different question."

"My Lady, you are alive!" Relief flooded him. "They did not misuse you?"

"They did not have time, Maker. They were busy misusing you." A deep sigh. "My son, I am so sorry about what they did to you."

"My arm?"

"Gone."

Gone? Lodin could not understand it. *How can it be gone?* But that scarlet-stained blade cut through the darkness in his mind, and he suddenly saw the curved fingers, the carved perfection of the hand as it fell. He turned and threw up violently, retching till there was no more in him.

"The lady here saved your life, lad," another voice told him when he was quiet again.

"Who's there?" Lodin asked nervous.

"Gamran. Keeper of the Locks as was; now just another refugee, same as you."

There was a world of sympathy in that voice, and it was almost more than Lodin could bear. He sat up again, and the whole surface on which he sat rocked. "Where are we? What is this place?"

"Careful, lad, you'll have us all overboard! Sit still and I'll tell you." There was a clicking of flint and the sudden flare of a lantern, revealing an old, bearded face in the darkness. "This is the undercity, lad. We are on the sewers and being carried along the river. You see?" Briefly he held up the lantern, revealing an arched roof not far above their heads, moving slowly away. Down towards the waterline unwholesome green moss clung to the pale bricks, and here and there was a plop and splash as rats jumped from their perches on the little ledge into the foul water. As Lodin glanced back into the distance, a light flicked on, and one after that, and in front another flicked on, and a second. Then Gamran extinguished the lantern and they were plunged back into darkness. "We dare not light the way in case the Ice Lord's men are following. Behind and in front of us, all the other sewer workers and lock keepers in their boats and rafts, and even the street urchins are guiding people along the pathways. Sooner or later the Ice Lord will find this escape, so we are keeping the lights covered, but with luck we should be away before then."

"Where to?"

"First to the coast. If the Ice Lord is already at the coast, there is nowhere else to go but the sea, and we are lost. But in any case, it is better to drown than to be herded up into the Ice Lord's prisoner wagons."

There was silence for a long time while they were carried along on the noisome waters.

Lodin shifted, trying to get comfortable on the hard wooden floor of the boat. "How did I get here? I don't remember anything after the alleyway. How long ago was that?"

"Not long," Queen Estrella replied. "It is difficult to tell in this darkness though."

"What happened?"

"They did not tarry much longer after they had hurt you. Why should they waste their time on a poor old lady, crawling in the mud?" She sounded tired, and her voice held the remnants of anger. He guessed that the humiliation had been hard for her to bear. "They were called away from us, and went back to the main street. One of them paused to urinate over me–they did not have time to do more–and they left. Shortly afterwards, help arrived in the form of our friend the lock-keeper here. The rest of the story I shall leave him to tell, for I am too tired to chatter, but I am glad that they did not manage to kill you, Maker. The old should not have to watch the young die, nor any beauty wither but their own. At least I know that wherever you are, there is a chance for beauty to return."

"My Queen--"

She interrupted him. "Queen, am I? We are now people of no land, with no belongings but those we carry and no family but those about us. That is why I call you son. It is not the blathering of a tired old woman, but the truth of our situation."

"Lady, I am honoured..."

"Yes, Maker, you are–but deservedly so." She was too tired to be waspish, but in the darkness, a withered old hand patted his arm. "Now I need to rest. Gamran, the tale is yours to tell." The boat rocked as she shifted into a more comfortable position, and fell silent.

"There is not much more to add." Gamran kept his voice low so as not to disturb the Queen. "Antor set those of us familiar with the sewers to hide down here while the city was ravaged and come out in the darkness to find survivors. A few of us were hiding in the tunnels beneath the square and as the streets grew quieter, we ventured out.

"A couple of times soldiers looked down the street, but covered in blood as you were, they saw only corpses. The lady here had daubed herself with blood. She made a tourniquet for your arm with strips torn from her headdress, and when anyone came near, she lay as one dead. As for me, I was making my way along the street and thought the pair of you were dead too."

"But you stopped?"

"Yes. A little green bird swooped and dived at me. It was oddly persistent. It would not let me pass."

"Tiris?" Lodin was interrupted by a chirp. "Is he here?"

"In the fold of my shawl." Estrella's voice slurred with drowsiness. "Our other remaining companion. Take care of him, Lodin."

"I will, Lady."

She sighed deeply in the darkness, and was quiet.

"I was afraid that the bird would call attention to me," Gamran went on, "so I turned back. All at once he was not diving at me but flying in front. He went across the street and flew down to the lady. I saw her eyes open as it landed on her, and realised she was alive, and so were you. Some of the others helped me to bring you away."

"Thank you." Lodin shivered. He pulled the heavy blanket more closely around him, but the movement jerked at his injured arm, and the pain made his head swim. Slumping on the uncomfortable boards, Lodin lost himself in the river's rocking, a slow wash and hush as he was carried away from the death of his city, and out to the unknown stretches of the sea.

He woke, chilled to the bone. The movement of the boat had changed, now running on long waves rather than the regular sway of the cavern's swells and eddies. Gradually he became aware that he was no longer in pitch blackness.

Huddled under the blanket, Lodin watched the sky pale to charcoal grey, to white and the most beautiful delicate blue. The little mackerel clouds were touched with rose, which spread until they were pink and red, strengthening to flaming orange. As the river carried him on, he was blinded by the first burning sliver of the sun as it crept over the horizon and swelled to a fiery arc. After the darkness, the colours were dazzling, and the sun on the water was painful to his eyes. Lodin looked away and saw Gamran, a small, wiry man with a jutting grey-streaked beard and kindly eyes.

"We came out of the caverns and onto the river a while back." Gamran stretched briefly, his movements betraying his weariness. "The current is too strong for us to stop. The Ice Lord must have opened the reservoirs under the city to have the water rushing through this strongly. Still, if he means to empty the river for his troops to march down, that might take a while." He chuckled.

"We cannot stop?" Lodin's head was still muzzy with sleep.

"We will be washed out to sea on the tide. If it is rough, we might sink, or be overturned in the breakers, but if it is calm, there is a chance that we might be washed into calmer waters."

Lodin considered this. "We can die as easily in any of those places, and if there is little left to live for, it does not concern me. But the lady?"

"Is still asleep." Gamran shrugged. "Leave her be, I reckon. No point waking her just so she can worry."

There was an indignant chirp, and after some struggle Tiris wriggled out from under the Queen's shawl.

"Hello, little friend." Lodin held his remaining hand out to the little bird as he had seen the King do. He did not dare try the whistle in case he woke Queen Estrella, but the little bird considered him and then hopped onto his hand, cocking its head to one side to regard him gravely. "How things have changed since last I saw you! But you are a welcome sight."

Tiris chirped again. He pecked at Lodin's palm lightly once or twice, then spread his wings and preened. In the sunlight, the iridescent sheen of his emerald feathers and the delicate scales of his feet were as vivid as love. Suddenly he launched himself, winging high into the blue. Lodin cried out in dismay, but Tiris did not leave them. He looped around, swooping and diving in the sheer delight of flight, and after a while, dropped lightly back down into the boat and perched cheekily on the bow.

"You have a friend there." Gamran smiled. "I was sure he'd be off into the wide blue yonder."

"You and me both! Though perhaps it would be better for him if he did. If we are drifting further and further out to sea, there is little chance for him to fly back. I wish I had thought of that when we were still within sight of land." After a thoughtful pause, Lodin roused himself to look round. There were no more than a couple of boats in sight, widely scattered. "Are those all that got away?"

"We were among the first." Gamran shaded his eyes from the brightness of the sun, trying to look at those behind them as the coracle was pulled this way and that by the capricious waves. "I have no way of knowing how many remain in the tunnels. There were more around us when we left, but once out of the tunnels we became widely spread. Those nearer the riverbanks may have found their way to a landing. Others may not have made it this far. As for us, we have little choice. This coracle was made for riding the cavern-river down to the locks. Normally they are pulled back upstream by the horses that bring down the provisions, so it does not have oars or paddles or a rudder, only a pole for fending off obstructions in the river. Out at sea, we are at the mercy of the wind and waves."

Lodin lay back again. He should be able to devise something, but he was so tired. It was difficult to care about anything but the tight chain of agony gripping his arm.

The sea grew wilder and the little boat began to dance. Tiris hopped nearer, and settled on Lodin's shoulder. *It's all very well for Tiris,* Lodin mused. *He has wings. What the boat needs now is a set of wings, so that it can fly back to the shore. Wings....* "You have the pole still?" he asked at length.

"Yes, though it is little good now."

Lodin lay awhile longer, looking at the scudding clouds which fled across the sky. "The Queen has a shawl. Could we steer if we had a sail?"

Gamran ran a hand through his beard. "The wind is blowing inland. We could certainly use it to get nearer the shore."

"Her shawl is a triangle shape, with tassels. I think it is silk. The tassels could tie it to the pole."

"I can break the pole to make a boom, though if I'm not canny about it we'll overturn the boat." Gamran was catching on now. "We can lash it to the seat with the mooring rope. Do you think the lady will mind if we wake her?"

"I'll do it." Tiris protested as Lodin heaved himself upright to wake Queen Estrella. *She's been sleeping for a long while.* "Your Majesty?" He put a hand on her shoulder.

She did not respond.

"Lady? My Lady?"

But when Lodin shook her, she slumped forward, limp.

A HAPPY MYSTERY

G amran leaned over and held his hand in front of Queen Estrella's nose and mouth for a few moments. "She's not breathing. It's too late, lad."

The coracle lurched as Lodin shook her harder. "It can't be! We got out of there. She saved me. She was alive. We got away!"

"She's gone, lad. Leave her be. She was old, and the flight from the city was a terrible effort for her. But she saved your life and she was proud of that." Gamran grabbed him, pulling him away.

The jolt of pain in his arm made Lodin fall back in the boat, white stars dancing in front of him as he hit his head. "But I was to keep her safe," he murmured, dazed.

"She said that you had done just that..." But Gamran's voice was lost in a swirl of chaos and terror.

ON THE DAY IT HAPPENED, Lodin had been consumed by feverish grief, and now every time he dreamed about it, it always ended with that sickening sense of nausea and loss. He dared not sleep at night, trying to stay awake as long as he could to avoid reliving those last days. But all the same, he had woken weeping from the loss and horror over and over every night for months.

Lodin jolted awake in the sickbed, numb amid the stench and semi-darkness of the hall. He was cold, despite the layers of thick furs on the uncomfortable cot. He was always cold in this gods-forsaken place, and every part of him hurt, though whether that was sickness or the uncomfortable bed he had been lying in for— how long? He did not know. He waited while his breathing calmed, and shifted uncomfortably, but there was no position in which he could lie without aching as thoroughly as if the Skrals had spent all night kicking him.

There would be no improvement, either. In the Skral Islands the earth was barren and livestock were few. They did not have the soft-feathered little ducks whose down made Lyrian beds as soft as a dream, nor the interest or invention to find a way to make the wooden cots and prickly straw pallets comfortable. At best they padded them with furs, but with the sick and injured of many nations gathering here, furs were in as short supply as everything else was.

He turned onto his back. His arm was gone, lopped off just below the elbow but still the ghost of his limb itched and stung and he had no way of scratching it. *Some Great Maker!* The contrast was bitter. Now he could neither scratch his itch nor construct something to use to scratch it. A mere child could do better.

This is as far from the Gardens of Paradise as it is possible to get. Kuhrin was wiser than I knew. If only I could find a way to join him. There was a potion they used to dull pain, but they measured out the doses and watched him drink it. *And really, genuinely, would I have the courage to kill myself now? Even now? Of course not.*

The few times he had had the opportunity, he had been afraid to go through with it; not afraid of dying but afraid of not managing to quite kill himself, and surviving to feel the scorn of those around him. In Lyria, perhaps he would have met with understanding, but to the warlike barbarians who lived on these islands, suicide was the ultimate shame and Lodin was afraid of the punishment that would follow a botched attempt. He had not dared to ask.

The few Skral in the hall were women, those who acted as healers. They moved around like ghosts, pale in the dimness. Lodin shuddered. Of course in Lyria they knew about these cold lands where the people were pallid, like creatures that lived under stones, but when the fever gripped him it was difficult to remember that they were living beings. *They look so much like the wights my Grandmother used to describe that haunt the catacombs, guarding the dead.*

One of them approached now: Alaera her name was. She spent most of her time in the sickhall, and now that the strangeness had worn off, he had come to see that she was a kind lady.

"Good morning, Lodin. How are you today?"

He searched for the right word. "Not too hot. Thank you. The bitter juice is good." *Useless! I can't even express myself properly!*

Alaera smiled and came over to lay a hand on his forehead. "You're quite right. There's no fever today. That is good."

"Fever." He repeated the word. He had never felt so far from home, so bereft.

"And your arm?"

He turned his face away. "Burning. I hate it." It itched and burned like fire in the night so that he could not sleep and if he did, all he could dream about was his hand falling to the mud, but he did not have the words or the energy to say so.

She nodded and came to sit at the stool by his bed. "Let me check it." She began to unwrap the dressing as gently as she could. "*Oh.* Maskal, can you prepare some poppy, quickly please?" Alaera hurried off and nausea assailed him as he watched her set a knife in the fire. His arm stank like rotting meat again, and there was a slow trickle oozing down what was left of his forearm. It was utterly revolting. *I can't bear it. I can't bear it one moment more!*

Maskal approached with a goblet. She hesitated, unsure whether to hold it for him to take left-handed, or put it to his mouth for him.

Snatching it awkwardly from her, he choked down the bitter poppy and held the goblet out again, trying not to retch. "More. Please more."

She refilled it from the pitcher she held, and again he drank it down, wiping his mouth on the back of his sleeve. Again, his gorge rose, but he was determined. *It is time.* Again he held it out. "More." *Two will not be enough.* "More! Please!"

Maskal cast a dubious glance at Alaera who was returning with the knife, held in a thick padded glove against the heat.

"As much as he needs," Alaera said softly, and that scared him, almost as much as the knife did.

Maskal filled the goblet.

TIME PASSED and Lodin's arm healed over, but his heart did not. The loss of his friends and his city roared in him like a void, drowning out everything but the itching of his cursed arm. Kuhrin had been part of his life for over a decade, and Bellara had been a good friend for nearly half that time. Antor had been a friend of sorts—not in the sense that they spent much time together or socialised, but the council meetings had been rendered bearable by his wry wit, in kinder times. Even Casim... Lodin's eyes filled when he thought of Casim's little daughter. *Is she safe? What will they tell her when her father doesn't come home?* The idea of the little girl waiting while her father lay dead in the gutter haunted him.

"Lodin? Are you in pain?" Alaera was doing the rounds this evening, and in the dim misery of the sickhall, her light was something to hold onto.

"I can't sleep. Will you stay awhile?"

"Let me check on the others, and then I'll come back."

He watched the glow of the lamp as it moved from bed to bed. It was always dark in the sickhall, but night was when his demons really taunted him. *It would have been dark in the caves of Laerzinan all the time. But not when they swept through with fire and blood. So much death, everywhere. Even the Dowager Queen. Why did I survive?*

Alaera returned. "Having trouble sleeping again?"

"Yes." Lodin wracked his brains for words. "Please. Help me. I don't speak well. Understand some but not to speak. I don't see your letters. Show me how to speak."

Alaera cocked her head. "I'm not a teacher, but if you want to practice talking I'll happily help you. And you want to learn runes, is that what you mean?"

"Runes. And…" He did not know the word for books, or stories. He was too tired to explain. He shrugged. "Runes."

"Certainly." Alaera jumped to her feet as the doors to the sickhall slammed open and a Skral came in, supporting a second who was bleeding profusely. "Olann? What's happened?"

"Bran got in a fight with Drankar, of course." The Skral shrugged. "He's been pushing it for a while now, and Drankar got fed up."

"Right." Alaera hurried across the hall. "Lower your voice. Everyone is asleep, or was."

"The *unSkral* parasites? I'm sure they are." He did not lower his voice. "All they do is lie in bed and eat our food. None of them adds anything. They were too weak to defend their own homes. They will eat with anyone's knife, friend or foe! I don't know what the Shantar witch did to get control over the Clan Elders, but she must have cast a spell on him. That's the only reason I can think of that we didn't just leave them all to drown. And now look! There isn't enough food to go round or enough beds for the actual Skral Warriors —"

"Stop your grumbling right now, Olann Endersonn." Alaera

hissed fiercely. "I have a patient to attend to, I assume, apart from your wounded pride?"

Olann looked angry but took his friend over to the nearest bed. "You. Out."

The inhabitant of the bed, woken suddenly, threw back the covers. The slight, swarthy man was Gai Renese, Lodin was startled to see. *Just how far has the Ice Lord got?* It was a new thought.

"Don't you dare!" Alaera grabbed Bran's arm and dragged him to her own bunk. "Ardmin, you get right back in that bed and get back to sleep if you can. Olann, bring Bran in here. And I swear by the Twins, if you ever try to drag one of my patients out of bed again, I will give you a dose that will have you soiling your pants for a week."

"Not needed, just cook me some mutton, from your cursed *unSkral* sheep. They make me sick to my stomach!" He spat on the floor in the direction of Ardmin's bed, but did allow himself to be drawn into the sleeping cubicle.

Alaera fetched poppy seed and sutures and patched up the man, all the while, Olann, drunk and vitriolic, went on about the stupidity of wasting resources on the refugees.

Lodin realised uneasily that he had had little to do with anyone outside the sickhalls. *Are all of them like this? Have we ended up in a different kind of slavery? Surely not, or they would not keep us alive, those of us who are wounded. But once we are better, what will we find waiting for us, outside these four walls?* The thought terrified him and suddenly he felt utterly drained.

Lodin lay back on his cot. *Why did I survive? All this, to find myself here at the far end of the world, alone in the cold and dark in a country whose inhabitants call us animals but behave like primitives themselves! I should have died with my city.*

He closed his eyes, tried to slow his heart, still his brain, let go and drift into death… but the burning of his arm kept him firmly anchored. Tears leaked under his eyelids and traced hot lines down the sides of his face and neck. *Truly I am as weak as they say.*

"Sometimes it is a mercy that they don't understand the language." There was the clang of the door closing and Alaera's voice came across the hall. "All of us were surprised when the Elders agreed to help the outlanders, I know, but it's a matter of numbers. Even if they can do little more than hold a sword, against numbers such as the Ice Lord commands we cannot win with the few of us that are left."

"The younger ones resent it as a slur on their manhood," Maskal replied. "They are all injured pride and no sense. It goes against everything we know to accept *unSkral* as equals. But when the Bards bring word from the shipspirits, even the Elders must stop and listen."

"Aye." Alaera sighed. "There are times when I have wondered what it would be like to know more about the unSkral, but this was not the way I imagined finding out. Ah well." There were the soft scuffs of feet on the rushes underfoot as Maskal went back to what she had been doing, and Alaera returned to Lodin's bedside. "Lodin?" Alaera whispered.

But Lodin did not open his eyes, and thinking him asleep, she slipped away.

SLOWLY LODIN'S ARM HEALED, and each night after the other patients were asleep, Alaera or Maskal would help him learn the Skral language. The guttural sounds did not come easily to his tongue, and there was no beauty in the language, but at least he could express a little more clearly when he was in pain or hungry.

His mood did not lift though. Every day blurred into the last, in one long dreary cycle of waking and sleeping and waking and sleeping, with little to interrupt it but the occasional incursion of a wounded Skral, often drunk and bleeding, and frequently cursing the refugees. It did not help.

One morning, a man entered the hall, obviously a Skral, his face lit with the brightness of youth.

Lodin watched uncaring. The Skral wandered round talking to people and paying attention to everything he saw, a sharp contrast to other Skrals. This young man was calm and cheerful in a way that seemed to lift the spirits of those with whom he spoke.

Alaera was passing and he caught her attention. "Alaera, who is that?"

"That's Maran. They say he is of the bloodline of the Kings who once ruled the Skral. He's our youngest bard, a great pride to his clan. He has completed his learning at the Halls of Lore."

"Halls of Lore?"

"Yes. Students who wish to be bards live in the Halls of Lore for seven years. They learn the wisdom of a thousand years of Skraldom, from the Old Kings when the Skrallands were one country ruled by one man, to the songs made about the current wars. Many start the training but only the best get in. It's a battle of the mind, Maran says."

"Oh." Lodin looked at the young man with new respect, embarrassed that he had thought the Skral had no education. "When he has finished what he is doing, would you ask him to come over here? I would like to know more about the Halls, and your country and customs."

"You're not up to long discussions yet."

"Perhaps not, but it would take my mind off this benighted itching."

"Very well—but I will tell him not to keep you talking too long."

Alaera bustled over to Maran. From high above, a solitary ray of sunshine lanced through the obscurity of the hall. Motes of dust danced in the light. As Alaera spoke to him, the young man brushed back a lock of the unruly blond hair which curled to his collar.

Maran was slender where the warriors were bulky and muscular, and his face was thoughtful and fine of feature. He reminded

Lodin of the beautiful statues of Lyria. Even in the dimness of the sickroom, Lodin warmed to him on sight.

Maran walked over to the craftsman's sickbed. "Let's see... From the look of you, you're Lyrian, I'd guess," he said in the harsh Skral language.

"Yes. I am Lodin."

"Welcome to the Skrallands," Maran switched to flawless Lyrian, to Lodin's utter bemusement. "I am sorry that you come in such unhappy circumstances, but I wish you joy of the visit."

"Joy is born in the company of friends." Lodin finished the politeness. "My preconceptions of your country may be sadly awry. I had not expected to find such learning amongst swords and axes."

Maran laughed, taking a seat on the stool next to Lodin's bed. "Your preconceptions are arrow-true, alas. My countrymen do not share my interest in the *unSkral*. They consider it unhealthy." He grew serious. "But you wished to speak to me?"

"Yes." Lodin shifted in his bed. "Alaera tells me you have much learning. I would love to know more. Tell me about your people, or your culture, or anything. I have been lying in this place forever, and I am floundering in darkness. Give me something else to think about, I beg, or I will go mad. I cannot free my mind from the murder of my city. It whirs round and round in my head until I cannot think of anything else."

"Have you spoken of it to anyone?"

"Who would I tell? All of us here struggle under the weight of our own stories, never mind anyone else's."

Maran nodded. "Then tell your story to me, my friend, to stop it from buzzing in your head. Make room for better things. Today, tell me your tale, and tomorrow I will tell you of far-off places where they have never dreamt of the Ice Lord. Is it a deal?"

"There is no pleasure in this tale." Lodin was reluctant to talk of his flight, but he itched to hear Maran's stories and songs.

"In Lyria they record things on paper, do they not?" Lodin

nodded, and the bard continued. "Here parchment is scarce and rarely used. We do not write, we remember. We bards are not just here to entertain, though we enjoy doing so. We are the repositories of knowledge for our people. You have libraries; we have bards. Please, tell me your story. Add to the knowledge of the Skrals. It is not an unworthy cause."

Lodin lay back in his bed and closed his eyes, trying to visualise where to start. *Kuhrin? Bellara?* "The fall of my home is raw and vivid with the loss of my friends. Do you want all of that in your chronicle?"

"They belong in your story. Tell me what you remember. No-one's tale is unimportant."

"My city is dead, my King, my friends, even the Dowager Queen I was tasked to protect. There are no other Lyrians here, even. I hope that the rest found a way to hide along the coast, but there has been no word of them..."

"...I was unconscious when Gamran erected the sail. They tell me that a tender from a Skral ship stole into the coast, and rescued everyone they could find. Gamran climbed aboard the tender to look after me, and they laid out Queen Estrella in her coracle with the shawl over her, and left the coracle to sail to the World's End. They tried to rouse me, but I was raving with fever by then." Lodin fell quiet for a moment and turned his face away. "I regret not having said goodbye to her. She was a lady of some character. When circumstances turned against her, her strength and determination could not be quenched. I was honoured to share her journey, and I would have liked to have made the new palanquin, so that she could have travelled anywhere she wished."

Lodin surfaced from the telling of his tale, and was surprised to see that the hall was dark, lit by the fatty candles and dim oil lamps that the Skral used. He turned his head, a little disoriented, but the young man Maran still sat beside him, his face sad.

"And then?" Maran prompted.

"Of our little party, I alone am left. When Gamran had seen me safe, he took one of the tenders and went back up the river to help those who had arrived too late for the boats and were trying to make their way down the sewers on foot. It was honourable, but foolish. The ship waited for some days, but he did not return. I hope and pray that he landed somewhere that the Ice Lord's soldiers will not find him, but I do not think that there will be many such places left."

Maran nodded sadly. "With the fall of so many other countries, Skralland is the last refuge we know of."

"As for me, I am left weak and useless. Gamran and his friends cauterized my arm while I was insensible. It was a brutal but effective means of saving my life; though I did not realise it, part of the sewers' stench was from my own arm, which had become infected. I was fading in and out of consciousness on the Skral ship, but I remember when they took the dressing off. It was not pleasant. The smell... I don't know that I shall ever forget the smell of my own flesh, cold and burnt, and the stench of rotting from the infection."

He swallowed a few times before continuing.

"I lie day after day listening to the cries of the sick and wounded of many countries. With my hand I have lost my craft and my passion. If I can no longer work metal and craft the devices that were my world, what shall I do? I cannot farm or paint. I can write in Lyrian but I have no skills with words, and there are few Lyrians left alive to read the beautiful windings of our script. I have some facility with languages but have never left Lyria before, and the primitive barbarism of the Skrals bewilders and appals me." Lodin suddenly recalled his audience. "I'm sorry, that's terribly rude."

"I know a little about Lyria." Maran smiled. "And if what I have heard is true, then my people must seem almost without culture, education or art. In fact we have all three, but none of the subtlety your people delight in."

Lodin pulled at his cover irritably. "The other thing I find difficult is the Skral obsession with war. In Skral war is everything, and peace is just for soft foreigners. In my country we abhor the waste and bloodshed of war. I am not sure there is anything we can contribute to a society which does not even believe in love, the central axis of Lyrian culture. Marooned here, I can only be a burden on your resources, which must be already stretched thinly with so many refugees to feed. What is the point? Surely it would be better for everyone if I just went to sleep and never woke up, like Queen Estrella did? And yet every morning I wake to another unwelcome day."

"My friend, I am truly sorry to hear of your troubles," Maran replied slowly. "There are many differences between your country and my own and you have lost much, but there is more to this land than you realise. Although we do not have your subtlety, we have a history that spans thousands of years, many tales for the telling and many songs. First get well, and then help us."

"Help you? How can I help?"

"You have knowledge and craft that we have yet to discover, or have forgotten. You have skills that would be valuable to any people. We are the remnants of a shattered world gathered here in the last refuge left to us. Your skills and knowledge will be vital. You can show us how to make stronger weapons, harder armour, more accurate arrows."

"I cannot." Lodin turned his face away from the younger man's impassioned plea. "I made a vow to Queen Estrella, and to help in the war effort would be to break that vow. I cannot reconcile it with myself to do so."

"Ah." Maran leant back on his stool. "To Skral ears, that is a very odd vow indeed, but I can understand why you would make it."

"Even if I had not made the vow, how could I help? You forget this." He waved his stump at the man, and then stopped. "Wait!"

"What is it? Are you in pain?"

"No, but my arm is not itching. It has been itching and burning for days, and now it has stopped!"

"A sign perhaps?" Maran cocked an eyebrow.

Lodin could not tell whether he was serious or in jest. "More likely that I was distracted from it–but still, it has stopped."

Alaera, who had been hovering for some time, approached. "Maran, you promised me that you would not tire my patient."

"I'm not tired!" Lodin protested, but the young man was rising.

"Alaera is right, my friend. We have talked much and you are not yet well. I will take my leave of you for today, and tomorrow I will introduce you to the culture of the Skrals. But there is one mystery which I believe you may have solved for me."

"A mystery?"

"I will not say more until I know the answer is the right one– but I will leave you to exercise your mind upon that, perhaps. Alaera, you are looking radiant as always!" And the bard departed, leaving the motherly Skral primping her hair.

GIVEN that Lodin would not help in the manufacture of anything to do with the war, he did not expect the bard to return, but the next day Maran reappeared shortly after they had broken their fast. He waved at Lodin from the door and strode across the stuffy hall. "Alaera! I need to borrow your patient."

"I beg your pardon?" Alaera hurried over.

"Lodin, my friend, are you up to a brief visit to one of the other clan-halls?"

"But he hasn't left this hall in weeks! It's only a few days since he started sitting up!"

Maran paid no attention, but perched on a stool nearby, a sparkle of mischief in his eyes. "How are you this morning?"

"Alive." Lodin smiled cautiously. "And puzzled over your mystery, if you must know."

"Just as I thought! Would you like to help me solve it? It will mean a trip over to the next hall–about as far as the fireplace and back. Are you up to that?"

"I don't know..." The words quavered out of Lodin's mouth as if an old man was speaking, and suddenly he was exasperated at himself. "What am I saying? There is nothing wrong with my legs. I would like to come to the other hall, but I am weak from staying in bed. I might stagger like an ancient, but if you will help me, I will go."

"Good man! I don't think you'll regret it. Apart from anything else, if you've been cooped up in here for weeks on end, to get out in the fresh air will do you a world of good. It is quite breezy outside, though, so we'd better wrap you up warmly."

Lodin looked at the floor, keenly embarrassed. "Even in autumn, Lyria is a hot country. I don't have any clothes but those I am now wearing, and they were given to me."

"Then take one more item." Maran took off his own thick-furred cloak and laid it on the chair. "I have another, and your need is greater than mine. Besides, I am impatient to have you come across the way."

They helped Lodin to stand. Though weak, he was not so weak that the idea of leaving the hall appalled him. He wrapped the cloak around him, revelling in the softness of the fur against his cheek. "Your cloak is wonderfully heavy."

"I like to be warm. Alaera?"

"Oh yes, I'm coming. All this mystery has me intrigued, too!" Alaera hurried off to find her own cloak. She came back with two, and passed one to Maran. "Maskal says you've to borrow hers."

"How they look after me!" Maran winked at Lodin.

"And me..."

They pulled back the curtain in front of the doorway. It was noticeably cooler than the hall, and when Maran opened the door, the light seemed so bright that Lodin threw his arm up to shield his eyes. He was a bit disconcerted to find that he had to move it across–there was no hand there to shade his face. It was a very odd feeling, but was quickly lost in the freshness of the wind that whipped his hair across his face. He took a stumbling step out onto the path outside, and another and another. Then he threw back his head and just breathed, glorying in the wild air. It felt as if he had been holding his breath for a month, and this breeze was blowing away the shadows and darknesses with which his brain had been filled.

"Lodin? Are you all right?"

He beamed at Alaera. "Yes, I am–or I will be. And this is the first moment that I have known it."

Maran took his uninjured arm companionably. "This way."

As they walked slowly along the path, Lodin's eyes became more used to the bright sunshine. Coming from the dark hall, filled with the stench of illness, the day was unutterably beautiful. He paused to look at the hall behind him. It was very similar to the others dotted around the plain, a long building with a high thatched roof sloping down to just above the ground. There was one large chimney at each end, each carrying smoke from three or four of the hearths set into the walls, and the gable ends were made of wood, heavily carved and painted to resemble beasts of some sort. "What are the animals?"

Maran followed his gaze. "The carvings? Those are the clan-spirits. Each clan is guarded and guided by a spirit which appears to them in the shape of an animal. The hall that we now use for the sick was once the home to the clan of the Snow Eagle. There were not many of them, so the oldsters and the children sailed with the adults, in order to keep the clan ship adequately crewed. Few of them were warriors. We found their ship in the bay, barely afloat. The Ice Lord's ships had tried to burn it but it valiantly made its way home, with the remains of its clan. We saw them on their way according to tradition." Maran fell silent for a moment.

"When we realised that this war was taking over the whole world, the clans were given guidance that refugees should be brought to the island, and that the empty clan halls could be given over for their use. It is a momentous decision for the Skral to agree to such a thing, but this is no ordinary time of peril."

Lodin looked around him. "Your people are skilled workers of wood. The carvings are beautiful."

"Aye—we are not all barbarians, you know!"

Lodin blushed, realising that he was being teased. "Yes, well that remains to be seen. If your idea of a puzzle is the one about how to get the farmer and the sheep and the lion all across the river, your barbarian status will be assured."

Maran laughed. "No, that is not the nature of our puzzle today."

"What's a lion?" Alaera asked.

Lodin was tiring fast now, but they were nearly at the other hall. "I may have to sit down for a while when we get there, but I'm glad we came out. These days, even walking across the way feels like a real achievement."

"For anyone who has been as ill as you have, it is an achievement." Alaera was entirely in earnest. "It was a terrible injury. Your arm was badly infected. We didn't think you would live."

They guided him up the stairs to the other hall, and once through the curtained atrium he was taken to a low comfortable chair by the fire. He sat gratefully.

"Catch your breath for a few moments, friend. I must go and see if I can chase up the mystery for you!"

Sitting in the warmth, Lodin relaxed back against the cushions they had put behind him. He stared into the fire, and watched the flames jump and smoulder.

A sudden ruckus startled him out of his thoughts. Children were shouting and laughing in excitement.

Alaera, excited, called "Is it here?"

"Yes. Look out!"

Alaera shrieked, but not in alarm. A crowd erupted out of the middle of the hall following Maran, who came over to Lodin at a half-run, his face alive with laughter. "Can you stand while I turn your chair around?"

Lodin stood as his seat was turned to face into the main body of the hall.

Maran gestured at him to sit down again. "I may have found your mystery but it might take a moment to show up. While we are waiting, would you tell the children about the Aviary Courtyard, please? They have never seen such a wondrous place, and they would love to hear of it."

The children clustered round, chanting "Please! Please!" There was clearly more to it than this, as they were all excited and laughing, but he could not guess what was going on, so he held up his hand for silence. With much shushing and whispering, the children shoved and hustled until they were all sat cross-legged on the floor in front of him.

Lodin began to speak, and this time he tailored his words to young ones. The children all fell quiet in wonder, at first giggling, but as he spoke, they became lost in the story. There amid the smoke and furs and dimness of the Skral hall, he spoke of the trees, the flowers, the delicate tracery of glass panes and the song of the fountain. He spoke of the tiny humming birds, like little living jewels, dipping into the great scarlet flowers which hovered amongst the lush greenery.

But when it was time to speak of the King, Lodin fell silent. That grief was too recent in his mind.

A tugging on his cloak made him look down. A little girl sat there, and she tugged at his cloak again until she was sure she had his attention. "Was there a bird?" She shot an accusing look at Maran. "He said you had a pet bird."

Lodin smiled down at her. "Yes, I had a pet bird." It was not the literal truth but he was glad that Maran had told them so. This way he could tell of the wonders they wished to hear without touching on his grief for the King's death, and that of the rest of his city.

"What was it like? Was it a gull?" one of the older children asked.

"No! Gulls are big and vicious!" Lodin smiled a little, remembering the delicate colours, the swooping flight. "My bird–Tiris was his name–he was not big and vicious. He was tiny. He could sit in your hand."

The children considered this, and the boy asked "And did he? Sit in your hand, I mean?"

"He did. He would even come to the whistle–not always, you know, but when it suited him."

"What does that mean, come to the whistle? Did you have a whistle that you used? Was it like mine?" A third child waved a wooden instrument with evident pride.

"Not a whistle like yours, though that is a very fine one. I used to just whistle, like this." He whistled the notes that the King had shown him.

The children nearly bubbled over with excitement. "How did it go again?"

Lodin could not work out why this was amusing them so much, but he dutifully whistled again, this time more clearly, and suddenly there was a glad little chirp amongst the rafters and something dive-bombed him. The children shrieked and laughed and shrieked. Lodin shielded his face from the creature as it swooped down at him again, but this time, it slowed to a flutter and two sets of delicate little claws clutched at his raised hand.

Lodin froze. There was another little chirp, and slowly he lowered his hand.

"Tiris!" He could not believe it. "Tiris!" The little bird was thin and his feathers were draggled, but as he lowered his hand it leapt cheekily onto his chest and settled there. The children *ooh*ed and *aah*ed.

"That, my friend, is the mystery of which I spoke," Maran said quietly. "He stayed with you, in the ship or around the rigging, all the way from Lyria. You were moved here first from the ship, but he must have lost you when they took you into the sickhall. He has been lurking in the rafters since. Pickings outside are pretty scarce, but he seems to have survived on leftovers. The children have been looking out for him though, so he has not starved."

"Thank you, children! Thank you with all my heart." Lodin's eyes stung. "You have saved for me something of the beauty of Lyria, which I had thought long lost. You have saved my friend."

"You're welcome," the little girl said solemnly, and others joined in.

"Now, children, let's go get a boiled egg, and see if we can't get Tiris fine and plump again. Go on! Whoever brings one back first can choose the story in their hall tonight." Maran ushered them away and, laughing, they scattered. "Shall I leave you there for a while, my friend? That was more tiring than I intended."

"Yes, if you would, just for five minutes." Lodin sat back in the chair. The bird was a little bundle of warmth on his chest, and he felt knots there loosening in more ways than one. It felt as if a little piece of the Gardens of Paradise had fallen from the afterlife into this stinking, primitive place, and his heart soared. It was stupid, he told himself. Tiris was only a bird–but that did not matter in the slightest. A friend had survived the journey, someone glad to see him, and if that someone wore feathers, that did not make him any less dear to the lonely craftsman. It felt as if an eternity had passed since the last time he had given thanks to the Eternal All, but this time his thanks were heartfelt and sincere.

A few minutes later, a little girl came back with an egg, boiled and mashed into a paste, and by then, Lodin could smile and let her hold the plate for Tiris, agreeing when she exclaimed in wonder at the sun-shimmer on those startling emerald feathers.

Eventually, Alaera decided that Lodin had had quite enough excitement for one day, and with Maran, she helped him back to his feet. Lodin held the little bird close, but the minute they left the clan-hall Tiris took off, a flashing green dart against the blue sky. While they walked back, he hovered on the wind, landed on the roofs and took off again, twittering all the time in sheer exhilaration of the wild, windy morning. When they reached the door of the sickhall, Lodin whistled, and the bird landed on his shoulder, scolding and chattering while the craftsman stumbled, exhausted, back to his bed.

Alaera took the cloak from Lodin and pulled the cover over him. He was very tired now, and relaxed back onto his pillows thankfully. His eyes were closing despite his best efforts, but there was something else he had to do... *Ah yes.* "Maran?"

"Yes?"

"Thank you. That was a happy mystery."

"You are welcome, my friend. Now rest, and I will see you tomorrow."

A DIFFERENT WAY OF SEEING

M aran was as good as his word. The next day he returned
as he had promised, and this time he brought others with
him, the oldsters who had little to do but sit tending the fire. They
chatted to the sick, taking their minds off their situation, and
made them feel welcome with brightly coloured blankets and
cushions to make the room cheerful and the beds more comfortable. Maran brought his harp and sang merry songs, and the
mood lifted in the hall.

"How did you know what to do?" Alaera marvelled.

Maran shrugged. "I could see the despair, the hopelessness
whispering in their ears. The loss and horror that they fled has
come with them, haunting their dreams. How can a man get well
when all he wants to do is die?"

"We do our best with the hurts of the body, but we do not
know how to help with the hurts of the mind." Alaera shook her
head. "For all our work, your medicine seems to have the stronger
effect."

Maran nudged her. "It only works on the living, Alaera, and
without you and the others many of these people would not be
alive now."

Alaera blushed. "Get on with you, my lad! You'd charm the stars out of the sky if you wanted to!"

Maran bowed grandly, making her snort with laughter.

Lodin's interest had been piqued by something else, however. "Maran, what do I need to know about using someone else's knife?"

Maran's eyebrows went up. "It is not something we would do, but I know that in other cultures the sharing of eating implements is not looked on in that way. Why do you ask?"

"It was a comment one of your people made. I think they do not think well of doing so?"

Maran glanced at Alaera. "Do our friends here still share utensils?"

"Yes." She shrugged. "We asked them if they wanted their own personal sets, but they didn't see any point."

"I can't speak for the others and perhaps I am very ignorant, but I didn't realise there were any implications to it." Lodin picked up the spoon from his table. "In Lyria, provided it's clean, there's nothing more to be said. Many would have a knife to use for everyday tasks, but we would not use a tool-knife to eat with."

"Ah. That is not quite how we look on it."

"No?"

"For us it is a very personal thing, and in part to do with family and history. It would be like a man offering to share his wife with others."

"Oh! That's something we did not know! I think once it is explained to them, everyone here will want their own utensils."

Alaera blushed. "It did not occur to me that they would not know what it meant to be knifeless. I will pass word round."

As Alaera bustled off, Maran was lost in thought. "Lodin, do you know if there are those who can work metal and wood here? Asking the smith to make knives for *unSkral* might be a problem, but I can't see anyone objecting to us providing you with the means to make your own."

Lodin felt bitterness rise up in him like bile. "You are asking the wrong person, I'm afraid. Once upon a time I would have solved the problem in short order myself, but I shall be no good to you now."

"Could you ask around? If there are those who are willing to learn, perhaps you could teach them?"

Lodin looked away. He wanted to refuse, to shout that he would have nothing to do with it. *Bad enough that I cannot make things myself, but to watch others doing it badly? That would rub salt into every wound I have! And yet...* It was a chance to be of some use, at least, to disprove Olann's drunken words which rankled and festered in his brain. He had once found joy in the sharing of knowledge. Besides, Maran had been kind to him and what he asked was for the good of all the refugees including Lodin himself.

Lodin looked back to find Maran's compassionate gaze lingering on his face.

"I ask much," the bard said softly, "but you are best placed to get this done, and done well enough to make my kinsmen wonder if perhaps they have underestimated those of other nations."

Lodin smiled crookedly. "It shall be done. Oh... and just to be clear, a man sharing his wife against her will is always a bad thing, but what if the wife wishes to share herself voluntarily?"

Maran's shout of laughter drew a lot of startled glances. "This is acceptable in Lyria?"

"Some partners keep only to each other. Most allow each other what freedoms they like. It all depends on whether the marriage is for love or for business."

Maran sat on the bench nearby. "Tell me more. It seems there is much to be learned. It may be that we will need to have a conversation with the Potentate of Gai Ren and the Mother of the Shantar, so we are able to avoid giving needless offence."

GRADUALLY THINGS BECAME EASIER. The oldsters revelled in the grateful friendship of the refugees, and much was learnt from the intermingling of the various nationalities.

The children liked to come and hear the stories of many nations. They brought with them little handfuls of grasses and flowers from the plain to put in beakers around the room for those who were too weak to go out there themselves. As the autumn progressed, the flowers were fewer, but the graceful tassels of the grasses brought a little of the outside world into the hall. The hall gradually emptied as the sick felt better. The past faded from their eyes as they engaged with the present, and begin to think about how to make a future for themselves.

As for Lodin, though his mood was still dark at times, his arm was healing. With the presence of Tiris, there was something else to occupy him. The little bird was thin and bedraggled, so he set himself to bring it back to full health. Tiris spent a certain amount of time lurking in the warmth of the rafters. He became a great favourite amongst the children, and the other inhabitants of the sickhall were cheered by his gleaming feathers and mischievous spirit. As he became stronger, Lodin would sit outside, or go for short walks with the bird, who dived and soared in the brisk winds that blew from the plains.

TIME PASSED but no more refugees arrived. Some thought it was a good thing, that perhaps the war had ended, but Lodin saw how grim Alaera looked when it was discussed. It was more likely that the Ice Lord had destroyed everywhere but the Skrallands, he thought, but he did not voice this opinion even to Maran. He told himself that thought was just a feverish night terror; but he could not bring himself to believe so.

One day Maran came in looking unusually sombre. "My friends, I come to say farewell for the moment. I have been sent on a journey of finding, and it may take a while. I do not know how long at the moment, but I leave very shortly."

"Where are you going?" Lodin asked, and a chorus of others chimed in.

He raised a hand to still the questions. "I cannot tell you without dispensation from the Elders. It is the custom of the Skral. This is something of which we do not speak to strangers. I shall be away for some time but I rely on you all to stay hopeful and heal as fast as you can. We may need your strength in the near future." He paused. "Wish me a pleasant journey, friends! I have cold and uncomfortable days ahead of me."

"Good fortune!"

"Safe journey!"

"Luck in your travelling!"

A chorus of good wishes followed him out into the cold of the evening. Dismayed, Lodin watched him go. The young bard's visits brightened up the days and it was such a pleasure to talk and banter with him. The others were pleasant enough, but none had Maran's sly wit. He would miss spending time with him.

"Hello, Lodin." One of the children approached.

"Hello, Saskia. And how are you this morning?"

She considered this, chewing the end of one flaxen braid. "I'm a little sad. Maran's going away, and no-one tells stories quite like he does."

"That is true. But don't you have a bard in your own clan-hall?"

"Well, there is old Ranulf, but he always tells the same stories. I already know the story about the widow's son, and the story about the King's feast, and the story about the boy who killed the giant and--oh, all the other ones. I want to hear a new story!" She petted Tiris, who leapt onto her shoulder and pecked at the beads of her necklet.

Lodin smiled. "Do you know the story about the princess and the marmoset?"

She turned curious blue eyes on him. "What's a marmoset?"

"A marmoset is a little monkey." She looked blank. "Hmm. It's a little creature about so big, with very soft fur and great big eyes."

"Is it like a dog?"

He laughed. "It isn't like a dog, no. But if you want to hear the tale, I have promised to tell it this evening after we have eaten."

"I will come and hear it. Thank you for letting me talk to Tiris." She nodded gravely and went on her way, leaving Lodin thoughtful. Perhaps there was something he could do for the Skral, after all. Being Lyrian, he had a good stock of tales to tell.

THE DAYS WERE GETTING SHORTER. Lodin's health improved enough that he could not bear to be in the sickhall, still stale-smelling despite all the fresh reeds they put down and the scented herbs they burnt to lighten the atmosphere. He moved his sleeping quarters to one of the other halls and Tiris went with him, though both went back to visit often. Sometimes Tiris would appear there on his own, darting through the door to find whoever had food. He was plump and shining now, not least because they had discovered that he had a terrible fondness for the dried berries that the Gai Renese had brought.

As for Lodin, in the course of his walks he caught sight of something that intrigued him, a league or so over the plain. From the clan-halls he could see the top of some kind of structure. It was far too regular to be natural but it reminded him of something familiar, something he should recognise. He could not work out what, though. Until the war he had never left Lyria, and Lyrian architecture was more inclined to be delicate than this blocky stone. At first it was too far away, but as he gained strength it began to nag at him. He became restless and eventually set out across the plain to investigate.

It was longer than most of the walks he had attempted of late, but the grasses of the plain were soft beneath his feet and the way was easy. Before long before he found himself standing by a circle of standing stones. Much to his confusion, he knew it as intimately as he knew his own workshop, from the strange recurring dreams that had plagued his sleep since his childhood.

For a long moment he stood and stared. *This is definitely the place in my dreams. How can it be?* He looked at the stone nearest him. *There should be a small pictogram of an axe scratched into the corner of that stone...* He walked round the monolith, and was awed to find the pictogram there, just as he had known it would be. *But what kind of place is it?*

He backed out a short way so that he could see the whole structure. Great slabs of blue-grey stone, the uprights capped with a running circle of lintels, exactly as he had dreamed. The more he looked, the more baffling it became, though. *How was it made?* This level of engineering was unknown to the Skral, and it had clearly towered over the plain since time immemorial. *There's no other stone of that kind anywhere near. Why are the stones here? Where did they come from, and when? What is it? A meeting place? A burial? A statement of power?*

Most intriguing of all, never having been there before in his life, how was it that he knew every nook and cranny of it in such detail? *I have to know more.*

Returning, he went to find Alaera. She was in the sickhall, cleaning the bleeding gash in a young Shantar's arm. With them was a small, hawk-nosed woman with grey running through her hair.

She was scolding him heartily. "You're a fool, Edan! You know what the Skral are like–they start playing with swords as soon as they can stand upright. What were you thinking?"

"I was thinking that it would be good to learn how to use such a weapon." He glanced at her. "A bow is good from a distance, but once they get too near for arrows, I have nothing to defend us but my dagger."

"And what will you be doing defending us, my lad? You are all of sixteen–in the homelands you would be barely old enough to join the adults at meal!"

"I know," he replied softly. "But this past year I have not lived the life of a child, and if there is a year to come, it will not be filled with wrestling or vying for the attention of girls. I need to learn how to defend myself–and you. Father is not here to help us. If the Ice Lord comes here, I will not stand with the children, boxed in by the elderly and infirm."

"You will if I say it shall be so!"

"I love and respect you, Mother, but even if you say so, I will not be there. I have defended you once, and it was not enough. I will not run that risk again."

His mother dropped her eyes. "My son, I am still alive and I still have you. If I could see well enough to fight, if your sister had not run the wrong way, if the soldiers had got to us a few moments later, then perhaps we would have got away. But all these ifs and maybes do not change the past. We are alive and we have each other: that is what matters. As for the sword, perhaps you are right. But be careful, Edan. I do not relish the thought of war. I cannot bear the idea of sitting useless and sightless while my people fight, but what I fear is losing you. I have suffered the loss of your father and sister already. You are all that is left to me and you are more precious than anything else in this world."

"And you to me." Edan fidgeted on his seat. "But the war has made a man of me, and you must let me be a man."

There was a silence.

Alaera tied off the ends of the bandage. "All finished!"

The Shantara smiled a little crookedly. "Go then. Learn to be a man. But try to do it without losing anything important, will you?"

The boy rose. "Shall I take you back to the hall?"

"No, don't worry. Someone will help me."

"I will take you back, if you like." As they turned towards him,

Lodin saw the boy's eyes fall to the stump of his arm. "That bit about not losing anything important? Sound advice, boy."

The boy did not know how to respond to this. He settled for nodding politely and dashed out of the sickhall.

Alaera stood. "Was that a joke, Lodin?"

"Actually, I think it was." Lodin was a little surprised at himself.

"Lodin? The Maker?" The Shantara peered in his direction. "I'm sorry. I wasn't making a personal comment. My sight is not good and I didn't know you were there. I hope I have not caused offence."

"Not at all, madam."

"Asri. I am Shantar, of the clan of Raelith."

"Well met, Asri of the clan of Raelith. I am Lodin, originally of the dead city of Laerzinan, and latterly of the Lyrian Court and the Skrallands." He did a courtly little bow, forgetting that she could not see it.

"And how are you today?" Alaera bustled about, getting a stool for him. "Is your arm hurting? Do you need poppy juice?"

"No, I'm fine, thank you. I had a question for you though."

"Oh, here we go!" Alaera nudged Asri. "Ever the Maker, this one! He never turns up but he has another question to ask."

Asri cocked her head on one side. "How else should he learn? Edan was the same when he was six."

Alaera laughed out loud. "That's put you in your place, Maker! What was your question?"

"The standing stones–there's a huge circle of them on the plain. What are they? What are they for?" He leant forward, eager for answers.

"What are they for?" Alaera was puzzled. "They aren't *for* anything, I don't think. They just... are."

"Where did they come from? Who made them?"

"I don't know. It's not something I've ever wondered. Just goes to show the difference between a Maker and a healer, I suppose."

Alaera thought about it. "You might ask some of the oldsters. Ranulf in particular knows a fair bit of history. Failing that, Maran will tell you a bit more when he gets back."

"Ranulf of the Tusken Seal?" Asri asked.

"Yes, that's him."

"I know Ranulf well." Asri stood, feeling for her cane. "If you wouldn't mind taking me across to the clan-hall, Lodin, I'll send one of the children to fetch him for you."

They entered the hall of the Tusken Seal Clan, and Lodin set Asri in a comfortable seat by the fire.

Edan trotted over. "Thank you for bringing my mother across, sir. Mother, I'll be in the training ring with Eldred and Ranfrith. If you need me, the children know where it is."

"Edan, before you go, could you ask Ranulf to come and speak with the Maker?"

"The Maker?" Edan looked more searchingly at Lodin. "Are you Lodin, sir? I'm honoured to meet you."

"Joy lies in the meeting of friends." The boy hesitated and Lodin explained. "It's a greeting. It sounds better in Lyrian."

"Joy lies in the meeting of friends. I like that." Edan nodded. "I'll get Ranulf for you, sir."

"Thank you." As the boy made his way across the hall, Lodin turned to Asri. "He's a thoughtful boy, and very polite. You must be proud of him."

"I am, the more so as he's all the family left to me." Her face was sad.

"I'm sorry. The war?"

"My story is just like everyone else's. My husband and I were traders. We travelled through Maravel and Gai Ren, along the Sarag to the plains where the horsemen ride."

"They got that far?"

"Aye, before we did. We heard there was trouble on the plains. There always is, of course, but it was worse than normal. The homelands of the Nan-Turi had become a place of the most terrible desolation. There was little sign of the Nan-Turi. Their tents, even their horses had gone, and the grassland was burnt black. My husband went to the well–you would always find someone there–but he returned pale and shaking. The Nan-Turi were there, sure enough, but they had been staked out on the earth for the animals. We packed up our camp and left then and there, but the smell of smoke followed us, and death stalked the plains. By nightfall the horse was weary. We made camp in the foothills. In the early hours we were woken by the sound of many men and horses. My husband said their torches covered the plain like ants boiling out of a nest."

She sat back in her seat. "We could not outdistance them in the wagon, so we left it, let the horse go, and searched for a hiding place. We heard the shout when they found the wagon, and a short while later the horse screaming. My poor pony." There was a tear in her eye as she stared, unseeing, into the distance.

Lodin sat down quietly. He did not think she had meant to tell her story, but he knew well that, speaking about those dark events, it was difficult to avoid being caught up in them.

"Then there was shouting and cheering. My husband said we had to hide. There was no time to argue. I kissed my husband and Edara, my daughter. She climbed into a tree while Edan guided me into the cavity under the tree roots, and my husband made a screen over us of branches and earth. And that was the last time I spoke to him.

"Edan told me they were hidden just in time. There was shouting and a lot of crashing and stamping as the men came in endless waves through the wood. After a while I thought that perhaps we had a chance but then Edara fell out of the tree. She panicked and bolted. My husband shouted us to stay hidden, and ran after her. They must have run right into the soldiers. We heard their shouts and screams in the darkness."

"I am sorry." Lodin's heart went out to her. All the refugees told the same tales, differing only in details; always the smoke, always the screaming, and always the guilt.

"Edan wanted to help them but he could not leave me, and I? I could not see well enough to notch an arrow. In my youth, I could have done something. As it was, I sat in a hole in the ground, sightless as a mole, listening to the death of those I loved." Her voice dripped with bitterness. "Eventually all was quiet. When dusk came there had been no sound for many hours. We came out of our hiding place. There was blood, so much blood that you could smell it, but no bodies. There was a terrible smell of smoke and burning. It made my eyes sting. Even with the poor sight left to me I could see that there was a great line of light cutting across the plain. They had set it alight to ensure that there would be no survivors. We were cut off. There was nowhere to go."

"How did you escape?" Lodin asked.

"The river. It was Edan's idea." She turned her face to him. "The river was deep and it ran swiftly through the plains. There was a dead tree on the bank, very rotten. We tied ourselves to it and pushed it in. We did not know whether it would sink or float, but by then we did not much care. We tumbled and crashed down the river, but we passed through the flames safely. The river slowed when it levelled out on the plains, and eventually we were washed ashore in a marshy valley, too wet to burn. Cold, battered and lost as we were, it was a long while before we could do more than lie there, but eventually Edan roused me. The knots were difficult to untie and Edan drew his dagger to saw at the cloth. When he had cut himself free, he started to cut at my bonds. Then there was a shout—a shape loomed and Edan spun away with a cry. I was left tied to the log, struggling to untie myself. The river sounds around me were too loud to hear what was happening, and I did not know whether he was alive or dead, or if his attacker stood watching me and laughing at my feeble attempts to get free. After what seemed like an eternity, Edan returned. He told me he had killed the man with his dagger. I felt the wetness of blood on his face, but he said it was only a scratch."

"It has not left a visible scar," Lodin told her.

"That is good. He was a bonny child. I wish I could see his face again. We walked along the river for days until we got to the sea. There was a group of villagers making their way along the shore. They told us that the Ice Lord was coming, killing and burning. We travelled with them until the Skral found us, and we were brought here."

She was silent for a time. "I was glad to see that others of my people had reached the Skrallands, but also afraid, for if the Ice Lord's men have reached Shantar, many of my friends and relatives must have perished. And so here I am, blind and helpless, and a burden on my only son."

Lodin looked at the stump of his arm. "We have all lost friends and family, and yet sharing that anguish does not make it any less. It is more frightening to think that this is happening in so many places. Can we really be the only ones left?"

"I pray not." She shook her head. "But we have had no word of any others, and the Mother has not been given Sight of any other survivors. I fear that we are the last. Even the Skrals from the other islands are beginning to gather here."

"Because of the Ice Lord?"

"Aye. He will come, sooner or later."

Lodin traced the carvings on the arm of the chair with a finger. "You are very sure."

"I have heard the stories of many refugees. He does not take slaves. He takes prisoners to put in the front line of his army, but they are allowed to survive only as long as they fight for him, and they rarely survive the first encounter. He does not attempt to keep what he has conquered, but burns it to the ground and moves on. He leaves nothing and spares nothing and, worst of all, when they take a place, first they kill the children."

Lodin swallowed. "There are not many children here..."

"And most of them are Skral. There are only a few Shantar and some from Gai Ren."

Lodin felt lost and helpless. "The whole world is being swallowed up and there is nothing we can do."

"We are alive!" Asri snapped. "While we live, there is always something we can do. And if all we can do is survive, then that is what we will do, and I will tell you why—because if we give up, if we lay down and die, then we have given the victory to the Ice Lord. We owe it to our loved and lost ones to at least make him fight for it!" Her face was fierce, tears running down her cheeks as she stared towards him.

Lodin shook his head. "Where do you find your strength, Asri? You are right—but the thought of a long fight to a slow death fills me with dismay."

Asri wiped her tears away wearily. "I have no strength. I have despair. Grief and rage eat at my heart so that there is no room for fear. I sat by while those I loved *died*, Lodin... If I had the sight I was born with, I should have put an arrow in the hearts of anyone who tried to touch them; but my sight is lost, and I could not help them. If the Ice Lord comes again, I cannot keep my son safe. He will not escape if he thinks I cannot come too, but I will not be the reason for his loss. I will not sit, helplessly listening to the screams." Her face hardened. "I will go out into the battle and throw myself on the sword of some warrior, and if it slows one of the Ice Lord's soldiers for long enough that someone can kill him, I will consider it a deed well done."

There was a long silence.

"Asri?" An older Skral hurried across the hall. "Is all well?"

"All is well, Ranulf." She smoothed her skirt. "I wondered if you could help—the Maker here has questions about the standing stones on the plain, and Alaera thought you might know something about it."

"I can look in the manuscripts, certainly." He was called from across the hall and rolled his eyes. "The Gods know it would be more interesting than what I'm doing now, but Anfrith and her sister have come to blows because their father promised a golden torc to whoever had their child first. They both gave birth on the same day, at the same hour, but their father does not have two torcs. Let me settle the case for them and I will set my mind to the question of the Stones." He hurried off again.

Asri put her head in her hands. "The end of the world is coming and they are fighting over a necklet!"

"We never change, do we?" Lodin began to laugh. "A thousand miles I've come, through fear and fire and pain, and the people are just the same! In a way, it's quite comforting. Whatever the world may throw at us, humans will still be humans, for good or bad."

"I suppose so. We all cling on to that which is important to us." Asri sighed. "And what about you, Lodin? What are you holding onto?"

"Me? There is nothing left for me to hold onto, even if I had the hands to do it."

"Really? You surprise me."

"I beg your pardon?"

"You are the Maker, renowned across the world. Even in Shantar, we know about the Makers of Lyria. I cannot believe that you gain that sort of title and that sort of reputation without the talent and the passion to back it up. Are you not the skilled craftsman that we have heard of?"

"I was. I am not any more."

Asri leaned forward. "Make your mind up, man. Either you are or you are not."

Stung, Lodin snapped back. "I was when I had both of my hands. Now I cannot hold a tool, and so my talent is wasted."

"Who on earth told you that?"

"Isn't it evident?" He was getting angry now.

"No, it is not!" Asri steepled her hands in front of her. "Where is your skill, Maker? Where does it reside?"

"What do you mean?" Understanding that she was not taunting him, Lodin calmed down.

Asri paused in thought. "Let's see. Tell me of something that you invented that was clever, or made you proud."

Lodin gazed up into the beams of the ceiling. His eye was caught by a movement; Tiris had developed a habit of stealing berries from the plates of the Gai-Renese, and he was evidently at it again. "When I became Maker, the gardens in the Palace were sparse and a little scrubby. Lyria is very hot. To keep them green, the gardeners had to bring bucket after bucket of water and even then, some plants would not survive. The King asked me to devise a way of watering them. I went to the farms on the edge of the desert, and to those on the high mountains, and I spoke to those who lived there to see what they did and what they had tried. Then I devised a system of channels fed by the river, and diverted water into little streamlets that ran through the gardens, into the bathhouse to fill the tanks there, and then helped to wash the waste into the sewers. The Palace Gardener and I worked to make sure that all the garden was watered. We built tiny bridges and little chattering waterfalls into the streams so that they were beautiful as well as useful. The Gardener was able to set outside many plants he had gathered from other countries. It took some years but when I left, the gardens were lush and green, scented with many exotic flowers. The bath attendants did not have to go to the river for water and in addition, because the waste was washed away quickly, the palace sewers were much less noisome." He smiled sadly. "I doubt the gardens are still so beautiful now."

Asri nodded to herself. "Why was it that you had to do this?"

"Why? The King commanded."

"That's not what I mean. If the Gardens were dry, why did no-one invent this before?"

Lodin frowned. "They did not think of a way to make it happen."

"And how is it that they did not and you did?"

"The twelfth Maker tried to. He developed a kind of fountain that made it rain on the grass."

"So why did you not merely mend the fountain? What made you do a completely new thing?"

Lodin stopped to consider this. "The fountain did its job when it worked, but it was not the best solution. No-one could walk in the gardens while the fountain was on and so the garden could only be watered at night but Lyria is too hot and dry for that to suffice. Besides, it broke within a few years. It was too complicated, doing a job that should be simple. They say the twelfth Maker was an arrogant man. Certainly he made a lot of things too complex, I think to show how clever he was. I thought there must be a better way–a simpler way."

"If it was simpler, what made you able to find it when no-one else had?"

"I don't know. I spoke to those who had developed small irrigation systems. I took their ideas and put them together. I found a place where the river had a small offshoot that ran near that side of the Palace. It just fitted itself together in my head."

"Right." This answer clearly pleased Asri. "And how was your hand involved in this process?"

"My hand? It wasn't involved in that part of the process. That bit was later, when I was making the model to see if it worked, and the gates to let the water through."

"So without your hand you still would have had the idea?"

"Yes..."

Asri smiled. "Maker, your skill is not in your hand. Your skill is in your head, in the way you look at the world and see the things other men miss. It is in the ideas you have, and the passion that means you have to get things just right. It is in the curiosity that makes you ask as many questions as a child. Your hand is just the tool you use to assemble things."

"But what good are ideas if I cannot make them real?" Lodin gestured helplessly with his handless arm. "I cannot carve or hold something in place to hammer it. I cannot build a model or make a toy. The ideas are nothing until they are made into a reality, and I cannot make anything!"

"The ideas are *everything*," Asri told him sternly. "You left Lyria with nothing. Even if you had both your hands, how could you make anything without tools? You have not even a hammer!"

"A hammer I can borrow!" Lodin was getting angry again.

"And if there are no hammers in Skralland?"

"Then I could make one. There is wood. There is metal. And before you suggest it, if there was no wood, I would fell a tree and if there was no metal, I could go up into the mountains to find some ore and melt it down."

"So you would not lose your craft for want of a hammer, or any other tool?"

The woman was talking nonsense. "That would be ridiculous! I would make a new one, even if I had to make it from raw materials."

Asri smiled to herself. "Maker, your hand is just another tool. Perhaps you cannot make another hand, but you are the Maker. Invent another tool that works in its place."

"Invent..." Lodin exhaled. "Another tool! Why didn't I think of that?"

"You were so busy telling yourself you were no longer the Maker that you made it true. Now it is time to stop feeling sorry for yourself and start doing something about it."

There was a long silence.

"Your sight is keener than you realise, Asri. My thanks to you."

The Shantara's face softened. "You would have sorted yourself out sooner or later."

"I'm not sure I would–and think of all the time I would have wasted!" He hesitated. "May I ask about your sight, Asri? You were not always blind?"

"No, not when I was younger. Once upon a time I was the best archer in my clan. I could shoot the tail feathers off a quickling at a hundred paces."

"A quickllng?"

"A bird, a tiny one. I was a very accurate shot. At first, I started to miss things that were far away. I found it difficult to focus on them. After that–well, far away got nearer and nearer over time."

"So you can see a little?" Lodin leaned forward.

"I am not blind, but I might as well be. I can see shapes and colours, but no detail. I could see Edan's face when he was born, but I have never seen his face as a boy–or as I must now learn to think of him, as a man. I see people before me but I cannot make out their faces. Though my hands retain their skill, I cannot tell out the weights and measures of my spices, for instance, and I must identify one from the next by smell and touch alone. Sadly, there is no tool that you can make to return my skills to me, Maker."

"I'm sorry."

"These things happen. And you need to concentrate on yourself for the moment, not some silly old Shantara who is no use to anyone."

"You should not say such things of yourself. You have done me a real service."

"Then I am glad of it. At least today I have not been a burden." She cocked her head. "I hear Ranulf calling. Has he finished with his dispute?"

"It would seem so. He is waving a scroll."

"Then go find your answers, Maker. I am glad to have made your acquaintance. And if you feel so inclined, come and let me know how you are getting on."

"Thank you, Asri, I will." Lodin patted her on the arm, and went to see what Ranulf had found.

THE DRAGON'S TEETH

L odin was setting off to walk to the circle of stones with Tiris. It was the sort of day when the plains were at their best, fresh and sunny but not particularly warm due to the blustery wind which delighted Tiris so much. As he passed the Clanhall of the Tusken Seal, Edan and his mother were just coming out.

"Good day, Maker!" Edan called cheerfully. "Your bird is brave, to fly in this weather. If he's not careful he will be blown right across the plain!"

"Edan; Asri." Lodin changed direction to walk with them for a while. "Are you going anywhere specific?"

"Not really." Asri turned her face to him. "I wanted to feel the sunlight on my face."

"Edan, are you coming to do some training?" A Skral boy erupted out of the door behind him, a sword in one hand and an axe in the other.

"Not just yet. I'll be back later though." Edan plainly wanted to go but did not let it show in his voice.

Lodin winked at him. "Asri, I was wondering if you'd like to see the circle of standing stones? It's a little way out over the plain but they're so huge..."

"... that even with my mole-sight I might see them? I would enjoy that. Edan, do you mind?"

Edan winked back at Lodin. "On this occasion, Mother, I shall forgive you."

"You cheeky young whelp!" She elbowed him in the side, amused. "Get on with you! And remember, if anyone gets maimed or blinded, there will be trouble!"

"I'll remember! Enjoy your walk!" Edan ran back to the hall for his weapons, the Skral boy with him.

"Thank you," Asri said. "He's a good boy and doesn't begrudge me his time, but it must be terribly dull for a sixteen-year-old boy to be stuck with his mother all day."

"From the way you two talk, it's clear that he enjoys your company." Lodin took her arm and they walked on. Tiris came swooping down to land on Lodin's shoulder. "Oh, there you are. Have you met Tiris, Asri?"

"This is your bird, isn't it?"

Lodin let go of her to hold out his arm so that she could see Tiris properly. Tiris was happy enough to jump down and be admired.

"What a wonderful colour he is! They said he was green, but I never imagined he would be such a bright green. There are green birds in my country, but they are all a muddy colour to blend in with the sparse grass of the mountains. He is like a little emerald, shimmering in the sun."

"If you hold out your hand, he might come to you–he's very friendly."

Tiris considered her outstretched hand briefly before hopping onto her fingers.

"How light he, is, and how delicate his feet are!" she marvelled. "He must be very beautiful."

Lodin was curious. "What can you see of him?"

"Naught but a shining green blotch, vaguely bird-shaped. But such a patch of colour is doubly welcome after the darkness of the halls. They tell me that it is not wholly dark there, but in half-light there is not enough definition for me to see even shapes, and I am truly blind. Talking of the halls, did Ranulf have much to tell you?"

"Not an immense amount, but it was interesting." Lodin changed their path slightly to avoid a wet place amongst the harsh grass. "Can you make out much of the Circle?"

"Not from here, no." She peered forward.

"It is immense. There is a ring of stones, great blue-grey slabs towering higher than the clan-halls. They are many different shapes and widths, but always even in height. There is a layer of slabs laid over the top. These are immense, flat pieces stretching across four or five stones. They do not entirely roof the circle over–there is an open part in the centre, but they make a wide shelter all round the outside part of it. At this end, facing the clan-halls two of the uprights are much wider apart than elsewhere and there is a very definite lintel across the two. It is clearly the entrance–but to what?"

"What did Ranulf say it was?" The wind was whipping Asri's hair across her face and she combed it back with her fingers, pulling her scarf up as a hood to keep it in place.

"He didn't know what it was for, or who had built it, but he did find word of it in a manuscript copied from one in the Great Halls of Lore, which is apparently the Skral repository of knowledge."

"What did it say?"

"It was a folk-tale." Lodin guided her round to the front of the Circle. "Strange how much knowledge thought to have been lost is actually just disguised as story and told round the hearth by the old ones." He stopped again. "Can you see it more clearly now?"

"I see a grey shadow, with a darker part in front of me."

"That darker part is the entrance. I'll take you inside." He led her into the Circle.

"Is it damp? It is very cold." She pulled her shawl more closely about her, and looked up. "That bright circle, that is the sky, is it? How big is the gap?"

"You could ride a cart through it, but it is very high."

She shuddered. "It is waiting, this place. Let us go back outside. It is wild in the wind, but the sunlight is kind, and out there I can see that the plain is pale-coloured and the sky is blue."

"It is beautiful." He led the way back out. "The plain is covered in long silver-gold grasses with tasselled ends. As the wind blows, they undulate like waves on a great rushing sea. There are bursts of colour here and there where the little shrubby trees are turning orange and red, and amongst that the clan-halls bask in the sun under a high blue sky. It will not last, this bright autumn, and they tell me winter here is frozen in snow and ice, but for now the colours of this day make my heart ache. Shall we sit?"

Asri felt in front of her with the cane she carried, and sat on the boulder next to him. "Is this fallen from the Circle, do you think?"

"No; it is a completely different kind of stone."

They sat in companionable silence for a while. Asri turned her face to the sun, her scarf falling back as she did so. Tiris hopped about in the grass, pecking busily at the turf.

Lodin picked a stalk of grass, twiddling it idly between finger and thumb. "Ranulf told me the name of this place, you know."

"I thought it was called the Circle of Stone."

"It is often called that now, but that is not its name. According to him, in the olden times they called it the Dragon's Teeth."

"A strong name." Asri nodded to herself. "Will you tell me the tale?"

"Certainly. Here is something I can do well, and with no special equipment!"

She laughed, and he composed himself, and began. "It is the usual widow's son type of tale. A King has a daughter of great beauty, whose hand is sought by all sorts of suitors. The boy is of a small and insignificant clan. They have no ship–they were decimated in a war some years previously, when his father was killed and the clan ship was sunk. One day a great dragon flies down and takes up residence on the plain. He makes a lair there, but every day he flies out among the islands, roaring and burning ships and clan-halls. At the Skraelmoot the King declares that he shall wed his daughter to whoever can stop the dragon. The young men of the clans are very excited at this chance to impress the King and make their fortune. One by one they go out and attack it, and one by one the dragon eats them. Nothing can stop him. Axes bounce off his armour, swords cannot pierce it, and there are hardly any young warriors left. The King is thrown into despair.

Then one day the widow's son comes into the hall. "May I have your permission to deal with the dragon, Sire?" he asks.

"No-one can deal with the dragon, boy," the King snaps. "It has killed my finest men. It will kill you."

The boy shrugs. "I will go and speak with it, at least. If I am not killed, what will you give me?"

Well there is little enough chance of that, the King thinks, so he can afford to be generous. "I will give you your own weight in gold."

The boy bows. He trots off towards the plume of smoke where the dragon has taken up residence, and the King thinks no more of it–but much to the King's surprise, not only does the dragon remain in his lair that day, but also the boy returns, carrying with him a massive, glassy scale. It is like nothing the King has ever seen.

The boy bows low and presents the scale to the King saying, "Sire, I have talked with the dragon and I have taken from him this scale. It will be a fine shield, light and proof against sword and axe. May I have my gold?"

The King is amazed, but he is not necessarily inclined to part with that much of his treasure, so he stalls for time. "Boy, I have only your word that you have spent the day with the dragon. The scale might have dropped off him as he walked. Why should I give you so much gold?"

The boy cocks an eyebrow at him, impertinent. "Because you promised, and it would not be honourable to refuse."

"Do you charge your King with dishonour?" roars the King. "Have I not said that I will give you the gold? I wish merely to make sure you are as good as you say. Go back to the dragon, and if you spend all day with him tomorrow, I will give you your gold."

"And?" says the boy. "I earned the gold today. What will you give me for spending two days in the dragon's den?"

Well, surviving today must have been some kind of accident, the King thinks, and if he himself watches the boy stride into the lair, it would be inconceivable for him to have that sort of luck twice. He assumes a benevolent mien. "For two days in the dragon's den, you will earn your weight in gold and my own second-best axe."

"Your second-best axe?" The boy whistles. Customarily this would be given to the heir, usually the oldest son. It is quite a prize. "For that I will go back."

So the next day the King rides out with the boy and watches him disappear into the dragon's lair. There is a deal of roaring and the ground trembles. The King flees for his life, gloating that he has just saved himself a lot of gold. All the same, he watches the skies, and the second day passes without the dragon flying out of his lair.

Towards the evening the King is a bit twitchy, and never more so than when the doors to his hall burst open, and the boy walks in carrying an enormous fang, very thin and light but clearly from the dragon. "Sire, I bring you the makings of a sword that will never break nor become dulled. In return, however, I think you owe me your second-best axe, not to mention the gold."

The King is flabbergasted, but still he doesn't want to part with his gold, and he definitely doesn't want to give the boy his second-best axe. Fortunately he has a cunning thought. "You may have it on the third day. Spend one more day in the dragon's lair, and you may have the gold, the axe and my daughter's hand in marriage–but only if you can guarantee that the dragon will never again come out to burn the islands."

The boy considers this. "Some might think that the King of the Skral was trying to avoid paying his debts." But just as he speaks, the curtains beside the throne twitch aside and the King's daughter looks through. She sees the widow's son and smiles at him shyly. Her smile warms his heart as if the sun had bloomed inside him. For such a smile, the widow's son would do almost anything, and he will definitely brave the lair of the dragon again. He looks back at the King. "Will you swear to give me your daughter's hand, your second-best axe and the gold if I spend a third day in the Dragon's lair?"

The King beams magnanimously. "I swear it on my crown."

It is not a very satisfactory oath but as it's likely to be all he'll get, the boy has to be satisfied with that, and off he goes. Once outside, however, there is a tap on his shoulder.

The King's daughter draws him to one side where nobody can see. "He has given his guards orders to hide by the entrance and block the doorway when you are in the lair so that the Dragon will kill you in there. Please be careful."

"I will... and thank you."

She smiles and kisses him full on the lips, then runs away blushing scarlet. The widow's son returns to his home, happy as a bird in springtime, but he takes her warning seriously. He leaves early the next morning, and goes into the lair where the dragon is curled on his bed of gold.

"You're early today," the dragon snorts. "What are you after now?"

"I'm not after anything," the boy replies. "When have I ever asked you for anything? Two days ago, I extracted the sharp branch that was stuck under your tail scale. Yesterday I helped you knock out the tooth that was causing you so much pain. And today I'm here to warn you that the King's men are planning to block you in your lair, seeing as they can't kill you."

"They are, are they?" the dragon hissed. "I'll soon see about that!" He pokes his muzzle out of the door and breathes flames out in a great jet, setting fire to the trousers of the King's soldiers who all run away to the river yelping, and dive in.

The King draws up in a sled just at that moment with his daughter. Confronted by a live, snapping dragon, he throws his daughter off his sled to sprawl in front of the beast. He shouts "Take her! Leave me!" and takes off across the snow, whipping his dogs as if his life depended on it.

The dragon is not impressed. "Coward!" he roars, and taking off, flies across the plain and circles back, dropping down in the snow with the mouth open. The King can't stop in time–the dogs swerve away but the King is thrown right into the dragon's mouth and disappears down his gullet without even touching the sides. The dragon belches as he flaps back to his cave. "What a thoroughly unpleasant little man."

"That was the King!" the boy says.

"And I think he owed you some things." The King's daughter glances under her eyelashes at him, a little shy. "Some gold... And his second-best axe..."

"Yes." The boy smiles. "And your hand in marriage, if you'll have me."

The two were married the next day and though some of the other Clans were a bit disgruntled, the King had never been very popular so they were quite soon resigned to it. And besides, who could stand up to a King who rode to battle on his own dragon?

The dragon, for his part, never forgot how the boy had helped him when he had such terrible toothache. He was a source of much good advice to the King throughout his reign. When the King died, the dragon laid down on the plain and faded back into the earth, as dragons do. All that is left of him now is his teeth, turned into a circle of stones."

Asri laughed, applauding. "An excellent tale, Maker! But I'll wager that the original Skral version had more in the way of blood and glory."

"Well yes, but you can't expect a Lyrian to tell a tale badly, and we don't like the killing and the horrible bits."

Asri shook an admonitory finger at him. "You allow style to cloud the truth! What happens in the original?"

"The boy hammered a stake through the dragon's head, and that's the hole in the top. I liked the dragon though."

"Yes, I liked the dragon, but that sounds a lot more Skral." She snorted. "Little boys, the lot of them, standing round playing 'My axe is bigger than your axe!'"

"You don't approve of them?"

"Skrals think of women as toys to be used, at worst, and at best, bedfellows to be rolled and then left to look after the children."

"And the Shantar? What do they think?"

"We're probably just as bad, only the other way round," she admitted wryly. "We're happy for men to do the hard physical labour, but anything requiring brain and subtlety is considered a task for a woman. It is only when you meet other nations that you realise that there might be more than one way of thinking. I remember my shock the first time we went trading, and I discovered that everywhere worked differently to everywhere else! What about Lyria?"

Lodin's eyes were far away as he remembered. "In Lyria we loved beauty and hated violence. In the pursuit of love and the ideal, everyone did whatever they were good at. There was more of a divide between skill and ungainliness than there was between man and woman. Whether you were born a King or a cottager, if you had a skill to use, people appreciated it. Even those who lived by the sword were artists in their own way. We called them sword dancers. They were few, but greatly respected. They would duel to decide feuds and the like, but even one who is skilled can be defeated when attempting to fight too many at once. When the Ice Lord's armies came, that is exactly what happened."

"Much has been lost." Asri reached back to pull her scarf over her hair again. "But we are alive at this moment, and we cannot tell what tomorrow will bring. Until we know that there is no future for us, we must act as if there is one, or lie down and die of despair." She felt around for her cane and stood. "Shall we go back, Maker? There is that about these stones of yours which lies heavy on my mind. I cannot tell what, but they do."

"Do you think a bad thing has happened here? I used to know a woman who claimed she could sense these things."

"Perhaps it has. Or perhaps it will. I do not know but I cannot be easy here among them." She shivered. "Besides, the wind is chill, for all that it feels like a beautiful day. Shall we go?" She reached a hand out to him.

"Certainly." Lodin placed her hand on the crook of his arm above the stump and they began to pace back through the silver waves of hushing grasses together. "I thought about what you said, by the way. About my arm being a tool."

"And?"

"There should definitely be something that I can do. It's just knowing where to start. It would need to be able to do so many things."

"Or you could have one tool that is useful for many things and others that are more specific. You're not making one tool, but many. What is the task that you most dread these days, the one made most difficult by being one-handed? Or is there one that happens all the time?"

"There are so many!" Lodin stopped to think for a moment. "What I find really humiliating is trying to eat one-handed. Using a knife takes two hands—one to hold the meat in place, the other to cut it, so I have to ask someone else to help, and it makes me feel as helpless as a baby." Anger and bitterness flared high just at the thought. "That's directly as a result of losing my hand, and it makes me furious every time I have to ask."

"Then make something which will allow you to cut your meat." Asri turned her face to him. "It will give you a place to start, at least. How will you attach it?"

"I haven't worked it out yet. I could use some sort of metal bracing with an attachment, but there is only half of my forearm to wear it on so it would probably fall off. Either it needs to be jointed so that it can go up my arm past the elbow, or strapped on, maybe."

Discussing it, they returned to the Clan-hall to find Ranulf snoozing on the bench. A scroll had fallen from his hand. Lodin picked up the scroll and put it on the bench.

"Maker!" Ranulf sat up and blinked a few times. "I must have nodded off. They said you'd taken Asri to the Stones, so I thought I'd wait here. I have something for you." He felt around for the scroll. "When I was looking for information about the Dragon's Teeth in the old scrolls, I came across something you might find useful." He opened the scroll to reveal a picture; a strange contraption of leather straps and metal loops. "We are a warrior race, and injuries such as yours are not unknown to us, alas. This is a scroll from the Halls of Lore, a copy of some writings by the Master of Healing. You will undoubtedly be able to come up with something closer to what you need, but in the meantime, it will be better than nothing."

"What is it?" Asri was intrigued.

Lodin looked closely at the diagram. "It is a false hand."

"Aye. Edric the Smith will make it up for you," Ranulf went on, yawning, "but I thought you would probably want to make some alterations. The scroll says it will take a bit of time to get used to it, but you should be able to wear it constantly in the end."

"Thank you! Thank you, Ranulf, I cannot say how much."

"You're welcome." And with a bow, Ranulf wandered away through the hall.

"What is it like?"

"Rudimentary!" Lodin laughed, but there was glee in that laughter. "But my head is starting to fill with ideas and it will not be so crude when I have finished with it. It is a leather sleeve, a sort of half-jacket. It has straps that fasten around the chest and under the arm, and at the end of it a wooden hand, poised to hold an axe. The Skral are constant in their love of warring at least. But as a place to start it is further along than I had any right to expect."

"What will you do to it?"

"In the first instance, I will make it so that I can change the hand."

"You are not intending to wield an axe, then?"

"Probably best not. I would chop through the plate as well as the meat!" And as she laughed, Lodin tucked the precious scroll into his robe so that the wind would not snatch it away, and went to find a quiet place in which to invent his new hand.

MARAN'S RETURN

Over the days that followed, Lodin worked to perfect his prosthetic. He devised a fitting that would allow him to attach and detach different hands to the leather sleeve, and enlisted the leatherworker and Edric to put it together for him. The first attachment he designed was very basic indeed–a triangular piece of wood with a slot in it, and a knife that he had shaped for the task. Donning the sleeve, he took the knife and went to find Asri, who was sitting in her usual chair by the fire.

"I have a puzzle for you, Asri. Can you tell what this is?" He lifted her hand and placed it on the leather of his sleeve.

Her face lit up. She brought her other hand up and felt the straps over his shoulder, and down to the fitting at the end of his forearm. Her fingers found the slot at the end. "What goes here?"

"Guess!" He passed her the knife. "Careful, it's sharp."

She felt the knife. "The handle is very straight and smooth. May I?" Carefully she slid the knife into the slot, but it began to slide out again. "Does it stay in?"

"Twist the wooden bit." Lodin tried to keep his face straight, but he could not keep the excitement out of his voice.

Asri rotated the whole of the wooden triangle through a quarter turn. There was a click, and the knife stayed firm.

"What's that, Maker?" Edan stopped on his way past, intrigued.

"A new arm..." Asri breathed. "Edan, run and get us a piece of bread on a plate, please."

Catching their excitement, Edan dashed off, and when he returned, Ranulf and several others were with him. He handed the plate to Lodin. "Got it!"

"Well?" Asri asked softly.

Lodin set the plate on his knee. Holding the bread in place with his hand, he set the knife to it, at first gingerly but then with increasing force as the knife cut through the tough crust. When the bread was in halves, a cheer went up as he handed one of the halves to Asri.

"You did it!" she exclaimed, feeling the edge of the piece. "Well done!"

The gleeful onlookers clapped him on the back and filed away, chattering. Lodin turned the halved slice in his hand, and the tightness in his heart loosened. He had become so used to that tightness that he had forgotten that a man could feel any other way. "Thank you, Asri. You believed in me when I did not believe in myself."

"You lost your confidence; that is all." She passed the bread back to him. "Even these mole eyes could see that. Now, haven't you forgotten something?"

"Have I?" He frowned.

"Alaera? If you had already told her she would be here celebrating with you."

"Gods!" Lodin was smitten with guilt. "I was so excited I forgot to call on the way here! I'll go straight across now!" He leapt up from the bench.

"Do! And Lodin?"

"Yes?" He paused.

"It's a wonderful start. Now go away and work out what the next one will be."

SOME TIME LATER, coming out of the sickhall with Alaera's good wishes ringing in his ears, Lodin found Edan outside, throwing the knucklebones with his friends and chatting.

The boy stood. "You lot can finish without me. I'll be back for the next game. May I walk with you, sir?"

"Certainly."

They followed the path from the sickhall back to the plain. Lodin was itching to go back to the little bench in the corner of the smithy and get to work on another fitting for his arm, but the boy clearly wanted to speak to him.

"Sir–your hand–the thing you made. It will make it like having a normal hand again, won't it?"

"When I've made a few more fittings, I think so. It won't be as good as a real hand but I should be able to do a lot of things that I can't do at the moment."

Edan thought about this. "You invent things, don't you? Things that haven't been done before, to solve problems."

"Yes, I do–or I did, and I hope to be able to do so again. What is the problem you're thinking of?"

"My mother." Edan looked at the floor. "Her eyes. Can you help her?"

"Ah. Of course, I should have guessed. Eyes are difficult, Edan. I'm not sure what can be done to help her. I would love to, but I don't really know how."

"Will you think about it? Please, I mean."

"Yes, I will. For what it's worth, if I can possibly find a way of helping her you may be assured that I will do so." The boy opened his mouth, but shut it again awkwardly. "There's more?"

Edan blushed. "She likes you, you know. She likes that you

treat her like everyone else. She says you don't treat her like a blind person, just like a person who can't see."

Lodin waited.

"She loved my father very much. It's only two years since... Since he died. It still hurts her, how it happened."

Lodin thought he knew where this was going. "It leaves scars, that sort of thing, scars that do not heal quickly. But give it time. At first the memories sting, even the good ones, but as time goes on the sting wears away and the memories remain."

"The sting has not worn away for her yet, though."

"Nor for you, I think?"

"Nor for me. Sir... I do not mean to be impertinent, but you spend a lot of time with my mother."

So this is what he's getting at. Lodin cocked an eyebrow. "Are you asking me what my intentions are?"

"No!" Edan's face flamed. "Well..." He took a deep breath. "Well yes, I suppose I am asking just that. What are your intentions?"

"I have none," Lodin told him gently. "And unless I am mistaken, neither does your mother. She has told me a little about your father. She obviously loved him very much, and to me she does not sound ready to let go of him. I am not sure that she ever will, but that is not something that any of us can control or influence in any way. It happens or it does not. As for me, I enjoy spending time with her because she is an intelligent woman who has travelled to many places and seen many things, but if you are asking if I am romantically inclined towards her, then be reassured. I am not. For what it's worth, I once had a sister. Your mother reminds me very much of her."

"She is not here, your sister?" Edan fiddled with a rip in his sleeve.

"She died a long time ago, when I was about your age." Lodin squeezed the boy's shoulder. "I miss her though. She was good fun, and very quick. At first it hurt too much to think about her, but now remembering her makes me feel as if she is not entirely gone. It takes a bit of time, that's all."

"Do we have time? The Skral boys don't think so."

Lodin shrugged. "Who can tell? It was your mother who told me that we have to assume that there will be a tomorrow. I think she's right. We know it will be a hard, desperate fight, but sometimes you have to believe that it will all come right in the end."

They stood looking over the plain while Edan thought about this. Finally he turned to Lodin. "Thank you for talking to me, Maker. I was afraid you might laugh at me."

"But you asked anyway."

"My mother is all that I have left. I have to look after her."

Lodin nodded appreciatively. "Good man. I won't forget about her eyes though. If I can think of anything, I will let you know."

"Thank you, sir."

"Lodin."

"Lodin." The boy grinned suddenly. "And if you need anything, you know, for your new hand, come and find me. I know everyone here, and I can probably find you almost anything you need!"

"I shall take you up on that."

"I should get back. They'll be starting the next game..." Edan nodded to the craftsman and ran off to find his friends, and Lodin walked on to the Circle, where he could already see the bright flash that was Tiris, bobbing about in the grass before the entrance.

THE WIND GREW COLDER, and the sun began to carry less warmth. Autumn was nearly done, and winter beckoned. A slow trickle of arrivals had started—not refugees now, but the Skrals from the other islands coming together to defend their oldest clan-halls. The halls were crowded, but the numbers were not above two or three thousand Skral now, even including the women and oldsters.

Lodin was looking forward to Maran's return. Now that he had two or three useful fittings for his false arm, his curiosity about the Dragon's Teeth had become sharper than ever. He had a thousand questions to ask and he suspected that if anyone had the answers, it would be the bard.

Today he had come out to the Circle again with Tiris. The little bird fluttered down to the ground, investigating the clumps of grass and occasionally dashing off in chase of insects. Lodin watched his antics for a while but, as always, his attention was drawn to the towering stones.

He loved the way the light and shadows danced over them during the course of the day, and the way they never looked the same, as sunshine or cloud threw different parts of each stone into relief. Now the autumn mildness was fading from the plain, and every morning frost edged the grass more thickly. Ice-crystals were beginning to form on the great monoliths. He wrapped his furs more closely to him as best he could. He had yet to invent a fitting to make it easier.

"Lodin?"

The voice startled him, but realising who it was, he beamed. "Maran! It is good to see you, my friend." Lodin threw his arms around the bard, clapping him on the back with his good hand. "How was your journey? You have been missed in the sickhall–no songs, no music, and none of your improbable tales!"

"It doesn't seem to have done you much harm though. I leave you all weak and apathetic and come back to find you dashing about the plain!" Maran smiled, his blue eyes twinkling with mischief. "But what is this they tell me? You have made yourself a new hand?"

Lodin stepped back and pulled his cloak aside to show the leather sleeve. "Based on one devised by your own Master of Healing."

"And improved vastly, I see." Maran scrutinised the fitting closely as Lodin took off the hand he was using and re-fitted it again. "May I copy the details onto a scroll to send back for the Masters?"

"Certainly. There is more to do, though. I have only the most primitive fittings at the moment."

Maran nodded thoughtfully. "Well were you chosen Maker, my friend. It would seem that I have as much to ask you as to tell you! But what are you doing out here?"

"There is only so long a man can lie in a sickroom before he begins to believe that there is something wrong with him," Lodin said wryly. "I was beginning to think that it would be better for me to be up and doing anyway, and when I saw the Circle, I could not rest until I had had a closer look."

"Alaera says you are out here most days."

"Aye." The craftsman turned back to the stones with a frown. "It is an odd thing. Since my childhood I have dreamt of these stones. I know every nook and cranny of every stone. I have seen them from near and from far. I have seen them from above, even, but I have never been to this country before now, nor can I think of any painting or map that would have shown them. Now, at the ending of the world, I run to the last place where free men stand, and here is the circle of stones from my dream. I feel that there is something to be done here, some task that is meant for me and only me. It is a very odd thing."

"It is a very true thing, friend, for that is why I am sent to you."

"True? I dreamt it! To say it is true would be nonsense!" Lodin snorted.

"Nonsense or not, you dreamed of them and you are here. You dreamt of a task and here I am to give you just that. Let us go back to the warmth of the clan-hall, and I will tell you all about it. Apart from anything else, the sun is low in the sky and the day is cold enough to freeze the beard off a Clanfather."

Lodin shook his head. "What kind of Skral are you, Maran?

There are not many of your tribe who will even admit to feeling the cold."

Maran gestured grandly. "Ha! Warriors! Their brains are dulled by all the dents in their helmets. They think it makes them more manly to stand around in the snow and ice without grumbling. Me, I am a bard, a wise man—and the wise man knows that when it's cold the best place to be is by the fire with a mulled ale."

"I am no bard but to me your wisdom is obvious. So tell me about your journey. Where have you been the past couple of weeks?" Lodin fell into step beside his friend, his heart filled with that lightness that Maran's company brought him, and they made their way back across the plain to the clan-halls where fire and ale awaited them. Maran led the way into the great eating hall. Nodding to the ancient in her alcove, he pulled a couple of stools to the hearth and gestured to Lodin to sit.

As the bard went to fill a couple of tankards from the butt of ale, Lodin looked around the hall, long and low with a double row of tables and benches in between which fires burned in a long low pit. There were two great cooking hearths, one at either end, and it was in front of one of these that he now sat. The hearths were enormous, almost little rooms in their own right, and inset along the sides of them were the comfortable benches where the ancients sat. Too old to contribute in other ways, they sat and tended the fires, occasionally stirring the great bubbling cauldrons of stew or oatmeal that hung simmering over the heat.

Around the fires were little groups of stools like the ones he now sat on, and in the corner on a long trestle table were the platters and tankards used communally. There was no communal cutlery..

Maran returned and handed Lodin a tankard. In the alcove the ancient crooned wordlessly to herself, gazing mistily into the fire with age-clouded eyes.

"Thank you," Lodin said. "Skies above, but it's good to have you back! So you have heard all about Asri's flash of genius–now it's your turn. Tell me about your journey."

Maran took his seat by the fire, drank deeply, and began. "Seven days I travelled, at first on the plains and then over the snowfields to the Halls of Lore. The Clanfathers, the Mother of the Shantar and the Potentate of Gai Ren consulted with each other. They decided we needed to know more about the Ice Lord, and I was chosen to find out what the wisdom of the Skral could tell us. With my brothers and the elder Bards, or such of them as are left, I pored over scrolls and tablets going back a thousand years, but nowhere was there mention of such a being as the one we now face. There were wars, I grant you, and kings and empires rose and fell as they always have and always will. But even the most rapacious invader usually tried to keep what he had fought for, or at least raided it and then moved on. We did not once find anything similar to the death-dealing practices of the man we call the Ice Lord–and we did not find any mention of the black smoke that possesses him."

"Black smoke? I have not heard of that."

"It is why he is said to have many faces. He–or rather it–seems to possess people, moving from one body to the next in the form of black smoke. We have heard that tale several times and it is the only thing that remains consistent. Certainly we were looking for references to it at the Halls, but we found nothing, and time was pressing so after a while I left them searching, and went on my way." He sighed. "It was so good to be back among those old stone walls. In the entrance there is a great gnarled tree which, legend has it, was planted as an acorn on the day that the Founders laid the first stone. As the tree has grown in height and beauty, so have the Halls grown in wisdom and accumulated knowledge. I have spent many a day in the shade of the King's Tree, reading the old scrolls or composing songs and stories. I wish you could see it, Lodin–it is a place very dear to my heart–but I fear we have run out of time."

"What makes you think so?" Lodin set his tankard down. "Have you news of the Ice Lord?"

"After a fashion, yes, and I fear greatly that the Hall is something that he will not be able to resist destroying. All our knowledge, our Lore—nearly everything that it means to be Skral is preserved or recorded in that one place. It will not last long after he arrives."

"He is coming, then? It is certain?"

"It is."

Lodin gazed into the red of the embers, seeing in the darting flames the fire that had consumed his own city, his friends... "How could you possibly know that?"

Maran took a long drink before continuing. "I will tell you, but that of which I speak is the most sacred of our ancestral places. In more normal times it is forbidden to speak of it to one who was not born of Skral ancestors, but these are strange times. Even we Skral have come to realise that our normal customs cannot continue as they have done for countless years. The Clanfathers have given me permission to tell of this to a few specific people but it does not come easily to speak of Skral secrets in the company of an outlander, even a friend such as you."

Lodin settled back in his seat. "Take your time. I can wait while you find the right words."

"The only thing we found in the archives was one scroll, very old and fragile. It was barely legible and for some time I sat with the most ancient of the Masters while he translated from the most obscure dialect of Old Skral. It was a tale handed down through many generations from the time just after the dragons left, and though there were fragments of the story here and there, it made little sense. At the end, however, we discovered that the guardians of the clans knew all. It was a fragile thread to follow, but the only clue we had to follow.

"And so it was that I left the Halls of Lore and journeyed on for some days. It was not easy going and the dogs were tired. We had already travelled far and now our path led for another few days over the plain. When we hit the snowline, I fitted the runners to the sled and another day's travel took us to the ships' graveyard, the home of those presences who guard and guide our people."

"A graveyard?"

"Exactly what it sounds like. Our ships are home and shelter to our clan for generations. They protect us from wind and wave, and with their sails flared they fly us over the water, free as gulls in the sunshine. It is difficult to express it. They are not *things* like sleds are, but vital beings that love us and are beloved. No, perhaps it is more fundamental than that. They are part of the clan, like a wise grandparent, strong and always there for us. They are so much a part of our identity that the idea of travelling on a ship belonging to some other clan is slightly shameful. They are made of the finest iron-oak that lasts for lives and lives of men, but after many decades the wood becomes weak and the ship too old to ride the wild seas safely. There is a ceremony when the keel of the new ship is laid, and the figurehead is made from the base of the mast from the old ship, to ensure continuity."

Maran shifted on his chair, staring deep into the embers of the fire. "For a year or two the old ship is only used for easy journeys while the new is tested and finished. Eventually there is a great ceremony where the new ship is launched and the old is brought out of the water. As a sign of respect, the whole clan gathers. The old ship is mounted on a great frame with many wheels and many ropes, and we drag the ship across the plain to the graveyard. In the olden days this took a week or so as the ships were small and light, but as our shipbuilding has improved, our ships have become larger and heavier. Nowadays it is more likely to take us a month or more."

"You drag it there yourselves? That's an immense undertaking. You don't have horses, do you? Or oxen? Do the other clans help?"

"They don't pull the ropes, because it is not their ship," Maran explained. "They do help by bringing food and helping set up camp and light fires, that sort of thing. The ship is pulled to the hill where it will be set to rest, and everyone helps to shift it off the frame and settle it in its place. Few words are said there, but when all have taken their leave of the ship, we come back to the clan-halls and rest for a week. You are right that it is a huge undertaking but in times of peace it only happened every couple of centuries so it was a great honour to be involved."

"In times of war though... You have lost ships?"

"Yes." Maran looked away. "We have lost six of our ships in the past two years."

"Six? To different clans?"

"Yes, but still it is many. We cannot build new ones quickly enough to replace them. We have used all the keels which had been laid down to season and if we make new ships now it will have to be of new, untested wood. They would be weak, and would not last long but in any case, from what I saw, I do not think that we will have time to try it."

Lodin regarded his companion gravely, whilst in the alcove the ancient rocked and sang, her crooning an eerily tuneless counterpoint to the bard's tale.

"I went to the ships' graveyard to ask the spirits of the ships to grant us counsel in this time of death and destruction. Mostly they do not answer but this time they did. What I saw gave me much to consider. In the centre of the ships' graveyard is a pool of water, salty as tears, and as I looked into it, I saw the beginnings of the creature they call the Ice Lord." Maran leaned back in his seat, thoughtful. "What do you know of the Ice Lord, Lodin?"

"Little enough that is certain, and much that is probably untrue."

Maran nodded. "Until now we have never known where he came from. It was quite sudden, some years ago, that we heard that a King who had once been a petty bully had started a war which took over the world. The ships have shown me more though, and that was not the beginning of it. It all started with a man who lived in a forest. His name is not remembered..."

A bell rang, and Maran stood. "Time has flowed faster than I realised. That is the bell to bid us to the council table. I have to report to the Elders now. It is a long tale, and one you should hear—come with me and you may all listen at once and save me a re-telling."

"Don't worry. I'll wait till you've finished with the Elders."

"Not so, my friend. I was sent to fetch you along." Maran pushed his stool back into the corner.

Lodin was a bit taken aback, but he stumbled after the younger man as he led the way out of the warm, dark food hall and into the Great Hall, where the Clanfathers were assembled. There were twelve remaining Clanfathers, men of a variety of ages and heights. All wore their hair in the warrior's braid and had the stocky shoulders of those who had spent many years hefting axe and oar. They were headed by a tall warrior whose jutting nose would have dominated his face if not for the grey beard bushing out from a luxuriant moustache to separate into braids over his belly. Shrewdness glinted in his eyes, but he had a ready laugh which boomed out across the hall as he made some joke to the other Clanfathers.

With them were outlanders. There was an old woman dressed in shapeless black, with grey hair and a stare as hard as diamonds, and a short, graceful man dressed in robes of brightly coloured silk.

"That is the Mother of the Shantar—they have a woman to lead them!" Maran whispered in wondering tones as they drew near the distinguished group. "And the little man is the Potentate of Gai Ren."

They were gathered around the table deep in conversation but as the bard approached, they looked up. "Maran, did you find him?"

"This is he."

They introduced themselves to the baffled craftsman, and gestured him to a seat.

"Go on then, lad, tell us the rest of it."

Maran stood in thought for a moment and then began to describe what he had seen in the pool at the centre of the ships' graveyard. And as the young bard told his tale, Lodin saw it as vividly as if he had been given the vision as well.

THE ICE LORD

Aman who lived in a forest found a strange creature lying in the snow. It was a wizened little beast with naked grey skin. It wriggled and squalled, but seemed helpless.

He picked it up and looked at it closely. "I have never seen your like before, and I have been trapping in these forests for many a year. Let us find out what sort of pup you are, and what beastie you grow into. If you have a decent pelt on you, it'll make an expensive pair of gloves for some pretty lady or other."

The beast sank its long rat-like teeth into his hand. He yelped, and threw it to the ground but as it hissed at him, he hesitated. "There's many a creature that would have earned a swift death for that, but there have been sightings of the silkenfox in these parts, and no-one has seen their young. If it were to prove a silkenfox, what riches I should earn. And then, if I should find another to breed it with... Yes, then the townsfolk would not look down upon me, nor Katya be so churlish in the bed!"

Taking off his cloak, he wrapped the creature in it so that it could neither wriggle nor bite. He took it home and kept it in a wicker hutch by the hearth where it would grow fine and large.

The Spring thaw came, bringing as it always did the first great Gather at the local town. It was a bare little place, with few shops and one hostelry, but always after the thaw all the trappers and traders gathered to restock with food after the winter and to trade their pelts. Trappers set up in the same place year after year, and the women went from one stall to the next to catch up on the gossip. This time the market started but there was no sign of the trapper or his wife Katya.

"Has anyone seen Katya's baby yet?" one of the women demanded. "Last time I saw him he was barely born, a sweet little thing with the most beautiful curls, and such clear blue eyes! They had not agreed on a name for him. I suggested that they call him Iniska, after my old uncle. I yearn to see little Iniska again!"

"They are not here." Larek's wife was as abrupt as ever. "That ne'er-do-well promised my husband a load of bearskins and beaver-pelts, to be delivered at the first fair of the season, and do you see his stall here? No, neighbour, it is as I told Larek. There are some debts which you might as well write off as soon as you've handed over the money. We'll not be seeing them here for a while, I'll warrant."

Behind her back one of the children imitated her sour face and had his ears boxed by his mother, but not very hard. Larek's wife was not popular.

By the end of the three days of the Gather there was still no sign of them, and concern was growing. Eventually Larek held up his hands in exasperation.

"Ladies! I am sure that all is well with them, that Katya has a cold or that the baby has scraped his knee or some other trifling ailment which has prevented them from travelling. However, to allay your anxiety I will drive to their homestead myself and see why they are not here."

"You're a good man, Larek!" the grand-dames called as they went past, nodding to each other. "He's a capable man, too. If anything is awry, he will mend it or come back for others to help him."

"You are too kind, ladies!" In fact, this was true. Larek liked the trapper well enough, and the wife was easy on the eye, but it was not a trip he would have considered making had there not been the question of the bearskins and beaver-pelts to consider. He clambered onto his cart and set off, wondering what his options were if the trapper had nothing to offer.

IT WAS NEARLY DUSK when the clatter of the cart's wheels sounded along the quiet village, and from many homes the women came out to cluster in the street. Larek pulled up beside the hostelry and helped a man down from the cart. He was wrapped in a blanket, stick-thin and staggering. Larek guided him into the hostelry and sat him on a chair by the fire.

"Bring out the strong spirits!" Larek's shout reverberated through the open door and across the street. His mule, white-eyed and skittish, let out a hideous bray and then fled.

Larek snatched up the bottle and downed nearly a third of the raw, burning alcohol before pouring some into a glass for his companion. He lifted the glass to the other man's lips and the blanket fell back to reveal his face, distorted with agony and horror. Larek tipped the glass, but the man simply sat slack-lipped and the alcohol spilled down his chin.

"What has happened to him?" Larek's wife lost her sharpness of tone, looking at that expression. "Where are the others?"

"Dead. *Very* dead." Larek downed the rest of the glass himself. "Looked like wild animals did it, probably some time ago."

"And he just left them there?"

Larek drank again. "There wasn't enough left whole to bury; just flies and bone fragments and the smell of death, so strong it was a greasy taste in the back of the mouth."

The trapper moved then, looking around him slowly. "Where...?" His voice grated with lack of use.

"It's me, Larek. I brought you to the town." He put the glass of spirits to the man's lips again. "That was no place to stay."

"The town?"

"You need to be with people. Lots of people to look after you. You look like death warmed over."

The trapper seemed to pass out and fell forward. Larek and his wife lunged to catch him but he was utterly limp. In the chaos of people trying to help, no-one noticed the faint black tendrils of smoke that escaped from the trapper's gaping mouth and disappeared into Larek's skin.

"He's dead." Larek straightened, and his voice was harsh and unfamiliar.

Larek's wife stared as the trapper fell to dust before their eyes. "What in all the hells just happened?" The trader smiled, and there was something about that smile that scared her. The others gathered in the room began to make their excuses and leave, muttering about witchcraft.

"Larek?"

A FEW WEEKS after the Gather, another trader arrived at the town. He was puzzled to see that many of the decorations that were normally up for the Gather still hung limply, faded and tattered by the weather. No-one was to be seen, but wild dogs slunk in and out of the houses as he passed, and the crows sitting on the fence watched him all the way down the street with a proprietorial air. He went to knock on the door of a friend's house, but at his knock the door swung open, letting forth a terrible, rank smell, and revealing the remains of the family, scattered about the room.

Reeling back, he went into the next house and the next, and to his horror, all he found was building after building of corpses. At last he made his way into the hostelry in search of alcohol, and there he found the one man remaining alive, whose face was remarkably horrible to look at. That one man collapsed into a pile of dust, and the little tendrils of black smoke sank into the trader, who left that site of death the following day to continue his journey onto the next town.

And so a trail of death and horror spread over the land, always starting with the arrival of one person whose face was terrible to look at, and never leaving more than one survivor, who would leave in search of new victims. As stories spread of people who came to visit their families or traders and found only the sites of old horrors, fear spread, and there were those who would not allow strangers into their towns or who fled at the first signs of unfamiliarity. As time passed, their tales began to coalesce into a story strong enough to pay heed, but by then it was too late.

Eventually just such a man staggered into the camp of an army on the plains where the horsemen made war, one tribe on another. Thinking he must be an enemy spy, they took him out to be hanged. As the rope snapped his neck the assembled soldiers were startled to see great ribbons of black smoke come pouring out of his body. The smoke felt its way across the field to where the King of the tribe, a ruthless man, stood enjoying the spectacle. The black smoke enveloped him, and when he opened his eyes, there was a monster looking out of them.

MARAN CONTINUED, "The King waged war on the tribes nearest to him, and slaughter and blood washed over the land. There were those who opposed him, but many more who did not. Terror washed like a deadly tide before him, and fear of him made strong men weak. His armies swelled with the assimilation of each tribe, and when all the tribes on the plain were conquered and all the plain burned, he attacked a city, and another. He has conquered half the world, and still he is not content. He does not appear to want to hold that which he has conquered, but destroys the land and the livestock, kills the people and leaves the earth smoking and barren behind him. It is rumoured that he seeks to end all life, and pare the whole world back to bare soil. His face is becoming more and more hideous to look at. He is hardly recognisable as human. Those nearest to him call him the Ice Lord. Several times in battle his body has received a fatal wound and has crumbled into dust, but always there is the black smoke which takes over another body. He they call the Ice Lord at any given point is merely the host in whose body those strange ribbons of black smoke reside. It always talks with the same voice, like blades over slate, and death and horror look out of its eyes. It is unclear what the black smoke is but it seems to be some sort of parasite, always looking for a new host body in which to take residence, and getting stronger with every new host.

"The Ice Lord has acquired a group of officers loyal to him. They call themselves the Ice Guard. He required them all to prove themselves by slaughtering their own friends and family so that they have no reason to hold back in battle. The wars are ever more horrific and country after country has fallen to them. If the Ice Lord and his armies are not to succeed in their quest for domination, something must be done."

There was a silence in the hall after Maran finished speaking. A small crowd had drawn near to find out what tale Maran was telling, but this one had no happy ending for them.

The Clanfather of the Tusken Seal rolled his eyes. "We know that something must be done, lad. That's why you find you us here in a hall together, Skral and *unSkral* alike."

"*UnSkral?* You are too flattering." The dry comment came from the Mother, whose matriarchal presence in the hall was greatly disconcerting to the warrior Skral, not least as she knew a surprisingly large amount about them and their language.

"No offence meant."

"It would be pointless to take offence at such details in the face of the threat that faces us." She shrugged. "Shantar and Skral working together is a twist of fate fit to make the gods laugh, but it must and will be so, for otherwise the world will drown in blood."

"Indeed, and we are grateful for the hospitality of your halls," the Potentate of Gai Ren chimed. "With so much of the world fleeing or in exile, there are few other places we could have gathered."

"With the freedom of the seas left to us it matters little if all the rest of the world goes up in flames, for the Ice Lord shall not catch us with his potbellied sluggards of ships!" Edan's friend was shushed in shocked tones and shoved back behind his father for daring to speak of any ships in such coarse tones.

"We have decisions to make without the benefit of your cheek, young Ranfrith!" Tusken Seal snapped. "Everyone, leave us be. That which we decide you need to know, we will tell you. Be about your business and leave us to ours!" The Clanfathers glared round and with shuffling reluctance the people quietly exited.

When they were left to themselves again, the Mother continued. "The question is, how do we fight the Ice Lord? We cannot kill it–we can kill the body but it just takes over another and becomes stronger in the process. We cannot defeat armies of that size with the few fighters we have, either."

"We can attack his ships." Tusken Seal spoke reluctantly. His people valued little above a glorious death in battle, and this slow rear-guard action felt shameful. "That young pup Ranfrith might be cheeky, but he has a point. On the sea we can sail better, faster, fight more artfully than the Ice Lord's ships can; but he has endless numbers and we are few. At the moment it is all we can do to keep this island clear. We cannot engage him on the mainland."

"I do not think that there is anything of this world that can contain or damage the Ice Lord, for he is not of it."

Tusken Seal turned to the Mother with a grimace of distaste. "You have information on this?"

"Only that much. My sources can tell me little more than that."

The atmosphere prickled with an odd tension and Lodin sent a questioning glance at Maran as Tusken Seal paced back and forth.

The bard murmured. "She has dreams that are true, or finds things by scrying. It is not something the Clanfathers can accept but her knowledge has proved true several times. So she implies spies have told her and they pretend they believe it, and the decencies are preserved."

Lodin snorted.

The Potentate gestured helplessly. "If there is nothing of this world that can hurt him, are we to despair? Surely we cannot give up?"

The Mother snorted. "Of course not! I said there was nothing *of this world* that could contain him, not that nothing could contain him."

"What in seven hells do you mean, woman?" Tusken Seal was losing patience.

"The graveyard of ships to which yon young man has been has already supplied you with much. The ships that lie there now were not always rotten hulks."

Tusken Seal leapt to his feet, outraged. "How dare you speak so of our clanhomes, the vessels of our spirits?"

The Mother held up her hand. "I meant no disrespect, Skral. My apologies if it sounded so. But these warrior spirits, you sent to them for guidance."

"It is unseemly to talk of it in front of a woman!" Tusken Seal saw her expression and subsided slightly. "Yes, we did."

"Have you asked them for more than guidance? Have you asked them for protection?"

"Protection?"

"Those ships are more than wood. They are life and battle and blood and clanspirit. For many lives of men, each ship there protected its clan from the storm, and from death in the waters. What is this if not a storm of mighty proportions? No weapons *that are of this world* can harm or contain the Ice Lord. It would be foolish not to ask for help from any who can give it. Ask the ships!"

"You have seen this?" Tusken Seal was frozen with the onset of sudden hope.

"My sources suggested it." The Mother twinkled at him.

There was a silence, and then the Potentate spoke. "Let us send those who are best prepared to take up that guidance."

"Warriors?" Tusken Seal cocked an eyebrow.

"Artificers and loresmen." The Potentate looked from one to the other. "Men who will best understand and be able to communicate what they see, and men who can make whatever is needed to contain the Ice Lord. Who is your most cunning artificer?"

"Artificer?" Tusken Seal shrugged. "My people make weapons and ships of great beauty, but if you speak of gadgets and devices, we are not clever in that way."

"Nor are the Shantar, especially." The Mother nodded. "So shall we send the Maker here?"

The Potentate nodded agreement. "Lodin, would you be prepared to go to the ships' graveyard if we asked it of you?"

"Me?" Lodin was totally unprepared for this.

The Mother smiled at the look on his face. "Why don't you think it over?"

RETURNING TO THE FOOD HALL, Lodin sat down on his bench. "That was a lot to take in."

"I am aware that much of it will be troublesome to your beliefs. If you do not believe in dreams or spirits, this must sound like madness to you." Maran paused in thought. "I will not try to persuade you to believe, but you have dreamt all your life of the

Circle and you have now found it. We have need of a man of your abilities. If you are amenable to going to the graveyard of ships with me and fashioning that which we are guided to make, you will be well paid, I will see to that--"

"Money is not the issue." Lodin swilled the ale around in his tankard. "Your clansmen have taken me in, healed me, fed me–I owe them a blood-debt. If it can be repaid in this way, so much the better."

"You will come to the graveyard?"

Lodin drank deeply before replying. "Bard, I think you and your people are mad to pay heed to dreams and spirits, but that is nothing to do with me. If we go on this wild-goose chase, I am fully convinced that we will come back empty-handed and looking more than a little foolish, but if it is important to your people that I go, then I will undertake to do so. After all, I have little else of interest to be getting on with, so yes, I will go along– if only to discover what quirk of fate has produced a Skral who acts like a sensible human being."

THE SHIPS' GRAVEYARD

They spent the next couple of days packing. The late spell of
fine weather had finally passed. The sun hid and the clouds
drew in. Without sunshine the shortness of the days was more
pronounced and Lodin realised that autumn had finally surren-
dered to the icy fingers of winter. He was not looking forward to
experiencing the ice and snow they had here, but the thought of
travelling with Maran kept him cheerful. He was drawn to the
bard, and found himself wanting to know more about him. A
shared journey would be a good way to spend time together.

Alaera bustled between himself and Maran, finding out what
clothes and supplies Lodin would need and taking him to the
people who could provide them. Finally they met the Potentate,
the Mother and a few of the Clanfathers for last-minute
instructions.

While Lodin was in conversation with the Mother, Tusken
Seal took Maran to one side. "You know how important this is,
boy."

"I do."

"That which has long been treasured amongst the Skral, that

which makes us Skral, all that will be lost if the Skral are lost with it."

"I know it, Clanfather."

Tusken Seal hesitated. "It is hard for us to say it but we have agreed, the other Clanfathers and I, that if the shipspirits wish it so, the Maker should be allowed to enter the Heart of Wood."

Maran's eyebrows shot up. "The world is indeed changing!"

"Aye, lad. I am too old to keep up with it." Tusken Seal glanced over at the Mother. "But when races appoint women to lead them, and foreigners are allowed into our most sacred places, it must surely be the end of the world! Who knows what we will be faced with next?"

"If it is merely letting go of our traditions, we may count ourselves lucky, I suspect."

Tusken Seal shot him a glance. "You know something?"

"No. I fear something. But I would not spread a fear until I know that it is not all in my imagination."

Tusken Seal nodded. "Well, travel safely, and bring back what answers you can."

Maran and Lodin made their farewells and, climbing onto the sled, they were off. The dogs were excited and soon the Clan-halls disappeared from view behind them. Lodin, having never driven a sled before, was merely a passenger. Maran, a seasoned traveller, knew not to tire the dogs too much this early in the journey. He slowed them to a more sustainable pace and they made what progress they could, travelling as late into the evening as the light allowed.

The journey was arduous. The skies were dull and the wind vicious. The oiled leathers they wore kept the worst of the wind and drizzle off them, but the cold sapped their strength and made Lodin's arm ache. Maran was hopeful that something would come of their mission, however, and his high spirits were infectious. Lodin listened to his tales and jokes, and told some Lyrian tales in return; the travelling was easier because of their enjoyment of each other's company.

When they left the chilly plains, they changed the wheels for runners and set off into the snow and ice of central Skralland. As the evenings closed in, they sat round the fire and chatted about the people and cunning artifices that Lodin had seen, or Maran played the harp until his fingers were cold and stiff. Then he would wrap it carefully in its cover and then sing songs of such beauty that they forgot about the night and the cold and the exhaustion of the journey. Lost in Maran's songs, time fled unnoticed and Lodin's heart was the lighter for it.

Eventually, when the fire burned low they retired to their tent, huddling close in the cold so that they could set both sets of furs under them and both blankets over. Between the shared warmth of their bodies and the doubled warmth of their bedding, they slept through the icy nights as relaxed and snug as children.

On the last morning, Lodin woke early. Warm and comfortable under the bedding, he lay contentedly. As light began to filter into the tent, he watched his companion's face go from a silhouette to a living shape. *Maran is a work of art in his own right.* Savouring every contour, he was pierced through by the beauty of that face. *As a craftsman, if ever I carved something so perfect I would consider my life's ambition reached.* The hollows at temple and throat, the graceful feather touch of eyelashes on cheek–there was nothing that could be improved, for it was flawless. In a world that had so suddenly filled with the ugliness of war this quiet, warm moment of peace was a balm to his soul.

A potent mix of happiness and dismay filled him. *No,* he breathed to himself. *Not now! Not this one!* But his heart swelled inescapably. With utter inevitability, Lodin realised that he loved the bard, had loved him for some time, could not un-love him, no matter how hard he might try. He had tried not to fall in love at all, but he was drawn to Maran's joy in life like a flower growing to the sun, and with as little choice.

Foolish, with the Ice Lord on his way. More foolish still to develop feelings for a Skral! Maran might not be a warrior but he was a Skral, and in this country love was a woman's indulgence. *Between men there is fighting and drinking ale, but nothing more intimate. Nothing! This will never, can never develop into anything.* The thought was a thorn in his breast, but was balanced with the precarious happiness of being so close to the man who, he now realised, he loved. It was a dangerous pleasure though. *I must never let it show.*

For a moment he wanted to weep for the loss of Lyria–there, this would have been a happy ending, not the beginning of a sweet torture. But he would not do that right now. Sheltered in this one precious moment as the first rays of sun outside painted everything in the tent with a ruddy glow. Lodin was content just to gaze upon the young man who felt like the other half of his soul. *No, more than content. Happy.*

Eventually Maran woke. He stretched luxuriously and shuddered at the cold outside the covers. "Another cold morning! Are you hungry?"

The day began, following the pattern of the previous three. They breakfasted and packed up the tent. Lodin swapped the knife fitting on his arm for a more generic one with two curved hooks which curved like fingers, and a straight bar that hooked between them, spring-loaded for grip. He struggled to pull up the pegs that held the oiled cloth of the tent in place. *This one is fine for holding things lightly, but I'll need to fashion a stronger spring to get a better grip.* The fitting gave and he staggered backwards. *I could add leather pads, or reshape the prongs. In any case, if I make a wooden cradle that cups my arm from stump to elbow, I should be able to pull or push things with more force than is possible with the leather straps.* He dropped the peg into the pile next to him and went on to the next one. Maran watched unobtrusively, ready to help if asked but with instinctive sympathy letting the craftsman work to get things done.

Finally all was packed. Mounting the sled and hitching up the dogs, they set off again. For a time, the sled was silent apart from the occasional yipping of the dogs and the swish of the sled over the snow.

Maran glanced across at his friend. "You're quiet. Are you in pain?"

"Not from my arm. Distraction would be welcome though. Tell me of the Skrals. Tell me of your culture. It is so different from Lyria. There is so much that I do not understand."

Maran laughed. "Ah, my friend, what can I tell you? We are warriors, we Skral. We have always been and I cannot imagine the day when Skrals lay down their weapons. Me, I am not a fighter and I've never felt this mad rage that turns Skrals into berserkers, madmen who do not notice wounds in battle and go to glory in short order. I would make a very poor warrior, but my weapons are not swords and axes. For the Skral, the bard is at once law-maker and lore-holder, wise man and Fool–we remember, we teach and we entertain. For our whole people, we remember what has gone before and what will come after, and we sing it at the Skral hearths so that each clan has the memories of its forefathers to guide it. But fortunately for us, because all the warriors keep getting bashed on the helmets with axes, it rattles all the wisdom out of their skulls and so they need those of us who are too puny or too sensible to fight to give them the answers they need!"

"And what do you sing for them?"

"Of many things, my friend. Of the gods and their adventures, of clans and their histories, of the future and what it means to be Skral." The merriment faded from his face. "And more recently, we sing the death songs of peoples and clans alike, of the death of all things and of what it is we fight for."

"And what do you fight for?"

Maran was silent for a moment as the dogs yipped, the snow hissed and the cold bit at their cheeks. He reached up to wipe his eyes, which were watering from the icy air. "We all fight for different things. Many are fighting for survival or revenge, because there is nothing else to do but surrender. The Skral are fighting because that is what they do, and they don't know how else to react to all this death and war. But me, I fight for life. Not just to survive—I mean I fight for life and love and joy and sharing. Togetherness and compassion, all the things that make it worth being alive. These are what the Ice Lord would take from us. These are what his soldiers have lost, men who are already dead without realising it, who have lost what it is to be human. These are what we need to save from this unholy mess. And that is why I am heading across this frozen waste now, to do what I can in the service of life and hope. But you, Lodin, why do you fight?"

Lodin squinted in the harsh brightness as the sun came out from behind the clouds and glinted off the crystals across the snowfield. "I have seen my friends killed, my country burned and my livelihood taken from me. I have lost my arm to the unprovoked warmongering of the Ice Lord, and have fled into exile in fear of my life. I have survived this far on stubbornness. It was all very simple. But now I am losing my way."

"Losing your way?"

"It is all so confusing. My country has gone, its culture smashed to a million pieces and its people scattered, but here at the end of the world, all of that is lost amongst so much other destruction. I cannot see how it can end in any way other than death and burning for all of us. And yet it makes this present moment so much clearer and more vivid that each glint of sun on the snow is as precious as gems. I am not thinking of anything else any more. The sled is whispering through the snow to a destination which is mysterious to me, and I am waiting for a task I was given in a dream. That is not a situation I have ever been in before."

"You will not lose your way, though, I am certain of it."

"How can you be so sure?"

"My friend, you are accompanied by the best bard in all Skralland!" Maran was only half in jest. "I will keep you on the right path."

The sled bumped and jolted as they drew near to an immense snow-covered hill, and eventually Maran called the dogs to a halt. "From here we go on foot."

The hill was cloven deeply, and they made their way to the gap in the cliffs. The path wound inwards in wide, smooth curves.

Lodin frowned. "The proportions are strange on this path, as if it were made for giants."

"In a way, it was. It is a graveyard of ships. If the path were any smaller, how should they get through?"

They followed the path until it came out into a vast bowl-shaped valley. Snow lay thickly on the ground. As his eyes adjusted to the bright sunshine, Lodin saw that the sides of the bowl were made up of a series of terraces, covered with small hillocks. They were of different sizes but all were long and thin. Lodin suddenly realised just how many of them there were.

Here under the shroud of snow lay ships that had sheltered clans of the Skral for countless years. Some of those at the bottom had collapsed in on themselves with age but up on the higher terraces the ships were less battered. Then, at the top, four that were badly smashed, along with two burnt, blackened shells, shockingly dark against the snow.

There was no wind. It was very still and silent, but not an empty silence. A sense of raw outrage and grief clutched at Lodin's throat as if he had no right to see those derelict hulls. He felt the weight of many watchful presences, and it was not a comfortable sensation.

"Come."

Lodin followed his friend closely through the skeletal vessels, along the slowly widening pathway until it ended in a flat space where thirteen keels lay intertwined, the remains of their ribs so interwoven that it made an enclosure. They were ancient beyond belief. All Skral ships had a figurehead carved into the shape of some incredible beast, but these were so weathered that their shapes were long worn away. The only details that could be seen were the black glints deep in the eye-pits, which watched him, hostile.

Maran walked round the intertwined keels. "This is the Heart of Wood itself, and our most sacred place. Do as I do and follow."

Warily, Lodin stepped over the keel to enter. As he did so, his clothing brushed against the uprights on either side of him and suddenly he was frozen in place.

"Skral ships, vessels of our spirits, I beg your attention." Maran's voice rang out, overloud in the silence. "This man is *unSkral* but he is not of those who have scarred our ships. He comes to aid us in our fight against the ship-killers. I pray you, let him pass."

Slowly, reluctantly, Lodin felt himself released and stumbled forward into the Heart of Wood.

Maran held up a hand. "The ships have allowed much to let you enter. Best to stay silent and watch until summoned."

Summoned? Lodin shifted uneasily. Until they had entered this valley he had believed that this was a waste of time, but he could feel the power here on his skin as if it were snowburn and his disbelief was fading fast. He took his place in the centre of the wooden structure next to Maran as the bard set polished metal mirrors to catch and focus the sunlight that slanted through the shattered ribs of wood. The beams of light were all focussed on the little pool of water in the exact centre of the Heart of Wood.

"Ships, guardians and protectors of our people, we have asked much counsel of you, and have come away the wiser. Now we are in desperate straits. Country after country has fallen, whole peoples are slain and scattered, animals slaughtered and fields burned. No-one and nothing of this earth can stop the Ice Lord, and it is coming to this island to finish the Skral. Our armies are few and his are vast. They are not honourable fighters, nor will these be the fights to win us entry in to the Halls of the Forefathers. There is no glory in this war, only despair. This is not the way that the Skrals wish to leave the world."

The sense of anguish and helplessness emanating from the ships became more intense now, searingly so.

Maran continued. "You have shown us that the Ice Lord wishes to bring about the end of the world. We cannot kill him, and nothing on this earth can even contain him. We are at a loss to know what to do or whether it is time simply to acknowledge that the Skral people have come to an end.

"We do not know what to do, and so we come to you. You are spirits not of the earth. You have spent centuries protecting our people. Once again, we come to you for aid. Can you guide us? Can you guard us? We must find a way to stop this being from sending the whole world to such a death that the Halls of the Forefathers are closed to us forever."

There was a silence. The wind hissed over the snow, and the sun glinted through the gaps in the wood. Where sunbeams hit the polished metal mirrors the bard had placed so carefully, it shed a soft light over the pool in the middle of the circle of beams.

And then one solitary drop of water fell from the arched wood, sparkling in the sunshine, and broke the mirror of the pool beneath into a dance of colours. As the ripples faded and the water subsided into stillness again, there was something odd about that reflection.

The colours are wrong. Lodin watched, fascinated, as the picture slowly coalesced and this time it was not the reflected ship-skeletons criss-crossing above the pool...

"LODIN? Lodin, man, are you all right?"

The craftsman opened his eyes slowly. His vision swam and settled. *A roofing of beams. The glare of the sun. Maran.* Lodin sat up with an effort. "What happened?"

"You tell me!" Maran helped him stand, and they staggered out of the Heart of Wood. "You looked in the pool, and you wept. Then you fell in a heap and I haven't been able to get any sense out of you ever since. Are you well?"

"Yes... No... Why is it so cold?"

"It's cold because you've been lying in the snow and the sun is nearly down. I hope that you have some answers, because the spirits didn't tell me a damn thing."

Lodin did not answer.

"Come on, let's get back to the tent. If we have to, we'll try again tomorrow." Maran put an arm round his friend and took him back to the tent, where the bard lit a fire. He heated the last of the ale, and the two of them sat in silence. They ate some dried meat, fed the dogs, and as the sun fell below the horizon, clambered into the tent and rolled up in their furs to sleep, back to back.

For a while all was quiet, but in the darkness tears were coursing down Lodin's cheeks and his breathing grew ragged with sobs.

"Lodin, tell me what you saw." The furs went slack as Maran turned towards his friend. "Is it a lost cause? Will the world end?"

"No..."

Maran put his arms around the craftsman, holding him as he would a child.

Lodin wept unashamedly. Eventually he subsided and lay trying to make sense of it all. "They showed me Lyria, the fall of the Court and of a million other countries like my own. They showed me the death of a whole world, and the burning of the last green field. There were no plants or birds or animals, just that monster standing there. And when the plants were gone the air grew thin, and the creatures in the sea were poisoned and floated to the surface. Everything that was alive was destroyed utterly and when the world was a dead rock with stinging dust blowing in the wind, the body he was using fell to dust and black smoke expanded to choke even the air. That is the end to which will we come." Lodin's voice trembled.

"Is there nothing that we can do to stop this?"

"Yes. Yes, there is. There is the Heart of Wood, and there is the Circle."

"What does that mean?"

Lodin cleared his throat and rolled out of his friend's embrace, throwing off the covers to sit upright. *I cannot stand to be in his arms for a second longer. It is breaking my heart. And I can't even tell him all of what I saw...* "They said that with a Heart of Wood and walls of water the Dragon's Teeth by the clan-halls can be made into a trap from which the Ice Lord will be unable to escape. To protect the clans they once carried over the deeps, the ship-spirits have agreed to move. I am to rebuild the Heart of Wood within the Dragon's Teeth."

"To move them?" Maran paused for a long moment, awed. "I don't know how we are to do that. And they have spoken to one who is not a Skral—such a thing has never been heard of! These are strange times, my friend...." He hesitated. "Was it the vision of the end of the world that caused you such sorrow?"

"No." Lodin tried to keep his voice light but even to him it sounded full of tears. "No, that was only a part of it. There will be so much death and so many sacrifices to be made, win or lose. There is no happy ending, whoever wins. It makes me wonder why we are fighting."

"How can you talk like that?" Maran flared, and it was the first real anger that the craftsman had ever seen in the bard. "Life is sacred! If what we do saves one life, it is worth everything! Remember that the countries are not dead yet—there will be bands of rebels and refugees scattered about in hiding. My people are sheltering many outlanders on this island alone. Once the terror has gone people will start reappearing from hills and mountains and woods, and from ships on the sea, and all sorts of places where they are hiding in fear for their lives. I have no idea how we are to get thirteen ship-skeletons from here to the plains in time, nor how we entice the Ice Lord into the Heart of Wood, but if this is what the spirits tell us, this we will do! And we will do it in defence of life, and hope, and happiness. And of love, Lodin."

"Love?" Lodin stammered before he could stop himself.

"Yes, of love."

Lodin was heartily thankful that the burning of his cheeks could not be seen in the dark.

"You Lyrians, you are a strange people, so open." Maran sat up, pulling the furs close around him. "I think that is why you are such great craftsmen and artists, because your emotions are as finely-crafted as your sculptures. The Skral are not so. Among them, it is considered a little womanly just to be a bard because emotions, which are so important in what we do, are among the weapons of the woman. You, your emotions are not weapons, but tools, and they put the heart into what you make. I think that you and I are as similar in some ways as we are different in others."

"What do you mean?" Lodin could barely breathe. *If only Maran was Lyrian, it would be so simple. I would tell him of the need that makes my heart clench in my chest, and ask about his feelings, and we could share the joy of togetherness. But in these cold islands men look upon each other only as brothers or rivals.*

Maran went on, "We are similar in our love for life, and in how we instil it into that which we make. I have only known you for a short time, but I feel that you and I fit together as neatly as the planks in a hull. We are as brothers born from the same birthing, my friend, and together I believe that we can do what a hundred thousand others have tried and failed. You and I, we can stop the Ice Lord."

Lodin felt himself smiling despite the fact that he sensed that there was more to come.

"We are different, though, in that though I love you in my own way, I cannot love you as you wish to be loved. I am, for all that, a Skral. Many of my people will never have even heard of men who are in love. It is not the Skral way. I am sorry that I cannot return your regard as you would wish, for you deserve all the happiness in the world. It is only that I am not the man to give you that kind of love." For a while they sat, quiet in the darkness.

Eventually Lodin spoke. "It does not come as a surprise that you do not share my inclinations. At this end of the world love between men seems to be considered shameful, for reasons that I do not understand. It saddens me greatly that a whole people should so restrict their chances of finding happiness, but happiness does not come solely from possession. I had no expectations that you would view it kindly..."

"Have I ever spoken harshly of love?"

"Far from it. But you should never expect a man to go contrary to his people's values; only hope that it may be so."

"And in this you are going against your own people's values, are you not?" Maran teased gently.

Unseen, Lodin's smile was bittersweet. "The Lyrians do not exist as a people any more. But, no, I am not going against our values. In Lyria there was much study of love–poems, ballads, discussions in salons, learned treatises and philosophical studies... The philosopher Anandel taught that there were many types of love. There is the passion that leads to the bed, the esteem that a child feels for a parent, the nurturing instinct that the parent feels for the child–so many kinds of love. But he also spoke of those who align as smoothly as two halves of one greater soul. He referred to these people as soul-twins, and this joining can be between people of any age or sex, and can include the pleasures of the bed or not."

"That's a fairly wide definition, isn't it?"

"Perhaps, but it is the rarest of all the kinds of love. It is when a person meets another person and it is as if they are two halves of the same soul, when one person's strengths complement the other's weaknesses. Anandel says that when a person meets their soul-twin, he will be drawn towards him or her as the tide is drawn to the moon, naturally, unwittingly and utterly inevitably. When the beloved walks into a room it lifts the heart as if the sun has come out from behind a cloud. Soul-twins go about the world in each other's company because that is where they are happiest. That is the wisdom of Anandel, at least..." Lodin's voice faltered.

"Your Anandel sounds to have been a wise man. Though we do not have names for the types of love as he does, or even recognise them as such, I cannot disagree with his definitions. Perhaps we Skral are not so unloving after all." Maran mused. "We are no strangers to lust and passion, I grant you, and all know of the bonds between parent and child–but this soul-joining is something we would understand. Between Skrals it is a brotherly feeling, but many a warrior swears an oath with his true friend, a bond to make them shield-brothers. In battle they are like right hand and left hand, and there is not a Skral alive who would leave his shield-brother wounded on the field. Among we who are not warriors it is much less common, for there is less to bind us that closely, but still it happens sometimes. I believe it is similar to what you describe, though we lack the aid of philosophers to define it. As for myself, I have often thought that this pairing of the shield must be a wonderful thing. I have never been one to leap from one bed to the next, and this kind of love seems much more natural to me than the furies of lust that make madmen of those around me. This is the kind of love that I feel for you, brother."

"Do you think that passion would awake in you if you met the right person to ignite it?" Lodin asked delicately.

There was a silence.

"In all truth, I don't think that I am made for that sort of emotion. I have experimented a little with women, but I have never met a woman whose body I felt an urgent need for. I have never felt the need for a man's body either. I am not driven by lust the way many people are. That is just my nature. I am sorry."

"I understand," Lodin replied dully. "There were also those of that nature in Lyria. I understand it better here, perhaps, than I did there."

Maran reached forward and gripped Lodin's shoulder in the darkness. "I do not lust after your body, Lodin, but I value your company and your friendship above that of anyone else of my acquaintance. I do believe that we are one heart in two bodies, one soul divided in two parts, and this will endure for all time. You offer me that which I cannot accept, but it is the lesser thing. If you can accept my limitations, do not ask me to be other than I am, for I cannot be what you wish."

Lodin had to swallow a few times to get past the lump that had risen in his throat. "My friend, if you understand that I love you and are comfortable that it is so, simply to spend time in your company would make me happy."

"In that case, soul-twin by your definition and shield-brother by mine, it is good to have you in my heart."

Lodin exhaled, feeling as if he had been holding his breath all this time. He could not say how thankful he was that this had not alienated his friend.

Though the darkness masked Maran's face, there was a smile in his voice as he continued, "Talking of no need for discomfort, it is cold now and in the morning we have to work out a way of transporting thirteen ancient and fragile ship-skeletons over four days' travel to the Circle by the Clan-halls. I hope the spirits have given you some guidance on that matter as well!"

"There is more, I promise you, but let us sleep now and talk about it tomorrow." Climbing under the furs again, Lodin treasured the touch of Maran's back against his own.

THE HEART OF WOOD

The following morning, Lodin slept late. He woke to find the tent empty. From the sound of it, Maran was pottering about outside, humming to himself gently. He did not sound worried or as if their exchange the previous night had upset him. Lodin listened to him for a while, and allowed himself to relax. He did not know what to do, though. Happiness and sadness warred in his heart. He had found his soul-twin, finally–but the future which the shipspirits had let him glimpse bore down on them with heavy inevitability. Where it would end he did not know, but he was afraid that the bard's light would be somehow quenched.

Even so, he would not mention it until it was too close for doubt. *Let him be merry and carefree till then,* he prayed to those spirits which he felt brooding nearby. *Let him be happy. I will tell him in time to prepare for it, but he should not have to live in fear in the meantime.* But though the weight of the ship-souls burned heavy in his mind, harsh as sun on the snow, they gave no answer.

As he lay there, he realised the sounds of the morning had changed. Lodin sat up. Maran had stopped humming and the plain rang with the barking of dogs. There were other sounds as well–shouts and the snapping of material in the wind. Crawling out of the tent, he blinked in the sunlight.

"We have visitors, it would seem." Maran was sitting by the fire. "But who? I've never seen their like–do you think it is the Ice Lord?"

Lodin shaded his eyes to look, and laughed out loud. "It is the Potentate, or at least some of his people."

"How do you know?"

Lodin gestured at the strange craft out on the plain. "In Gai Ren they have deserts, great waterless seas of sand that stretch for mile after mile in undulating dunes. Their trade routes go right across the middle and every few weeks they put together a caravan, a great group of traders who all have goods to carry. In times long gone, they would assemble on beasts of burden, but the journey took weeks. Sometimes there was a sandstorm, or the beasts died, or they ran out of water. A million things could go wrong, so being a cunning folk, they found a better way of travelling."

"And that is?"

"As you see–ships that ride the sand. Only here they have put them on runners for the snow. They are light and fast, and if my eyes do not deceive me, there are thirteen of them."

They watched the strange fleet come whipping across the snow to the cloven hill by which they stood, and as the ships got nearer, Maran and Lodin waved and shouted. The lead ship tacked as it got nearby, and dropped its sail. As the others followed suit, the momentum kept them skimming the last few yards until they drew up by the camp in a ragged line.

The Clanfather of the Tusken Seal was first to descend, laughing like a little boy. "Such speed! Your people are indeed cunning, Potentate. Those are exhilarating vessels!"

The Potentate was walking from the next ship down. "Your wind-sense is keen, my friend, to outrun a Gai Renese in his own craft. Alas, we will not be so swift on the way home if we are more heavily laden, but there is not much that is as exhilarating as a good run in a sandship."

"Or in this case, a snowship." The Mother joined them.

Tusken Seal turned to Maran. "We were informed that you would need haulage. I for one am convinced that it is mistaken." He glared at the Mother who rolled her eyes. "I was overruled, though I told them that there is nothing but snow in this area to haul."

"Ships that run on land!" Maran breathed. "This is truly a time of wonders!"

Tusken Seal glared at the bard.

"It is true that we need help–but how on earth did you know?" Lodin was puzzled. "There is no-one but us for miles!"

"Well, that's not strictly true, is it?" The Mother cocked an eye in the direction of the ships' graveyard.

"Do you mean--?"

"I have you now!" Tusken Seal interrupted, overloud. "It is trained birds, is it not? Your messengers are trained birds!"

The Mother exhaled in exasperation. "Some might consider that a half-witted suggestion; but yes, that is exactly what my sources are. *Birds*."

"You said it was spies before," the Potentate objected.

"Yes I did, and I will continue to agree that my sources are whatever he needs to believe until such time as he can accept the truth."

"You were saying?" Changing the subject pointedly, Tusken Seal turned to Lodin, who hesitated. The Clanfather might be advanced in years but he was still considerably taller than the slight craftsman and, with his braided beard and bristling brows, he had an intimidating glare. Lodin was not at all sure that he was the right person to explain that they were to desecrate the Skral's most sacred site.

"I think," Maran's voice cut through the hubbub of activity as the crews descended from their ships, "that you need to come with us."

"All of us?" Tusken Seal was outraged. "Surely not the *unSkral?*"

"Yes, all of us." The grave look on the bard's face was unusual enough that the Clanfather acquiesced, and thirteen crews of three followed Maran and Lodin along the path as it wound into the hill. They paused in the centre in awed silence, and after asking the goodwill of the spirits, Maran stepped into the Heart of Wood, with the Clanfather of the Tusken Seal beside him.

"Heart of Wood, preservers of the Skrals, you have led Lodin to believe that we must move you from your long resting place here." Maran was interrupted by shocked exclamations from the Skrals, but he held up a hand and they fell quiet. "We are here to do your will, but to move you we must break up the Heart of Wood, and we are afraid to set axe to you lest we do some damage. Show us how to proceed, of your kindness!"

Tusken Seal erupted. "Break up the Heart of Wood? Are you mad? I sent you out here to get answers, not to—" There was a rumble, and Tusken Seal fell quiet.

"Stand back!" Lodin yelled as slowly, one of the intertwined keels leaned outwards and fell to the ground. Maran and Tusken Seal froze. The rumble grew louder as one by one, the other keels all began to splay outwards, toppling slowly–almost too slowly–to land in the snow with muffled thuds. A cloud of white snow obscured everything, and when it cleared, they all stood blinking in the sunlight.

"Well!" The Mother was the first to speak. "You did ask."

Lodin gazed round at the keels in wonderment. "They could not have fallen. I saw how they all supported each other. It cannot be!"

"And yet it is," Maran said softly.

"Aye–and even I cannot argue with this." Tusken Seal let out a long breath. "It is the passing of an age. Come, all; we have much to do. Maran, I should know better than to have doubted you. Maker, tell us what you need."

Lodin looked to the Potentate. "Sir, you know the capabilities of your craft better than I do. Is there one of your men who can supervise the loading of the keels when we get them out to you?"

"I shall do that." The Potentate bowed his head slightly. "Sandships have been my particular delight for many years now. I know as well as any how the weight should be distributed."

"Thank you. Mother?"

The Mother cast a measuring eye at the assembled Shantar. "We are a slight race. The Skrals will be able to carry more, and may wish to carry the keels themselves. Shall we clear the way of snow for you?"

"The Skrals will lift the keels. They are ours to carry." Tusken Seal nodded appreciatively.

"You see, Clanfather? Brain and brawn can work together quite happily sometimes..."

Tusken Seal began to nod and suddenly realised he was being teased. "You are a terrible woman, Mother of the Shantar, but for all that, sometimes you are right. Skral, to me!"

And as the Shantar and the Gai Renese began to clear the snow from the road, Maran and Lodin set to work, with the willing help of the others.

It took many hours to disassemble the Heart of Wood, gently untangling the ribs of the ancient wood and loading the pieces on the sandships. Each of the Gai Renese vessels carried an ancient keel and as many of the crumbling ribs as could be salvaged. The shards that remained were set carefully along the lines of the original Heart of Wood, around the pool.

At the last, Lodin paused by the water but it was still, reflecting only the sky above. *I will play my part as best I can*, he vowed to the watchful silence.

When he left the ships' graveyard, the first of the sandships were already pulling away. He climbed onto the last sandship, where Maran was waiting.

"Hold on!" the Gai Renese Captain called, and they did, Lodin clinging onto the rail with both his hand and the double-hooked fitting. The wind was blowing briskly and with a final flourish a crewman shook the sail free. There was a quiet boom as the wind hit it, and then they were off, shooting across the glittering snow as the sun fell lower. Maran's dogs had been settled on the sandship with them and they yipped in puzzlement and snuffed at the cold rush of air that whistled between the bars of the enclosure at the back of the ship.

At first there was a certain amount of tacking and changing to get the course just right. They settled down for the long run to the plains, skimming along the frozen snow so lightly that they barely seemed to break the icy crust. Everyone was quiet, either enjoying the run or lost in thought.

Maran and Lodin huddled under a fur, sitting on a spare sail at the front of the ship. There they were a little shielded from the bite of the frozen wind, and were out of the way of the crew, who would occasionally dart about making tiny adjustments, reading intricacies of the wind and correcting for them. Ahead and to either side, the other ships were dotted widely across the plain, each following its own path to a common destination. Lodin was quiet, savouring the touch of the bard's side against his own as Maran put a companionable arm over his shoulder. Lodin unclipped the fitting from his false hand, so he could put his arm round the bard's waist, leaning his head on Maran's shoulder. Maran tucked the fur round them, and they sat comfortably. Lodin's heart ached with longing for this moment to last forever, made more poignant by the knowledge that his time with the bard would be so short.

The sun sank lower and disappeared behind the low-lying cloud. Slower the ships went and slower, and the ground became more and more bumpy until the crisp silence was broken by the sound of a Skral horn, winded three times.

"We stop for the night." The Captain dropped the sail completely and allowed the ship to coast to a halt. He anchored it, roping it tightly to sharp poles on all four sides, and Maran let the dogs out. He and Lodin made a fuss of each of them in turn, and the hounds reared and dashed about gleefully, recalled only when he put down chopped meat for them.

"We should check that the keel is holding up under the stresses of the journey," Lodin suggested. They lit a lantern in the frozen dusk and he tugged on each and every bit of the strapping. All were firm. The keel was safely stowed, and would not slide. "I'll have a look at the others too."

As they made their way across the snowfield, Maran asked softly, "Do you realise the magnitude of what we have done, my brother? Do you realise the importance of this day?"

"What do you mean?" Lodin trudged along next to him, keenly aware of the bard's closeness.

"In all the ages of Skral, from the first Kings who are forgotten, to the last King who built the Halls of Lore, no outlander has ever been told of the existence of the Heart of Wood. And now not only have you been there, but the shipspirits have chosen you to take them back to the Dragon's Teeth. It is unknown in our history and our lore. I do not know what to make of it."

"I am honoured."

"You are, certainly—but I suspect the rest of us are also honoured. For the ships to agree to be moved—well, it is a possibility we have never even considered." They approached the next ship, where Skral stood at either end. "Standing guard, my friend?" Maran asked one of them.

"Truly. My mother was of the clan of the Snow Eagle and this was their clanhome. I recognise it from her tales. There are few others to see it home."

Lodin went on to look at the keel while Maran talked to the

guard. As he returned, the guard turned to him. "Maker, I would like to thank you. My mother spent many an hour telling the tales of our seven clanhomes, their names and the great glories won by my forefathers in these ships. I never expected to see one, but standing guard here, I am able to preserve the honour of a lost clan. I would not have had the clanhome of my mother's people left unguarded. I am deeply in your debt."

Lodin bowed to the man, and to the ship behind him. The Skral was clearly pleased, and as they walked away, Maran smiled. "Well done, Maker! We will have you a master of Skral etiquette yet!"

"He talks of the ship almost as if it were a person."

"Almost, it is. Every Skral knows the names of the ships of his clan. We know their descriptions, how they sailed and where, and who sailed in them. We recite the names of ships and captains for a thousand years. These are not just vehicles. They have a sense of belonging, and of majesty. Yes, that is the word–majesty." Maran thought about this for a moment while they trudged on to the next ship. "Lodin, tell me of a famous hero of your people, one from so long ago that that he is right on the edge of memory."

Lodin considered this. "The first King Raghinan, perhaps. He was one of three brothers. An evil sorcerer from the desert kidnapped their beautiful younger sister Ysalia and laid waste to all the land. The youngest brother rode out to rescue her, but the sorcerer turned the boy into stone. The middle brother rode against the sorcerer, but was turned to stone as well. Finally King Raghinan went to her aid, and the sorcerer tried to turn him to stone, but King Raghinan turned his magic back on him with a highly polished shield. However, the shield shattered and the sorcerer threw a last spell with his dying breath, so that Raghinan was turned to stone as well. Ysalia took up residence there among her three stone brothers, but the sorcerer she chipped to pieces so that his evil should never again be released on the world. In time, her tears became a river, which watered the land so that it began to flower again, and the earth took into its breast the three statues, building up mountains around them. To this day, the horse lords say that if you climb Mount Raghinan in the first full moon in spring, you can hear Ysalia weeping for her loss. They say too that there is a cave on the mountain into which the shards of the sorcerer's statue were cast, where they melted into a fiery lake."

"And so the story ends?" Maran prompted him.

"Yes. The legend says that one day when their sister calls them, the brothers will wake from their sleep, and finally defeat the sorcerer."

"Imagine that these brothers did awake and that all this was real, to the last word," Maran suggested. "If King Raghinan himself walked in and spoke to you by name, and said that he was glad to see you and needed your help, it would be frightening, awe-inspiring... a great honour. That is how the Skral feel. Their clanhomes are speaking directly to them for the first time in a thousand years."

"Ah." Lodin digested this. "Then for Tusken Seal to allow us to dismantle the Heart of Wood..."

"You might as well have suggested poisoning Ysalia's lake! Nothing on earth would have persuaded him to allow it—except the shipspirits indicating that this should be."

"Then truly I am honoured." Lodin stopped. "The shipspirits—they are in the keels?"

"We believe so."

"Are they sentient? Do they speak?"

"That is a more difficult question, and one to which you will receive a different answer from every Skral you ask." Maran kicked at a lump of snow, which disintegrated in a shower of white. "I think they hear and answer, but not as you and I answer each other. They have communicated with me in concepts and pictures though, and I was never in any doubt of what they wanted to convey."

"They did the same to me in the Heart of Wood," Lodin agreed. "They do not speak out loud?"

"They are not humans. They do not use words as we do. And they are not made of the keels–they reside there."

"They do not move? The figureheads I mean?"

"They are made of wood, my friend, and wood may flex in wind or sea but it does not move of itself."

Lodin looked at the keel on the ship they were approaching, which had some kind of beast-head with glinting black eyes, deep-set. "Are you sure it isn't watching me? That one has been staring all the way across."

"Watching you? Ah, that's a different matter." And Maran went to chat with the guard, leaving Lodin paused in his tracks.

"I'm never sure if he's making fun of me or not," he told the figurehead irritably. "And why you're staring at me I don't know." He held the lantern high and went to check on the strapping for the keel. One of the straps had broken and the keel was tilted precariously. A good jolt or so would have toppled it over into the snow, he thought, calling for help. It took some time to get the keel straightened and safely stowed again, and when all was done he returned to the figurehead. "Was that what you were trying to tell me?" he asked it softly, feeling like a fool. There was no answer, of course, but he walked away vaguely unsettled. It did not seem to be staring at him so much anymore.

Having checked on all the ships, Maran and Lodin sat around their fire for a time. Maran was lost in thought, staring into the flames.

"What is that?" Lodin asked at last.

"What is what?"

"That chanting. It comes and goes." Lodin fell quiet, listening as another rhythmic songchant whispered through the frozen snow-silence.

"They are singing the old songs, the Lays of their clans. They are singing the names of all the clanhomes, to honour those that are with us."

Lodin listened to the eerie strains. "What about this ship? Should we be singing to it?"

Maran sighed deeply. "Yes, we should. You recall me to my honour, brother. It is the clanhome of my people." He stood and bowed to the keel. "I cannot give you full honour this night, ship-spirit, but I will sing you the Lay of Aron."

Lodin held out the bard's harp, but the youth shook his head.

"We sing these unaccompanied, the breath through our throats like the wind in the sails of the ship. This is one of the shorter Lays and it tells of this clanhome, the fourth of its line. The figurehead at the front was once a great bear, and his name was Aron. We sing of his making, the captains who stood at his rudder, and the ships who fled at the sight of him."

He composed himself for a moment, and then began to chant. The song was in a language Lodin did not understand, but he was carried away into a waking dream by the rhythmic beat of it underlying the chilly night. The melody stayed with him long afterwards, laced through with the tang of wood smoke, the heat of the fire on his face and the blue-black sky pierced with stars above him.

Eventually Maran fell silent. He bowed again to the ship and went back to his seat by the fire. Lodin was lost in fire-dreams of voyages and storms and sea-battles, but slowly they faded. The night was too cold to stay out long, and quietly they all filtered away to their beds, to lie shivering, fully-dressed beneath the furs.

Maran and Lodin went back to their tent, huddling back to back. Lodin wished that he could have turned to lie in Maran's arms as they sometimes had done on the trip here, but he was more self-conscious now. The bard's feelings were important to him, and he would not for worlds have made him feel uncomfortable, though it tore at his heart to be so close and not to be entwined as he longed to be.

"It's colder than it has been." Maran pulled the furs more closely over them. "It smells like snow."

"Isn't it a bit early for snow, even in this frozen rock of an island?"

"Yes. Yes it is."

Lodin thought his friend was saying more, but he was so tired that it all became a part of the dream that he fell into, of snow and ships and blood and brightness.

THE TALE OF THE SCARRED ARTISAN

L odin awoke to find the camp was busy with the sounds of
activity. He had slept late again, and as soon as they had
packed away the tent it was time to go. He hated this continual
weakness, but the healers had told him that it would take a long
time for his body to finish healing itself and even now, any particular exertion left him exhausted.

During the journey that followed, Lodin sat silent for a long
time. There was so much he did not want to think about. It was
painful to know what lay ahead and he did not want to dismay the
bard, but to keep the secret locked away from that perceptive
young man was very difficult. Eventually he felt he must burst
rather than keep silent.

"Maran, there's something the spirits told me..." Lodin faltered.
"I don't know how to tell you this, but I must because it is about
you."

"Did the spirits tell you in the Heart of Wood?"

"Yes."

"Do you not think that they would have told me if they wished
me to know?"

"I don't know... but this is important! This is something you have to know."

"Are you so sure that I do not already have this knowledge?"

Lodin looked sharply at his soul-twin. For a moment the bard's face was tinged with fear and sadness. "But how can you..?"

"How can I have some idea of what waits and still be cheerful?" Maran fiddled with the cover of his harp. "They haven't told me for sure what will happen. I have a little choice left in the matter, and that is where the danger lies." He leaned closer to his friend. "If I decide that the worst will happen, that I will die or be taken by the Ice Guard, I will spend the next days and weeks thinking of all the horrible fates that could overtake me. If that happens, I will either dishonour myself by running, or at best simply freeze and have my fate overtake me. I may not be a warrior, but I am still a Skral and I wish to end my days with honour. I do not wish to waste these last precious few days worrying about something I cannot avoid. How much better to savour every second of the time that is given to me, to understand what there is that is worth fighting for, and at the end of it to stride forward to my fate like a Skral."

Lodin looked out over the frozen wasteland, which suddenly seemed much drearier than before. "I honour your courage. It is far greater than mine. I wish you would run away now, that one good thing at least might escape the coming storm." He tightened the elbow strap on his false arm, tucking the end under the buckle. "When you are gone, there will be nothing left for me in this world."

"If the world is still here by then, my friend, we will need your help to rebuild it." Maran nudged him gently. "And in the meantime, I need you to help me keep my spirits up. Let us not think of tomorrow. We have too little time to waste. Let us simply enjoy these hours, this day. We are bathed in glad sunshine, flying over the snow as if we have wings. Tiris would love this, if he were here–he would be racing us! Have you ever heard of anything as cunning as these ships, Lodin?"

Lodin swallowed hard. He knew what his companion needed and set himself to lift the mood, but despite his efforts to keep it light, he found it difficult to speak. "Yes." He cleared his throat and tried again. "Yes, as it happens, I have." He cleared his throat again and his voice became stronger as he fell into the telling of the old children's tale.

In the great city of Laerzinan, there was once a very important old man called Imlan. He was very rich, and prided himself on his great inventiveness. To make sure that he never got complacent, every year he would challenge one craftsman from the city to outdo him in fulfilling three tasks. If the craftsman won, he received a valuable prize of whatever pleased him best–tools, land, horses, money, whatever he requested, and the cleverer his inventions had been, the more he received. If Imlan won, on the other hand, the craftsman would still get some sort of gift, but he also had to nail a plaque over his door for a year saying "Bested by Imlan". In truth, as time passed, it became such a privilege to be invited to participate that this became a badge of honour rather than a mild embarrassment. In the whole forty years of the contest, there had only been two plaques ever made that read "I bested Imlan", and these were treasured indeed.

This year was no different. Names were suggested to Imlan, and under the guise of an elderly merchant, his servant Brinam went to visit each shop to gauge the cleverness of the craftsmen. When he had been to all, he returned to the palace, and went to report to Imlan.

Imlan was in his study, poring over a map of the stars. When Brinam entered, the old man rolled up the scroll carefully and restored it to its tube. He stood stiffly, and walked over to the gracious window that overlooked the city. "So, Brinam, what do you have to tell me?"

Brinam bowed, and came to stand by his master. "I have been to see the craftsmen, my lord. Would it please you to hear my report?"

"It would indeed." Imlan looked out over the city which sprawled across the foothills before him.

"The first shop I went to was that in the merchant's quarter. It is a fine house with mosaic floors and a little stream flowing through the gardens. The craftsman made moving ornaments using golden tools with bejewelled handles. The man says there is no need to waste his time on the common people but that he has friends in high places who have guaranteed him an invite to this year's challenge."

Imlan snorted. "Ha! And the second?"

"Tools of brass and a pretty house with three floors and a shady courtyard. He makes interesting devices to amuse ladies, jewellery boxes which play a tune and writing desks with hidden compartments, that sort of thing."

"And the third?"

Brinam did not try to hide his disgust. "The shop right on the market place? As full of flies and children as you might expect. The craftsman, it turns out is barely a boy. Oh, he is talented enough, but will never make much of himself. His tools are battered old things, and he makes toys for children, and devices to chop food, and a well in the back of his shop with a mechanism to pump up the water without having to haul the buckets. Laudable enough for those who have to haul buckets, I daresay, but not of the sort of calibre to take part in the challenge."

"Did you speak to him?"

Brinam sniffed. "He claims that this sort of challenge is all very well but it does not result in anything useful. He says he is extremely flattered to be amongst those who might be chosen but he does not think for a moment that it was more than a mistake that he was included. And then he turned to a small urchin who was demanding he mend a toy donkey, and I could not get another word of sense out of him."

Imlan stifled a smile. "Thank you Brinam. I shall think well upon what you have told me."

.... In time, the names of Lyria and Ghiblin became a byword for excellence across the land, and when they became old they retired to a pleasant place near the coast. They were followed by many artisans and poets and dancers, who flocked to the court which did not judge them on who or what they were, but on what they were capable of achieving. And so excellence flourished, and knowledge that otherwise would have remained in darkness was brought into the world. And that, my friends, is the tale of the Lyrian Court." Lodin put on the voices of all the characters as his nanny had done, and mimed her inflections and actions as best he could remember. The other crew-members drew near to listen. Eventually the tale was done to much appreciation. Then one of the Gai Renese launched into a tale of the battle of wits between a dragon who lived under a lake and the fisherman who made his living from it. The time passed in laughter and tall tales, and the ship flew over the sunlit snow like a bird through the clouds. When the laughter died down and the day grew long, they fell back into thought.

After a while, Maran said, "Thank you. I knew you would understand."

"I love you. Whatever you undertake, I will help you as best as I can."

"You are a shield against the world, Lodin." Maran sat and watched the snow hissing by for a while and then absentmindedly picked up his harp. Humming to himself, he strummed quietly until he had a progression of chords just as he wanted them. He began to sing.

"My heart is in dry-dock, hulled empty, forgotten,
a ship set on high blocks, far from the tides' storming.
The deafening echoes of riptides come roaring–
amid such a maelstrom, I must lose my moorings.

Fearful I listened to dark waters swirling,
fearful as faintly the water came creeping.
Unnoticed it lifted, directed my drifting
till gently I floated, midst plaintive gulls' skirling.

Now riding the high swells, my sails are unfurling
to fly across oceans to the white waters' ending.
Washed free of my fear by the salt sea spray sparkling
I soar on the wind to my destiny's calling."

HE GLANCED at Lodin with that bittersweet smile as he sang.

"Yes, washed free of fear by the salt sea spray sparkling
I soar on the wind to my destiny's calling."

He strummed a while more, absently. Lodin watched the
bard's expressive face in profile against the whiteness of the snow,
hair golden in the sun and ruffled by the wind. *How little time I
have been given with this other, dearer half of my soul! But I will always
remember this.* He tried to notice every detail and commit it to
memory: the sun, the snow, Maran's faraway expression and the
tune winding itself around his heart.

A tear ran down his face. He wiped it away before the bard
could see, and tipped his head back so that more could not follow.
He shut his eyes. In this sheltered corner, the sun was warm on his
eyelids.

After a while Maran set aside his harp, packing it back into its covering. He walked to the rail. "That's odd. We should have come to the end of the snow long before now."

"We have come further than there was snow to travel on, two days back." The Gai Renese captain padded up behind them. "There must have been a mighty blizzard since, but we travel the faster for it, for it is smoother than the bumps and hills of the grassland."

"Does it normally snow this heavily here?" Lodin wondered.

Maran looked thoughtful. "Once in a while, I grant you, but the timing is much in our favour." He laid an appreciative hand upon the blunted head of the ancient keel jutting forward in front of him. "I wonder how far the snow reaches now."

They rode on snow right to the clan-halls. As the first stars came out that evening, the ships drew up and were besieged by Skral come to help unload the ancient ship-skeletons. They laid the precious cargo in a rough circle in the great Skraelhall, where the people gathered for feasts and celebrations.

That night, the hall was never empty. Throughout the darkness, Skrals were drawn to pay their respects to the shipspirits that had protected them for so long. People would slip in and in the half-light of the central fire's embers, they walked around the circle of keels, eventually coming forward to the ship that had sheltered their own clan. Men, women and children, all approached reverently, laid a gentle hand on the wood and stood for a few moments before leaving. They left as quietly as they had come, but their expressions had changed to wonder and awe from the weariness and fear that had lined their faces before.

"Do you see? The ships are sharing their strength." Maran too was watching them. "They are powerful allies."

"Have you been up to them?" Lodin had the sense that something sacred was happening.

"No." Maran turned over in his bedding and pulled the furs over him again. "If there is only one chance to be strengthened, I will wait until I need it."

WHAT CAN A BARD DO?

The following day Lodin was deep in thought, trying to put together his plans for the Heart of Wood, when there was a sudden flurry of noise and movement in the hall.

"He's coming! The Ice Lord is coming!"

A woman stopped to hush the boy. "Enough, child! He is not coming quite yet."

"What is it?" Lodin paused.

"The Ice Lord's ships have been sighted. That's all I know."

Lodin thanked her. *So soon? The trap is barely started.* He went in search of Maran, who was in conference with the Clanfathers, the Potentate of Gai Ren and the Mother of the Shantar.

"How long do we have?" the Mother demanded. "How long before they arrive?"

"It all depends where they put ashore." Tusken Seal shrugged. "Skral boats sail right round the island and land in the harbour down at the river mouth. The Ice Lord is unlikely to know this area. If he lands at the far side of the island and marches across, we have at least four days and probably seven by the time he has landed all his men and organised them for the march. If he sails round the island, he will lose half his army in the effort but those little potbellied ships of his could probably land on the headland yonder, and they could be here in maybe three days or less."

"Three days..." The Potentate sighed. "We have much to organise."

"What is there to organise?" Tusken Seal slammed his fists on the arms of his chair. "He will come, and we will fight to the last Skral falls!"

"Men!" The Mother rolled her eyes.

"Excuse me?"

"Sorry, Potentate, I meant Skrals. Tusken Seal, there is much to organise because if the Ice Lord comes and everyone is here, our peoples will be wiped from the face of the earth quite unnecessarily!"

"What are you suggesting, woman? Do you doubt the prowess of my warriors? Are you saying that we should hide like dogs? Then you do not know the Skral, for they are worth far more than your grovelling Shantar!"

"My friends," the Potentate interjected smoothly as the Mother drew breath for a scathing retort, "let us not be overhasty. We have all a part to play in this battle, and we all have that which we would wish to see outlast it." He turned to Tusken Seal. "The Ice Lord does not just intend to kill people and animals, but to exterminate cultures. All your lore and legends, all your knowledge and customs, would you have them erased from the face of the earth? If we sit blindly waiting it does not matter who wins, for no Skral will know that the graveyard of ships is anything but a hill with a crack in it. No-one will know more of the long, glorious history of the Skral than that there were some people of that name who once existed, and perhaps not even that. Your sons' sons and their descendants will be as ignorant of the Hall of the Forefathers as I was until I came here and heard the singing of your legends. Would you allow all the customs and culture that makes Skral unlike any other people to be trodden in the dust by this villain?"

"That would be a victory for him, indeed." Tusken Seal frowned.

There was a short silence and then the Mother spoke. "Man of the Skral, let us work like Aethir and Aethling on this."

The Skral looked up sharply at her invocation of the fabled brother and sister Gods of his people, and was startled into a rumbling laugh. "Maran has done his job well, if even an outlander knows of the Twins!"

"We have the same legend, though we know them as Etha and Elen. Let us each work according to our skills. You organise the defence and the fighters. I ask only for a few ships, to save that which is most dear to each of our peoples. Specifically, as much of the lore of our peoples as we can save, the children and the old people who cannot fight but are wise and canny enough to bring the young ones into maturity, should they need to."

"And the women," Tusken Seal added.

"The women have much to fight for, and much to avenge. Those who wish may go on the ships but some will want to stay and fight. Many of my people will, for certain. Shantar women are no strangers to war." The Mother met Tusken Seal's gaze squarely, and after a moment he nodded agreement.

LEAVING Maran to finish up with the Elders, Lodin went back to the Skraelhall to look a little more closely at the various keels. He walked round the hall slowly. Somehow the silence was welcoming. Lodin had been considering his task for some time now. Despite the numbing cold the snow had brought, he thought it would be best to transport the ship-skeletons to the Circle and assemble the Heart of Wood there. There was room to do it in the Skraelhall, and no doubt some kind of sled could be arranged to get it across the plain, but he was conscious that the wood was very old, and he did not dare risk it in any way.

"I do not understand the forces that you command, my friends, but I would rather work in the cold unnecessarily than end up with a broken Heart!" He patted the fragile keel of the ship in front of him and all of a sudden he could not move his hand away. A sense of friendship and strength was offered to him, and of understanding. The bleakness that overwhelmed Lodin when he thought of the fate they had suggested surged through him, but to his surprise it was countered with hope, and comfort.

"What hope can there be?" he whispered. "I cannot see any kind of hope."

"Do you think that all there is to life is flesh?" It was Ranulf. "Do you not know of the spirit, which leaps time and space like lightning or starlight? Do you think that he who you love will not exist any more when his body dies?"

"He..?"

"You love, Lodin."

Lodin looked into that old face, seeing only compassion and wisdom in Ranulf's eyes. "I am afraid that he will die, and I will never see him again."

"He will not be with you as you have grown accustomed to see him, but that does not mean that he is extinguished. My son, you are like a timid fledgling mourning the loss of its brother who is no longer in the nest, while the brother soars and swoops above on the warm air currents, waiting for you to join him! Look at the shipspirits. They have never had flesh as you understand it. For the moment they choose to inhabit these shapes, but when their wood has fallen to dust and ashes, they are not unmade, just as we are not when our flesh has fallen to dust and ashes."

"Where will we be then? What will we be?"

"We will be free, and that is how it will be for him you love, too. It is not an ending, but the beginning of a whole new adventure." Ranulf gestured at the keel before him. "The shipspirits have shown us. The furthest reaches of creation will be ours to explore, and when we tire of learning, we will find them sailing the silver seas at the world's end, and they will carry us to the Hall of our Forefathers."

Lodin leaned his forehead on the keel, unwilling to meet the old man's gaze. "Then I shall never see him again... The Skral Forefathers would not allow an *unSkral* in, especially a Lyrian. I am everything they would despise most."

"Maran will see the Hall of his Forefathers because that is what he expects to see. You, you will see your Lyrian Paradise, and he will be there to welcome you. Those that search for each other are brought together simply by the wish to be together. The ship-spirits are very amused at our idea of the afterlife, you know. According to them, it is nothing like any of our expectations, but after a while we grow past expecting things to be as they are in this world and simply experience them as they really are."

"I don't understand!" Lodin wailed. "How can that be possible?"

"Some things just are." The old bard smiled kindly. "You worry too much about logic and substance, Lodin. Neither reach further than the confines of that world we live in now. You play an important role here, both as friend and as craftsman. The fate of many lies in your hand. Have faith, and you shall do what is necessary." Ranulf patted Lodin on the back and went quietly on his way.

Lodin leant his head on the wood again, and whispered, "How can I have faith in the face of such a test as this?" For a moment his heart quailed within him. Then, with an effort, he rallied. *I will not let the man I love stand this test alone.* His determination grew to a steely core that ran through him. *I will do my part and do it well, regardless of what it costs me. Whatever support Maran needs to be able to make his decision, he will have. I love him without bounds, and if loving him means letting him choose to go, I will stand behind whatever choice he makes.*

Again, strength and approval flowed into him from the ancient wood.

Lodin took a deep breath. "Thank you."

AT THE END of the day, with the low sun drifting wearily round the Dragon's Teeth, the Elders came across the plain to see how the craftsman was getting on.

The first step was to rebuild the Heart, and it had already taken the efforts of many people to reload the keels onto the sand-ships and haul them across the plain to the Dragon's Teeth. Teams of men and women of all races had hauled on the ropes and now all thirteen keels were in place.

In the middle of the Circle, the keels were placed roughly as they had been in the ships' graveyard. Maran was striding round with the parchment on which he had sketched the original lay-out. Every figurehead was scrutinised–all were worn and amorphous but not so much that the bard could not tell one from another. Satisfied that they were all in the correct place, he shouted across to Lodin, who was paying close attention to the ribs of the ship and how they fit together in the tight space.

Though the Dragon's Teeth was large when empty, with the Heart rebuilt inside it there would be little extra room. Much work was needed and yet few could fit in to do it. The stronger members of each team stood ready to help lift the keels, and Lodin flitted from one keel to the next, working out how they would fit together.

He had a paintbrush in the latest version of his new hand–the smith had made him a stronger spring to keep the thumb-lever closed–and every so often he made a mark on a rib, muttering to himself.

"This one juts across there. If it were a hand span shorter it would lie flush with that one. The second one can stay as it is but here is a problem. Which of these should lie over which?

Hmmm..." He daubed on another blob of paint, and turned to greet the Elders. "Gentlemen."

"H'hmm."

"... and Lady."

"What do you think, Lodin? Will it serve?" The Potentate's face was tired and anxious.

"If I can do as the ships have commanded, it will serve." Lodin gestured at the skeletal shapes around him. "Not in the sense that it will physically trap him, but that is not quite what the ships meant. They will keep him dormant, I think. In any case the instructions I have are quite precise. I don't begin to understand why they want what they want, but I'm just the maker. As long as they know what's going on, that's enough for me."

"And this from a Lyrian!" The Potentate smiled at the others. "Will it be finished in time though?"

"How long do we have?"

"We're not sure. The scouts will light the beacons when the army is sighted on land, and that should tell us where they are coming from. We still do not know whether he will send his army through the straits, but even if he tries to march them across from the other side of the island, we have a week at best and at worst, days."

"How many days?" Lodin cast a measuring eye across the keels.

"How many do you need?"

"At least three for the Heart of Wood, if there are plenty of people to help."

"And for the rest?" Tusken Seal gestured vaguely at the towering stone monoliths around them.

"That is not something I can tell you. They will finish the construction." The craftsman nodded at the ship-skeletons whose deep-set eyes glittered in the red light of the falling sun.

"They will?"

"I don't know how."

Tusken Seal stroked his beard, thoughtful. "We will see what can be done to give you the time you need. I will have my scout ships do what they can to harry the Ice Lord's flotilla. It may be that we can lead them off-course. At any rate, every soldier that dies on the ocean is one less to fight us here."

"That is true, but be aware that the same applies to your own men," the Mother warned. "Bravado aside, we need every last warrior here. Every ship they sink will help but we cannot afford to let them risk their own lives."

"It will gall them. The Skral way is not to fight and run."

"They're not running away, though," the Mother snapped. "They're running to the next battle, that's all."

"Oh. They might do that!" Tusken Seal's face cleared. The Mother and the Potentate shared a glance that would have been amused in less serious circumstances. "When the Ice Lord gets here, what will happen? How does this trap work?"

Lodin hesitated. "I shall rebuild the Heart of Wood as it was in the ships' graveyard and around the Heart of Wood I am to make walls of water."

"Walls of water? Snow?" the Potentate ventured.

Lodin nodded. "The snow walls are to go over the whole of the Heart of Wood. The spirits say that when the Ice Lord goes in, we will be able to seal it off, and he will be trapped inside."

"For how long?" Tusken Seal rumbled but the Potentate cut in.

"Wait a moment. How do we know that he will go in here?"

"The trap will last for as long as it is needed. I suppose it could be opened from the outside if there were those who were determined enough, but it would have to be a Skral. The ships would not respond to anyone else. There are no absolutes, of course, but given that your clan-halls lie within sight of the Circle, the story should go into your histories so that people should know what lurks within. And if all the Skral are wiped out and the knowledge is lost, there will not remain any who would be able to get past the ship-spirits."

"You did not answer the Potentate's question, Lodin. Why

should the Ice Lord enter the Heart of Wood?" The Mother fixed him with a hard stare.

Lodin looked at his feet, clearly unhappy, but Maran laid a hand on the craftsman's shoulder. "We know that the Ice Lord will enter because I will call him in."

Tusken Seal snorted. "And what can a bard do?"

"What can a bard do?" Maran gestured widely. "I can play you a tune that will keep your feet dancing. I can sing you a song that will break your heart. And if I can speak with any man, I can play him a tune that promises all that his heart desires."

"And this will call in the Ice Lord? A pretty tune?" The Mother's voice dripped disbelief.

Maran executed a courtly little bow in front of her in a most unSkral-like manner and offered her his arm. "Come, the sun is down and we can do no more work in the cold of night. Back in the halls there is fire, food and ale, and we can discuss these things at leisure."

Raising an eyebrow at the others, she took his arm nevertheless and they all returned to the halls of the Tusken Seal clan, and sat at the long table to eat.

There was much banter and good-humour which at first Lodin found difficult to take. *With death approaching, how can they be so uncaring?* Gradually he realised that the jokes had a slight edge. Even the warlike Skral were doing just as he was, keeping talk light and laughter constant in an attempt not to think about the black clouds on the horizon.

When most people had finished eating and sat back comfortably on the benches to drink the last of their ale, Maran mounted to the dais at the top of the hall. There was much cheering and stamping of feet on the floor. He swept them all a deep bow and waited for the noise to die down.

"Warriors, ladies, and good peoples from the remainder of the world," he began, "I am sad to tell you that my professional reputation has been called into doubt!"

There were cries of "No!" and "What reputation?"

He went on. "What is a bard good for, I have been asked?"

"Holding my axe while I kiss your sister!"

"I have promised your leaders a jig that will have your feet dancing, a song that will break your hearts, and a tune that promises all that the heart desires. So—are you ready to dance, my friends?"

"I ate too much to dance!" someone groaned from the back.

"You'll dance regardless, man, with the tune I'm about to play for you," Maran quipped, and picking up his knee harp, he began to play.

In truth, there was something about Maran's playing that could not be denied. At first, they found their feet twitching in time. Then they beat their fists or tankards on the table to keep rhythm with him, and eventually the whole hall was up on their feet, dancing.

The music was wild and carefree. The beat lifted them. The swirls of the melody had them whirling up the hall to the dais and careering back down the lines of dancers to progress through the steps again. They whooped and laughed as far as they had breath to do so, occasionally staggering out of the fray to gulp down a drink and then diving back into it. The older members of the audience clapped in time, as they could not keep up with the dancing. Even the oldest grandfather stood and stamped in time, though he held onto the back of his chair for support.

Finishing with a flourish, Maran set down his harp and took a deep draught from his tankard. There was much cheering as the dancers stopped to catch their breath. Even the Mother and the Potentate had been caught up in it all, and returned to their seats flushed and breathless. Tusken Seal kissed his wife soundly before coming back to sit with them.

"And now a song to break your hearts." Maran looked out at his people with a twisted half-smile. Tuning the harp to a minor key, he sang of the maiden Fathellas whose lover was lost at sea, and the deal she made with the sea-witch to give up her own life if her lover could be saved. At the end, her lover was returned to her on the sea shore and after one sweet kiss, the maiden was stolen away by a rolling wave. As Maran half-sang, half-whispered the last part, it seemed to Lodin that he was there with her. He was stabbed through with sorrow as she let go of all that she held dear in the knowledge that only through her could her love be saved. He stifled a sob, and glancing around saw that tears dripped from the faces of everyone there, warriors, children and women alike.

As the last note faded into silence, the people in the hall took a deep breath and another. Experiencing Fathellas' sorrow, Lodin had been able to let go of his own fear. He was left feeling that perhaps something good could come out of all that they were going through. In the eyes of those around him, he saw those same tears of sadness and hope, that feeling of a future restored.

"A song to break your hearts," Maran said softly, "and a tune to promise all the heart desires." He glanced over at Lodin, gave him a smile of singular sweetness and paused in thought for a moment. But Lodin wiped the tears from his face and stood suddenly. All eyes turned to him.

"Elders, let us agree that this young man can do that which he has promised." It was a battle to keep his voice light and jocular but he did so. "And let us agree it quickly, for I am mortally afraid that he will play me a tune promising a beaker of vintage red wine from my homeland. I should never recover from the longing for it!"

The laughter dissolved into cries for more of Maran's dancing tunes. When the bard tired, he gave over the stage to musicians and storytellers from the Shantar and Gai Renese contingents, who kept the crowd entertained late into the night. Maran came back to general applause and Lodin handed him a beaker of ale, which he downed thirstily. He set his harp safely in a corner, and made himself comfortable on the bench to listen to the stories which were his passion, his currency and his trade.

Lodin sat next to him, slightly at an angle so that he could watch the bard's reaction to the tales as well as the storytellers on the dais. There were many stories that night from the three different nations, and this meant that no person there knew all the stories and each one was heard for the first time by many of the audience. It was a raucous, appreciative crowd.

Maran listened with easy enthusiasm, his expressive face showing his amusement. In the smoky, mead-scented warmth of the hall, he laughed and shouted with everyone else as the stories progressed, sometimes leaning over to make some quip or other. Lodin treasured his every touch. He knew he should not wish for more. Maran's reaction to his love had been generous and affectionate, and that trust was an honour that he would never tarnish. But to his shame, Lodin could not stop himself from yearning to kiss him. *I never will, though, and I must not think of it. There will never be any relief if I let it grip me, and besides, even thinking about him in that way is to betray his trust a little.* He crushed the thoughts ruthlessly, and made himself concentrate on the storytelling, but it did not help. He rose to refill his tankard, and when he came back, sat a little further away where the bard's touch was not such a distraction.

"I would have played for you," Maran whispered later that night as the crowd was dispersing. "I should have played you a few moments of happiness at least."

"I could not bear to hear about that which my heart desires the most, when I know I shall lose it." Lodin's voice trembled with tears, and losing control, he strode out into the cold night.

THE TALE OF THE LAST DRAGON

It was dark and crowded in the confines of the circle of stones, and tempers were fraying but Lodin worked on. The ends of the beams had to be trimmed to fit, and the keels bound in place. Even with his new hand he could not knot ropes into loops. However Asri pointed out that she did not need to be able to see to tie knots and so between them, the work went on until each keel was bound and supported in a nest of ropes.

By now the light was fading and the day was nearly gone.

"Is it secure?" Maran stretched.

Lodin tested the rope with his good hand. "Secure enough for the moment."

"It is too dark and cold to stay in here. Let us finish for the day."

"There is much still to be done, and the time is so short..." But Lodin hesitated. Maran's face was shadowed. *His future lies heavily on him here. Asri was right to say that the stones were waiting.* "Everyone, thank you for your help. We will need you back out here at first light tomorrow to finish." A general cheer went up, and slowly the cramped space emptied as the workers filtered out into the blue chill of the evening.

In the last light of dusk, the chamber was shadowed, the intricate ropes looped and relooped around the skeletal keels. The beastlike figureheads comforted him a little, but the stones breathed cold into the centre, and the thought of being here for any length of time... Lodin shuddered.

Maran laid a gentle hand on his shoulder. "Do not think about it, my brother. Come back to the clanhall."

That night Maran was subdued. When the people called for a tale, he had none to tell and remained quiet in his seat with Lodin.

At first there was a murmur of dismay, but to everyone's surprise Asri stood, and her son guided her to the storyteller's place, blushing at all the eyes on him. Lodin was amused and surprised–he had thought her too self-effacing to give such a performance–but soon he was carried away with the story and simply listened, as did the others in the hall

Asri felt behind her for the high seat, and once safely ensconced there, she began. "In these latter days I have discovered an amazing thing. Despite the miles that separate these islands from my own Mountains, many of the tales I have heard here are similar to tales that we tell at home. I do not think that this is a coincidence, because the tales of Gai Ren and Lyria are so very different. Rather it makes me think that once upon a time our peoples may have been more closely entwined, even as we are now. Be that as it may, I have heard your story of the Circle of Stones, more often called the Dragon's Teeth, and it reminded me of a story of my own land which tells of just such a circle. Shall I tell it to you?"

Roars of approval and interest greeted her question. She settled back on her chair more comfortably and began, putting on all the voices and expressions as if she was telling it to the children. "In the long ago and far away there was a large young a Dragon called Jorr. He was not a very nice Dragon, nor a particularly intelligent one, but he was very big and powerful. He was much bigger than the other little wyverns, and would bully them unmercifully.

At first the older Dragons thought that he would grow out of it but though he grew, his behaviour did not get any better. Eventually the Dragons called a Council, and all the Dragons in the colony gathered together in the great meeting place on top of the mountains to decide what should be done about this troublesome beast.

"The Council recognises Marr, mother of Jorr," one of the grayscales intoned.

Marr nodded respectfully at him. "Thank you. My friends, I have called Council today because of my son Jorr. When he was a hatchling, he was disobedient. Many hatchlings are, so I did not think much of it. When he was a wyvern, he was unruly, but when I remonstrated with him, he paid no heed. Now he is an adult dragon and his behaviour makes trouble for the entire Colony. I come to you today to ask the Council's advice. What should I do with this son of mine?"

The Dragons hummed and swayed their heads from side to side as Dragons do when thinking deeply."

LODIN LISTENED, carried away with Asri's words as she told of the dragon's exile and his slow journey towards understanding his loss, until at last the tale came to its ending.

"FORGOTTEN, Jorr fell into a deep melancholy. Eventually in the dark night of his soul, he began to sing. He sang of his loneliness, and of how he missed the friends and dragons that were no longer with him. He sang of sorrow and foolishness, and how his youthful hubris seemed shameful to him now. He sang of his mother and the other dragons, and of his wish to be back in the heart of the Colony, one among equals, asking their forgiveness.

Scattered across the hills, the humans came out of their houses to listen to the bronzed notes rolling across the mountains under the stars, and they wondered at the richness and the sorrow of it.

Jorr sang on until his tale was finished, then dropped his head, and lay hollow, but there was a glimmer around him, and his last note did not fall silent as had the rest. It swelled to a hum, a chorus, a great scintillation of sound, and the glimmering light became a brightness that hurt his eyes. Out of it, two sparks of fire coalesced into the eyes of Ghed, oldest of Dragons.

"Jorr." In that one word was all the love and acceptance that Jorr longed for.

"Please," he whispered. "Take me with you. I don't deserve it, but I know better now, and I am sorry. I will do anything you ask. Please, take me with you."

"Jorr?" A voice echoed across the Council chamber. Gemi's daughter helped her down off the litter, and she struggled across to where the dragon lay. "You found them? Your Colony?"

Jorr laughed, with such happiness as she had never heard before. "They found me."

"Then go." There were tears in her voice, but she was smiling. "Go to them. You will not forget me?"

"Never, my dear." Jorr gave her the most delicate of dragon kisses, and the same to her grand-daughter. "Thank you for being here. I would not have liked to go without saying goodbye to my friends." Speechless, the girl curtsied to him, for he was now a very large dragon indeed.

Jorr laid his head down and closed his eyes. The glimmering enclosed him, growing in brightness till Gemi had to shut her eyes. The humming grew intense, and then faded. The light was gone, and there was only a circle of standing stones where the dragon had lain.

"Goodbye Jorr." Gemi patted the stone sadly. "I will miss you, but not for long, I think." They took her back to her own bed, where she fell easily and painlessly asleep for the last time.

Gemi's daughter travelled widely, leading her people to a realm where they could live peacefully. Wise and blessed, she became the first Mother of the Shantar, and the virtues of dream-walking and wisdom bestowed upon her by the dragon's kiss were given also to her daughter, and to the oldest daughter in the line thereafter. So it has continued down all the generations to the present. That is why the Shantar walk paths not known to other peoples. It is because the line of the Mother was chosen by the last Dragon in the world to guide her people in the Dragons' absence."

Asri finished and there was a collective sigh as everyone came out of the spell of her tale. Then, after a moment, the hall echoed with applause and shouts of appreciation. She stood, found her stick and bowed to them all in the Shantar manner, flushed with pleasure at her success. Edan took her arm and guided her back to her seat, and then some of the Gai Renese went up onto the dais to play a lively song in their own language. The chorus was simple and everyone was soon stamping away and singing along.

Lodin turned to Maran. "I haven't heard that one before; have you?"

"Something like it, long ago and far away." The bard smiled sadly. "She told it well, though."

"It does seem to me that no matter where you come from or what language you speak, every country has its tales about dragons," Lodin continued. "Sometimes the dragon is foolish, sometimes wise. They can be good, bad or indifferent, but there are always dragons. I wonder what that means?"

"Maybe the tale is right, and dragons sang the world into being." Maran was obviously making an effort.

"Maran..."

"It's all right, Lodin. We're doing fine. We work through the day, and we distract ourselves through the night. That is how we will get through the next few days, and anything after that is out of our hands." The bard smiled, and this time it was an unforced smile. "That's an oddly comforting thought, isn't it?"

"Yes and no..." Lodin shrugged off thoughts of tomorrow.

"Let's not think of that now though. I came across something that might interest you."

It was an obvious change of subject but one which Lodin welcomed. "Tell me."

"Well, you see the Potentate of Gai Ren? The little man sitting next to him on the right?"

Lodin squinted over in the dim lantern light. "What has he got round his neck?"

"Precisely. He has little crystal windows, two of them in a frame. He puts them in front of his eyes and it makes what he's looking at bigger."

"Really? How do windows make it bigger?"

Lodin's interest was infectious, and Maran laughed. "Shall we go and ask?"

A TERRIBLE FEASTING

The following morning Edan brought his mother up to the Dragon's Teeth. Once she was settled, he took Lodin to one side. "Maker, Drankar has asked me to help with the defence. I know that what we are doing here is important but with the Ice Lord so near..."

"You feel the need for action."

"I can't just wait around here for the army to appear, when we have no means of defending ourselves!" the boy burst out. "I can't! Not after last time."

Lodin nodded gravely. "I think you do right."

"I do?"

"What we do here is important, but we will need time to finish it. If the Ice Lord arrives before we are done, all is lost. Besides, I do not know how any of us can be saved, but if it is possible it will be through men such as yourself."

Edan stood a little straighter. "Thank you, Maker. I thought that you might be angry."

"How could I be?" Lodin patted the boy's arm. "It breaks my heart that we rely on the swords of the young. I am horribly afraid of the losses we will suffer but we should each follow our hearts, for there will be no quarter when the Ice Lord arrives. Besides, there is little enough room in the chamber now, so we cannot fit in everyone who is willing to help. One thing, though."

"What?" The boy looked apprehensive.

"Be careful of yourself, Edan. Your mother has lost much in this war. When the armies come, do your best but do not take any risks you do not have to."

Edan nodded. "I am not a Skral. I don't look for glory in death. I just want to strike against the Ice Lord for my father and sister, and to keep my mother safe."

Lodin watched the boy leave. *War is a filthy thing when it involve children, but this is not war so much as a struggle for survival. That being the case, the children have as much to fight for as the adults do— perhaps even more. It's their future they fight for, after all.*

Lodin gathered his helpers together. "Everyone, we have much to do and not much time in which to accomplish it. The keels are all in place now but there are shards of wood everywhere. We need to gather it into sacks. The Potentate has got permission of the Skral Elders to use it in some of their contraptions. After this we need to make blocks of snow to pack the spaces between the Heart of Wood and the stones of the Circle. We will roll the snow into spheres, and when they are in place we will carve them flat and pack them with loose snow so that every bit of the space is filled. The top will be difficult to manage, but we will do our best."

He looked round at the faces surrounding him. "This will be cold, hard work. Make sure you have gloves on and try not to get too cold to help. If you are getting painfully cold, go back to the Skraelhall and thaw out by the fire, change into dry clothes if you need to, and come back as soon as you can. Time is getting short, and we need to use it as productively as possible, but bear in mind we won't be finished today, and at the end of it all we will have a battle to fight."

As the people dispersed on the snowy field, he went to find Asri. "Asri, is this something that you are happy to do?"

"Yes." Asri was decisive. "I can see the difference between the whiteness of snow and the dark grass. I can roll the snow if someone else will take it back to the Circle, and keep me from wandering away lost."

"That sounds like a job for me!" Maran volunteered. "We can work together."

First, every splinter of the wood from the ships that was not used was carefully collected together and sent back to the Skraelhall. The Heart of Wood was finished but as work started on building the great blocks, word came that the pot-bellied ships of the Ice Lord had landed on the island.

"Look," Maran breathed as they packed up for the evening. Far away in the darkness, a tiny spark flickered into being, and then another, and a nearer one. They grew and flared into tiny points of light, and as they did, more appeared, larger and nearer to.

"What are they?" Lodin laid a chisel into the leathern pack which held his tools, and rolled it together.

"They are the beacons. The Potentate had wood carried up to the tops of the highest hills when he arrived, that we might have more notice than Gai Ren did. At the top of every hill is a boy with a dog-sled, a supply of oil and kindling and three lanterns."

"Three?" Asri gathered together the last of the timber shards into a sack.

"One to stay lit at all times, one as a back-up for when he needs to refill the oil, and a third in case of mishap. When the scouts saw the Ice Lord land, they lit the first beacon and fled. Each boy is set to watch the previous beacon and when it fires up, to light his own brazier. When the one after him in the chain has been lit, he is to leave and head back. Somewhere along that line there are boys fleeing in the night, with only the stars to guide them back here and their sleds to carry them. And further along that line of fires, the Ice Lord's army has started the march to Skraelhall."

"Maran—over there!" Lodin pointed to another point of fire which flared on the other side of the plain. "More beacons?"

Maran caught his breath. "They come at us from two sides, maybe more! Come, friends, we need to be sure that others have seen this."

The three of them hurriedly gathered the last of their tools and made their way back to the Skraelhall.

"The Ice Lord has landed troops on several different parts of the island," Tusken Seal reported. "The beacons burn at all points of the compass. The troops will not reach us all at the same time, which is some little consolation, but they come in numbers such as will easily overwhelm us, even with the first wave of foes. As the rest reach us, all that will be left for them is to chase down anything that has escaped destruction. I say any *thing*, my friends," he looked around at the faces of the other Clanfathers and leaders who sat in the hall with him, "because I do not think that any one of us will be able to escape or retreat. They surround us utterly, or will do by the time they arrive."

"What shall we do?"

Tusken Seal looked at the Potentate gravely. "What shall we do? We shall fight to the last man, and when that last man falls, we shall hope that somehow Lodin and Maran have managed to catch the Ice Lord in that complicated structure of theirs. I think every Skral here knows that this is not a quest for glory so much as honour. None of us are likely to be remembered for our deeds on the battlefield as there will be none but the enemy left standing, but each of us can die with the knowledge that we have fought in all honour, and have fallen in the defence of all that was once good in the world."

"The people of Gai Ren stand at your side." The Potentate rose and bowed to the Skral.

After a moment the Mother did the same. "The Shantar will fight with you."

"Then let us forget all distinction of clan or race." Tusken Seal's statement earned a raised eyebrow from the Mother. "We are not

Skral, Shantar, Gai Renese. We are the last remnants of the world we knew. We are brothers."

The Mother cleared her throat pointedly.

"Very well, we are family." Tusken Seal rolled his eyes. "Now, enough words. There is much to be done. Are the ships prepared?"

"They are," the Potentate confirmed. "The *Gundal*, the *Dreda* and the *Aelfrith* are stocked and ready."

"Are the children and their guardians ready to leave?"

"They await the word to board."

"They should go at first light, and the Gods send them a clear journey and no sight of the Ice Lord's ships." Tusken Seal's sigh was echoed by many in the room, and with little more than nods of acknowledgement, they each left to begin their preparations.

ONE OF THE women was weeping quietly as she made her way back to the halls.

"Frida." Her cousin hurried up behind her.

"Olann, what are we going to do? I don't want to send the boys away, but Eldred's only fourteen, and Ranfrith is just twelve. I can't have them stay here and be killed! What are we going to do?"

"Shhh! Get Bran and meet me by the sleds."

She stared after him with burgeoning hope. Olann would come up with something. He always had done, ever since they were children. She fetched her husband, much to his irritation, and brought him to the long low building where the sleds were kept. Olann was waiting there by the smallest sled, bundled up for a long journey, with a pack on his back.

"What is this, Olann? What are you doing?" Bran, Frida's husband hissed. "Do you plan to run from the Ice Lord's men?"

"I am not doing it for myself, but for Frida and the children. And I am not running away. I intend to go up the mountain and spy on the enemy, Bran. It's just that if I'm up there and out of the way of the army, I should like to take Frida and the children with me." Olann hesitated. "I can teach your boys a bit of woodcraft, perhaps, and... and..."

Frida clutched at her husband's arm. "You and Olann can defend them better than the oldsters who will be on the ship. I don't have to come. Leave me, if you must, but take Eldred and Ranfrith. Teach them woodscraft. Teach them to kill the enemy one by one. Teach them... teach them whatever it takes."

Ignoring her, Bran turned on Olann. "Would you dishonour the clan? Would you drown our name in shame forever?"

"No. I would have it *continue*. Whatever shame you may feel now will be as short-lived as everyone here. Only we will be left, to earn glory and honour in dedicating our lives to killing as many of the Ice Lord's men as possible. Let me ask you this," Olann raised a hand to forestall the interruption that he could see coming. "What earns the most honour, a short brutish death or a long life fighting the enemy? Because those are our choices. If we do not blindly do what we are told now, will we not wash away the shame in the blood of the Ice Lord's men? In twenty years, or thirty, will that not make amends for it?"

Bran turned his back.

"It will make amends, Bran. They will be heroes, living up on a crag and raining death on the enemy. Living heroes, not dead boys!" Frida clutched at his arm.

He snatched it away from her. There was a long silence before he spoke again. "What is your plan, Olann?"

"I will go up to Fang Peak. There is a place I know there, a little hidden valley with game and water and shelter. I will scout the way and make sure it is clear. When I am there, watch for my signal. On the top of the peak I will light a fire. When you see it, come as fast as you can. Bring provisions as if you will never see this place again, for the chances are that you will not. Do not tell anyone, not anyone. We will just go, as silent as shadows, and your line will live on in Eldred and Ranfrith when you and I are long gone. I swear, Bran, by the sigil of my father, this will I do." He pulled up his sleeve to expose the tattoo on his arm, a complicated spiral that was the sign of his father's line, and echoed those painted on his shield and weapons, and embroidered around the border of his cloak.

Bran did not turn. "Go. My wife and sons will follow. I will not." He strode off into the night, as if trying to deny this surrender.

Olann bent to hug Frida. "Can you travel to Lamefoot Pass in the dark?"

"I will. I must."

"I will meet you there, and bring you up to the valley." He kissed her on the cheek. "I will take a sled tonight and send it back before morning. The dogs will come back here when they are hungry. Make sure all is set in place and put away before anyone else rises." He lifted his pack onto his back and shrugged his shoulders to get it settled properly. "Frida? Do not tell anyone, not your mother, not your sister, not anyone. The game will be scarce. We will be lucky if we do not starve in the winter. I would not have separated you from Bran, but the fact that he is not coming means we have a better chance of avoiding starvation. For the sake of your sons, Frida, do not tell a soul."

She nodded. "Be careful. The Ice Lord's men are on their way. I am placing the life of my sons in your hands."

"I know it. I will not fail you." He disentangled himself. "I must go. Watch for my sign, and when you see it, come with as much speed as you can."

Wiping her eyes, she nodded, and hurried back to the clanhall to tell her sons that they would not be embarking with the other children.

❄

THERE WAS little sleep to be had that night. There was much to be done as they finally moved everyone who was to leave to the shore and on board the ships. They were sending away the oldsters and the wounded, the children and those who would look after and defend them if they could not outpace the Ice Lord's ships. Everyone knew that these were likely to be their final good-byes. By torchlight parents took their children on board, found them a place on the hastily-erected bunks and set their packs down. They stayed till the last possible moment, with the wounded and the oldsters coming on around them and most of the remaining stores of food and water. Those staying did not expect to need more than a few days' supplies. As little as possible was to be left for the enemy.

Eventually, word came that the parents should gather on the shore. As the first light turned the sky from black to grey the quays were lined with silent faces, and the children stood along the rails of the ships. No-one shouted or waved. There was the occasional sniffle but none had words for an occasion such as this, and even the younger ones who did not understand were awed into silence by the sombre mood.

In eerie quiet the anchors were raised and the ropes cast off. The three ships moved away with only the hushing of the waves, the clank of the anchor chains and the booming slap of canvas as the sails caught the wind. No-one moved. They simply stood, husbands holding wives, friends with their arms around friends, throats locked tight with tears unshed, watching the ships that held their children, their parents, all their hopes for a future beyond the coming bloodshed.

Slowly the sun rose, its rays touching the far-off sails with white as they diminished into the green sea. In little groups, friends embraced each other. Silently they filed off along the quay and back to the halls with aching hearts, but a calmer resolve. If all else went badly, something at least might be saved.

At the halls, food was prepared. Few were hungry but they ate anyway, and gradually the noise levels in the hall rose to a more normal level, if still subdued.

"May I have your attention please?" The Potentate stood on the dais to address them, and there was a lull in the conversation. "Good people, what we have done today is a little miracle. In the face of overwhelming odds, we have saved a little of ourselves from the Ice Lord. The *Gundal*, the *Dreda* and the *Aelfrith* hold all that is precious to us. It has strained our heartstrings to watch our loved ones sail away, but there is no time for us to indulge in grief. Neither is there reason to do so. Our children have sailed with those who will give them a good chance of surviving this time of death and madness. We will not see them again in this world, but we do not have time to lie and weep. To preserve the ships, we must keep the Ice Lord's attention focussed here long enough for Maran and Lodin to trap him in the Dragon's Teeth, and that will take all the efforts of every last one of us." He looked round the hall. "Come, friends. There is little hope for us, perhaps, but we share a purpose. Let us work at our tasks with a ready will. We all have equal share in these times, and every task is as important as every other. We are only a ragtag group of exiles from different clans and nations, but we are all that is left. We stand between the Ice Lord and his wish to bring death to the world. Let us do our best to stop him."

A Skral stood in silent toast, and a Shantar followed. One by one all the inhabitants of the hall stood, and when all were on their feet, the Potentate raised his tankard. "To the *Gundal*, the *Dreda* and the *Aelfrith*. Safe sailing and an easy landing to them, wherever that may be."

All drank, and the tone in the hall eased a little as they filed out of the benches and went about their tasks. Warriors as they all now were, the various members and nationalities made peace with themselves and each other, making vows of brotherhood to their comrades, even those from other countries. Many of the women and some of the older children had refused to leave. The smiths were still hard at work sharpening blades and fitting them to staves cut down from the handles of oars, that these smaller ones might have a weapon with which to defend themselves. The Gai Renese were putting finishing touches to the contraptions they had fashioned to send into the Ice Lord's army, carrying fire and destruction in their wake. These were strange, complicated things with sails to catch the wind and propel them onward, and a space in their bellies where burning pitch could be set. Wood from the keels had been woven into their design and they were tethered by the Dragons Teeth, where their strange, angular skeletons thrummed and rattled in the breeze like headless warhorses raring to dash down into the fray.

As the day wore on, the sandships were sent out with the scouts aboard. They returned with several of the boys from the beacons on board, and reported that the army were indeed advancing on several sides. Time was short.

Night drew in, and fires lit the horizon. Snow was falling as Lodin, Maran and Asri returned to the clan-halls, and the misty flakes glowed with the far flames of the army's advance, burning everything in their path. The sandships skimmed through the snow like ghosts in the red half-light, returning ever more frequently to report how near the army was, what they had destroyed. The great stands of oaks which had been nurtured for generations to build Skral ships, and the shipyards nearby had gone. Maran wept to hear of the passing of the Halls of Lore. From the plain the scouts had seen the flames leaping high amongst the mountains, where the Halls had stood for a thousand years. Even the ruins of the old palace where the Kings of Skral ruled when the Skral were one tribe, even these had been razed to the ground. All that was Skral was destroyed. The rivers were befouled and where they could, the Ice Lord's armies felled trees into the harbours and blocked them with great boulders, cut the struts of quays, burnt crops and killed livestock.

❄

ELDRED AND RANFRITH had been working alongside Edan for most of the day, helping to fletch arrows, but as the darkness drew in, they were sent back to their various families.

"I never thought Mother would let us stay and fight," Ranfrith gloated. "Normally she treats us like little children, so I was certain they would send us away with all the babes."

"I wasn't sure my mother would let me, either, but I was determined not to go." Edan packed the remaining feathers.

"It was a bit unexpected, really." Eldred was thoughtful. "I thought it would take more than just saying we didn't want to go. But then we are nearly grown men—not that they usually treat us that way, but in age we nearly are."

"But it's too late now! The ship has gone and they can't send us after it!"

Eldred looked at his brother in some irritation. "This isn't going to be all mead and glory you know. Horrible things happen in battle, and they might happen to us too."

"To you, maybe!" Ranfrith punched his brother on the arm. "Great warrior like me, I'll probably win the whole war for you!"

"That would save us a lot of time. Get on with it then!"

Edan had to grin at that. "You coming to the food hall later?"

"I reckon so. Depends on how long it takes me to get away from my mother." Eldred grimaced. "I know everyone's acting strangely at the moment but honestly, my parents are the strangest of the lot. My father's striding round like Arn the Destroyer and my mother's looking guilty as sin."

Ranfrith looked up. "Talking of which..."

Frida hurried over. "Eldred, Ranfrith, hurry up and stop loitering about! There is a lot to do before we go to bed for the night. And it will be early tonight. Tomorrow will be a long day, so don't try and persuade your father's friends to give you ale until you throw up again."

Ranfrith pulled a face. He had suggested this very plan to Edan. "So much for being counted as one of the men!"

"Of course you're not men, you silly boy! It's just that you'll be much better here with your father and your uncle Olann than you will on a ship with some ancients who can barely see well enough to read a map, never mind manage a sail!"

"I'll see you later, Edan." Eldred followed Ranfrith in the wake of their mother, deeply embarrassed and a little resentful at the way she had talked to them in front of their friend.

They ate quickly and she had them go straight to bed. Ranfrith rebelled considerably at this, until his father, who was in one of the worst moods they had ever seen, suddenly turned and blasted him.

"What kind of warrior will you grow to be if you cannot take orders?! Will you dash into battle before the rest of them are ready? Do as you are told, boy, and do not shame me with your disobedience!"

Considerably taken aback, the boys went to bed in the little niche where their sleeping furs were. Ranfrith reached forward and pulled the curtains of their bedding place slightly apart. Through the gap they watched their mother hurrying about. Gradually they became aware of what she was doing: under the guise of tidying their ownings, she was gathering them together in one place, packing them in sacks and every so often, putting on a cloak to hide the sack she was carrying out of the hall.

Eldred did not know quite what to make of this. The night wore on, and others filtered in and went to their own bedding places, until the sides of the halls were one big wall of curtains, with the occasional gap where some drunken warrior had slumped on his bed (or off it) in a stupor of mead and anticipation. Then his mother drew aside the curtain to his own bedding place. "Shhh. Come."

Ranfrith started to protest, but Eldred hesitated. "Father?"

Bran was sitting nearby, but now he came into the bedding

place. "Do as your mother says, boys; but before you go, I want to give you something. Here, Eldred. This was your grandfather's. I think he would have liked you to have it." It was an eating set, the one his father used every day, and now Eldred was really concerned.

"What--?"

"Ranfrith, take this dagger. Look after your brother."

"Father--"

"Don't argue, boy. Just go. Take it, and remember me." He caught the boys to him in a brief hug. "And make sure you clean our slate in the blood of the enemy in the days to come."

"But Father..."

"Enough! Go. Frida, you have seen the sign?"

"I know the way, Bran. You will not come with us?"

"No. I will stay, and fight."

"But father, I don't want to run away!" Ranfrith interrupted. "I will fight with you!"

"Be quiet! Someone will hear and your mother will get into trouble!" There was no answer to that, and so the boys rose, put on their cloaks and slipped out of the warmth of the hall into the freezing darkness. Their father patted them on the shoulder awkwardly and made his way back inside.

Uncovering a shielded lantern, their mother led the way to the dog-sheds, where she had packed and readied a sled and team. "Get on, and hurry!"

The boys were bundled onto the sled with all the other baggage, bewildered. Frida strapped the lantern on, and climbed on the back. With a jerk the sled moved off across the plain.

FOR SOME HOURS they rattled on in the darkness, going slowly and always aiming for that flickering firelight on the mountain. The ground climbed up to the foothills, and they came to the road that wound over the mountains: Lamefoot Pass.

"Unload the sled. We will find somewhere to hide the food until we can come back for it. Hurry!" Frida loosened the dogs' harness from the sled and tied it to a tree so that they should not move away. Eldred had been asleep despite the bumping, but Ranfrith was awake and burning with resentment.

"You never meant to let us fight, did you? You told us we didn't have to go on the ship because you had already planned to run away like a coward. And what are we going to do here?" Ranfrith heaved a bundle off the sled and slammed it on the ground.

"Don't shout! Someone will hear you!" Frida moved the bundle over to a stone. "Your brother understands why I did it, though, don't you, Eldred?"

Eldred looked at her for a long moment. "I understand why you did it, but you have given away our honour without even asking us." He shook his head. "If any Skral survive this war, we will always be the ones who stole a sled and ran away. I can't believe that Father allowed it."

"Eldred..."

"You should have *asked*. It should have been our decision as well." Eldred picked up another bundle. "I will help you bring your load to wherever you're going, but then I will take the sled back. They might need it."

"But Eldred, you will die! They will all die! That is the only reason why we are here—so that someone will be left to fight the enemy when the rest of them have all died."

Eldred shook his head. "That might have worked on Father because he would want to believe it. It makes no sense at all though. You should have sent us on the ship if that was what you intended." He began to harness the dogs to the sled again, calm but determined.

"You can't go back now though, or we will all be in trouble, me especially." Frida stopped. "Do you want that? You know the punishment. If they sent me away now I'd be alone with that army coming along. How long do you think it would take them to kill me? No, it's too late now. We're here and we're going to meet up with Olann and we're going to go with him. Look, that will be him now." She nodded at a light that was coming closer. "Who else would be on the mountain?"

The dogs began to growl. Eldred exchanged glances with his brother. "The enemy?"

Frida backed toward the sled as the boys turned it round.

Eldred stepped onto the driving platform. "Get on, just in case!"

As Ranfrith and Frida tumbled onto the sled, the light came round the corner, to reveal three men, thin and wary. They all froze, and then one of the men came forward, speaking some language Eldred did not know. He smiled, and approached gently. The other two fanned out either side and edged forward. He was not holding a weapon. In his hand was a piece of roasted meat on the bone, hot and succulent. Juices ran down his hand and he licked at them. He said something to the others, who roared with laughter as he tore a big bite of meat off, chewing it as if it were tough.

Eldred stared. *That meat is strangely shaped. What animal is it?*

The dogs were snapping and snarling and as the man edged nearer, Eldred saw that the skin on the meat was marked with a convoluted spiral tattoo. He froze.

Then in a flurry of fear, he whistled the signal and the dogs were off and running, faster and faster into the dark. He could not see the way very well but the dogs were on familiar ground and knew where the clanhalls were, and all of them were desperate to be far from the Ice Lord's men and the terrible feasting on Fang Peak.

When they reached the halls. Eldred went round and knelt by the sled, where Frida was clutching at Ranfrith. "Mother. We're back, Mother."

Frida did not react. Tears were streaming down her face.

Eldred's brother struggled out from her grasp. "She's been like this all the way home."

"She was very close to Olann."

"What? What happened to Olann?"

"He's dead."

"How do you know?"

Eldred paused. *He didn't see or understand it? Thank goodness.* He would not leave him with that image which was burned into his own brain. "They had his axe, all covered in blood," he lied. "He would never give that up. Listen, we need Father. Go and get him—but quietly. No-one must know. Mother said so."

And as Ranfrith slipped away into the night, Eldred put his arms around his mother, holding her until help came.

"Eldred." Bran stank of mead, but was in control. He crouched beside them. "I am glad and sorry to see you."

Eldred smiled crookedly. "Is Ranfrith in the halls?" Bran nodded. "This is what happened. I have not explained to him." He went through the events of the evening, ending with the lie he had told Ranfrith.

"You did well tonight, boy. You are growing to be the man I hoped you would." Bran sat back on his heels.

"And I have killed you both." Frida still had that strange intense stare. "You should have gone on the ship."

"That's not important now." Bran pulled her to her feet. "Come. We must get you back to the halls. Eldred will see to the sled."

Eldred was left to unharness and water the dogs that had saved them that night, and then to make his way through the noises and whispering of the darkness into the temporary safety of the clan-halls. When he got back, Frida was in bed and apparently asleep and Ranfrith just drawing the curtain shut on his own bed.

Catching Eldred's eye, Bran came to the doorway. "Come. We need to tell the Elders what you saw."

"I do not want to get Mother in trouble..."

"Olann was the instigator of this foolishness, and Olann is dead." Bran held open the door of the clanhall. "Your mother will not be punished."

The clanfathers were not pleased at being woken, but once assembled, Eldred's story quietened their murmurings.

"You say only your wife and the boy here know?" Tusken Seal stifled a yawn. "Then I say we tell only those who need to know. There is no point in panicking everyone. On the other hand, we do need to pass it on to those manning the scoutships. If they see people on foot, we will make sure they pick them up. To be eaten is no death for a Skral." He paused in thought. "We will not need the sleds now. There is nowhere for us to attempt to escape to. Send Drankar and his people out, one rider with each sled. Make sure they are good fighters. Have them circle around as widely as they can, and get back quickly. We do not send them to die now. We need them back before the battle begins, and it will not be easy."

THE ROLLING OF DRUMS

The sandships came back with first light, reporting that though the greater part of the Ice Lord's army was still making its way over from the other side of the island, the nearer part was within a half-day's march. The ships would not go on long sweeps any more lest they return to find themselves trapped, and as the light grew into a grim dawn, enemy scouts were sighted.

With the coming of day, the first soldiers of the Ice Lord's army came into view and as the day progressed, the army came on and on, and no end to it could be seen. As the front edge of the army grew nearer, the Skrals and their allies spilled out of the clan-halls and went to take their places around the Circle.

Lodin, Maran and Asri worked like demons, but even so they paused every so often to glance round at the horizon. No word was spoken as the bowl of the plain filled to overflowing, the white snow trampled by the black tide of armoured soldiers who spilled into it.

"I cannot see them. It is bad, is it?" Asri's face was weary with resignation.

Lodin knew her well enough not to lie. "The Ice Lord's army stretches to the horizon."

"The Skral are few."

"Valorous as they are, they cannot stand against so many."

She fell silent for a moment, her every movement expressing a kind of fury. "Then let us hope that it is finished in time. You are sure that it will work, this trap?"

"The ships told me it would." Lodin nodded slowly. "I am sure, yes."

"And you can make the Ice Lord walk into it?" she demanded of Maran.

"Yes. I will promise him that which he desires. He will walk in. I have seen it."

"And then the ships will lock him in place." Lodin leaned on the snow wall in front of him. It all seems so simple. *Perhaps I was wrong to fear for Maran. If the Ice Lord is inside the Heart of Wood, how can he hurt Maran? Perhaps it was no more than a danger of something happening, rather than a definite prediction.* Lodin glanced across at his soul-twin, who looked tired and pale in the dullness of the morning. No matter what the ships foretold, if he could save the man he loved from this danger, he would–but still his heart wept within him with the fear of parting.

Maran met his gaze and came over to him. "Stay strong, my brother," he whispered raggedly. "You are my strength. You have seen what happens if we do not tread this path. You have seen what the Ice Lord did to Lyria at first hand, and the ships showed you what the consequences will be if we turn aside now." Maran held him tightly. "If you try to save me, you kill the world and I will die with all the rest of it. There is no point in that. If I am not to survive this, I would rather die here in the Heart of Wood of my own choice that at the mercy of the Ice Lord. Let me end my life doing something worth dying for! The ships have said that I am the means of freeing the world from the Ice Lord's threat, at least for now. That is a choice worth the making, my brother, wouldn't you say?"

Lodin could not speak, but swallowed hard, trying to get past the tightness of his throat.

"Lodin, you know as well as I that it is necessary. Help me to acquit myself with honour. Please..."

They embraced for some moments before Lodin was able to nod.

"Many have sacrificed much to allow this to happen, bard." The gentleness of Asri's tone belied the harshness of her words. "It is a hard thing you do. We will both help you, as far as we can."

THE ICE LORD's soldiers spilled over the plain, not attempting to engage with the rabble of warriors setting up a last defence before them. Further and further round they spread, until the defenders were completely surrounded and the enemy stretched from one horizon to another.

The leaders had set their defences in place. Closest to the Dragon's Teeth the weaker fighters stood with the few children who had remained, defending the areas set aside for the wounded. Round them, a ring of the crossbows whose bolts would carry furthest, along with a couple of mangonels fashioned by the Gai-Renese. In front of them, three rings of archers, each staggered slightly so that the children who were in charge of the arrows could dart through and keep them supplied. Outside these, the first circle of defence was made up of the better fighters among the men, women and the older children. Among these Alaera, Edan and his friends stood, Lodin knew. Once all were in place, it was just a matter of waiting while the plain filled and overflowed with the Ice Lord's army. *There is so little time!*

A rustle of robes heralded the Potentate, whose leather breast-plate contrasted oddly with his usual silks. He carried one of the lethal Gai Renese blades. "They have us surrounded. How long will it take you to finish the trap?"

Lodin set down the tool with which he was packing the snow and tucked his hand under his armpit to warm it. "I cannot say. We have finished much of the wall but there is still the area on the top to be done, and it is difficult. The net of rope will not support solid blocks of snow so we must slice slabs from the top and lay them on. We will finish as quickly as we can but..."

The Potentate finished his thought. "There is little chance for any of us. I had hoped that perhaps a few might break away and survive."

Tusken Seal and the Mother joined them.

"We will hold them as long as we can," Tusken Seal told them, "but how long that will be is anyone's guess. It is a question of how long they wish to play with us. If they decide to crush us now, we cannot stand against them."

"When they attacked the Court at Lyria, there were fewer of them and more of us." With so much that was terrible surrounding Lodin, the pain of the memory was lost amongst the rest. "They sent their champion against ours. Ours won, and they shot him down with arrows. Their herald challenged us for another champion, and another and another until no more would come forward. They taunted us as cowards and then attacked, but the point is that while they were calling out champions they held off from the main battle. They used it as distraction then. Perhaps we can do so now."

There was a silence.

"Now this is more like the Skral Way!" Tusken Seal boomed suddenly, startling the Mother and the Potentate. "While there are Skrals left standing, you shall have your champions!"

"But they will die, inevitably!" the Potentate objected.

"We all will, but that kind of personal glory is very much to the Skral taste, I should think." The Mother clapped Tusken Seal on the back. "They are assured of a place in the Hall of the Forefathers at any rate."

"Aye!" Tusken Seal looked positively gleeful.

The Mother shook her head, baffled. "You are a strange, macabre lot, you Skrals, but I am honoured to fight alongside you."

The Potentate thought for a moment. "Very well. A challenge... We need a herald, preferably with some sort of drum or horn, and we need to attract their attention quickly before they are all positioned for the attack."

"The Clanfathers have horns. I need them not to go in on the first wave in any case. When the battle starts the youngsters will go berserk too quickly if left unguided, and we cannot win by fury alone here. The Elders will take it hard not to be allowed to volunteer as champions but there are three things that a Skral never gives to another–his ship, his knife and his battlehorn. We will use the Clanfathers as a guard of honour."

"Very well. And the champion?"

"We may have to draw lots to find out who goes first. I shall go and tell my people." Tusken Seal nodded at both and left to organise this.

"Skrals!" The Mother sighed. "They are an extraordinary people. I hope this is not the last the world sees of them."

"We will do our best to make sure of that." The Potentate looked at the sparse lines of fighters between the Dragon's Teeth and the vast armies surrounding them. "Let us hope that our best suffices."

EDAN

"Edan? What are you doing here?"

Edan turned. "Alaera? I didn't know you could fight."

"I'm Skral." The healer smiled sadly. "We all learn to wield a weapon, even if we don't want to. In the old days the clans used to raid each other, until it occurred to them that if they raided other people the clan-halls didn't get burnt down every year or so. I'm no warrior though. And neither are you."

The boy looked down. "I did kill a man once. It was horrible, but I did it. And I'm not very good but they said we need everyone we can get."

Alaera looked out over the plain. "I know. I keep telling myself we aren't going to get out of this, so there's no reason to worry about it, but I must admit the sight of all those soldiers scares me."

"Me too. I must be a terrible coward..."

"There is no shame in being afraid." The Potentate paused, on the way to his place. "Everyone feels fear. It is part of being human. It is what we do when we are afraid that makes us brave or cowardly. The brave man accepts his fear and does what he has to despite it. It is only the man who allows his fear to rule him that is the coward, the man who uses fear as an excuse not to do what must be done. We are all afraid, young man, because we know that pain and death await us. All we can do is sell our lives dearly enough to win the time that is needed for the completion of the Heart of Wood."

"Will it work, sir?"

The Potentate looked at the boy standing before him, nearly as tall as he but with fear and uncertainty in his eyes. "I am no seer myself, but if the shipspirits have said it and the Mother of the Shantar agrees, then I think it will work. And if it does not, at least we will not be here to see it. It is a strange kind of consolation, but it makes me feel better nonetheless."

The boy's face eased a little. "Thank you, sir."

Around them the massed armies settled into place. The ranks stopped moving and a quiet descended on the plain, broken by the sounds of flags snapping in the icy wind and the faint shouting of men, almost beyond the edge of hearing.

Alaera fidgeted. "I hate doing nothing. I hate it anyway but more so when I'm nervous. Would you like to help me sort out the bandages while they're still getting in position? We made extra but didn't have time to roll them." She handed him a tangle of material.

"Thanks, Alaera. That might keep my mind off it for a bit." The boy began to tease it out so that he could roll it up, ready for use. "How quiet it is. The waiting is horrible."

"It is the calm before the storm, no more." They both jumped as a cacophony erupted within their own lines.

"What on earth is that?"

Further around the little circle of defenders, a procession was forming. A double line of Skral men blowing on horns were flanked by Shantars, bashing weapons on shields. The grey bearded Skral carried ornately ornamented axes and horns, and were led by Tusken Seal. Behind them walked a brawny warrior, strong and confident in his bearing.

Alaera wiped her eyes. "That is Rankar, of my clan. He is a mighty warrior. He deserves this honour."

"What honour? What is happening?"

"He is the first of the champions. He goes to a valorous death against the enemy."

Edan looked out across the seas of men on the plain. Tusken Seal led his procession out into the gap between the armies. The Clanfathers gave a final mighty blast on their horns, and Tusken Seal opened a great scroll and called out what was written on it, brief phrases in two or three languages.

"A challenge?"

"Aye. That'll be an addition from the Potentate," Alaera replied. "The Gai Renese have a good feel for effect."

"But what's the point? If he's going to die anyway?" Edan blurted. "Doesn't he just want to get it over and done with? I would."

"Perhaps so, but every moment that he buys for us is another moment that you and I get to live. Give us enough moments, and who knows what we may do?"

There was a thunderous roll of drums. From far back in the Ice Lord's army, there was a ripple of movement. Rank after rank of men parted to allow a party of mounted officers through. There were fifteen or twenty of them, broad-shouldered and powerful of build. Edan could not see their faces from that distance, but they cantered through their own men with a blithe disregard for life and limb. He saw at least two of their own soldiers trampled under the horses' hooves. The tallest officer wore the same black cloak as the others, but with a dash of red satin around the edges–the uniform of a member of the elite Ice Guard. He rode right up to Tusken Seal and spat on the floor beside the older man.

There was a brief exchange. Rankar shouted something that did not sound complimentary. The Ice Guard reared his horse, and galloped back through the enemy ranks, his men close behind him. The drums rolled again, and then settled into a heavy beat which hung in the air, stifling as thunder. It went on for a short while, and then there was another drumroll and crash.

"What does that mean, Alaera?"

"I think we're about to find out."

This time when the Ice Guard returned there was another man with them, wearing crimson armour and armed with a spiked mace and a spear.

"He has no shield," Edan whispered.

"He is not intended to survive. He is there only to entertain them." Alaera continued to wind her bandage as if that could hold off the fighting for another moment, just one moment more.

The drums were speeding up now, taking on a double beat that echoed the racing of Edan's heart. The Clanfathers saluted Rankar and drew back, as did the enemy officers. The Ice Lord's pennants snapped in the sharp wind.

The drums resounded across the plain. Rankar and the other warrior hefted their weapons and began to circle warily. Suddenly they lunged into action, feinting and blocking. A roar went up from both sides. The Ice Lord's man stabbed his spear at Rankar. The Skral deflected it with his shield and brought the axe smashing down. It missed the warrior but hacked through the spearhead. The warrior whipped the spearhaft round like a cudgel, beating the Skral over the shoulders. Rankar staggered and the warrior tripped him with the spearhaft. Rankar fell. The lethal spiked mace sank deep into the turf where Rankar's head had been as he lunged away, jerking his opponent's legs from under him.

They rolled and climbed to their feet, beginning to circle again.

"He's good." Edan could barely breathe. He did not want to see but could not tear his eyes away.

"He's very good," Alaera replied softly. "He will fight well and, I hope, die well." As the warriors lunged and parried on the field, Edan opened his mouth as if to speak, but did not. She caught the movement. "Does it shock you that I should say that? If we expected to survive, perhaps I should not, but Rankar does not expect to live. I would rather he died quickly and painlessly. Now, death is sure, and because the uncertainty is gone, it is to be accepted, not feared—but I cannot help but fear pain."

"I am glad to be standing here with you, Alaera," Edan told her suddenly. "My friend Ranfrith was talking like a mighty warrior, boasting how many he would kill and how we would win the day despite the odds. For all his talk, fear was in his eyes and his hands shook. It made me feel even more afraid. You are not hopeful as he seemed to be, but you are determined. That makes much more sense to me." He watched the champions as they wrestled on the sparse grass of the plain. "I do not think we can survive, either, but I will do my best to die honourably."

Alaera gave him a brief one-arm hug and released him quickly. "I had a son, you know. I sometimes imagine how he would be now. I hope he would be a bit like you."

Edan did not quite know what to say to this. "I wondered if

you had your own children, but it seemed rude to ask. You're like everyone's mother."

Alaera did not take her eyes from the bandage she was rolling. "I only had one child. My son died when he was a baby. He would have been a bit younger than you are now, I think. I never thought I would say so, but I am glad his little life was so short. All he knew was a few months of flowers and sunshine, and then he went to sleep and never woke up."

Edan looked at the ground. "That seems like a good thing to me now." He was thinking of his sister.

A roar went up from the Skrals as Rankar's axe went through the helm of his opponent. The Ice Lord's champion stiffened and fell. Rankar yelled his triumph, brandishing his axe high, and Edan and Alaera shouted with the rest.

Then Rankar stumbled and collapsed to the ground, an arrow in his neck. The Skrals fell silent. He lay still. Warriors came forward to carry Rankar back to the Dragon's Teeth, while men from the Ice Lord's army dragged their own champion to one side.

"Is he –?"

"He's dead." Alaera wiped her eyes again. "From the look of it, that arrow pierced the artery in his neck. But he died triumphant, just as he wished. The Forefathers will make a special place for him."

There was a moment's pause before the drums started again, and the rippling ranks of the army announced a new champion coming through. A second Skral champion stepped forward. Again the drums picked up that double beat, getting faster and faster, and again the warriors chose their ground.

Alaera turned to Edan. "Pass me another bandage, please. We will put up champions for as long as we can. We could be here for some time."

. . .

THREE TIMES THE DRUMS ROLLED, and three times a new champion came to battle, but if the Skrals won they were slain with arrows. By now the ground was trampled and so slippery with blood that it was difficult for the fighters to keep their footing, but still there were many young Skrals waiting and ready to volunteer. After the third champion was slain, bowstrings twanged and the victorious Skral died, but the pattern of the drums changed.

There was a prolonged roll that filled the horizon with thunder. Then, as the echoes faded, a new beat started, and now it was a fast marching beat. Horns brayed, and across the whole plain there was a shifting of black, as if the sea was suddenly flooding over the island.

"They have tired of their sport too quickly. I hope we have at least bought Lodin the time he needs." Alaera packed the last of the bandages into a basket and held it out to Edan. "Would you return this, please? And Edan?"

"Yes?"

She held out the weapon he had put down. "Take your sword. This may happen very quickly."

Edan glanced out at the enemy, from the ragged ranks at the front to the well-armed, uniformed soldiers ready behind. Taking the sword, he slotted it neatly into his scabbard. Then he ran for the centre, holding the scabbard against his leg so it did not trip him. He dropped the basket of bandages by the oldster who was closing the eyes of the last champion whose body had been brought to lie with that of Rankar and the other. The oldster crooned the Skral death-rites, but Edan had the feeling that that withered voice sang for all of them, Skral, Shantar and Gai-Renese alike. He nodded acknowledgment to her but she did not pause in her song. The Ice Lord's drums kept up that fast pace, and the horns brayed again, a great blare of sound which echoed across the plain.

Edan took a deep breath. He suddenly felt very young, but as he looked out over the great sea of black before him, there was a chirp.

"Tiris? What are you doing here?" Arrows thrummed out from the first ring of archers as he leant down and grabbed the little bird, which squawked in outrage. There was no time to hesitate. Edan ran back to the entrance of the Heart of Wood. "Mother!"

"Edan?"

"Mother, Tiris is here. He will get hurt. I brought him back so you can look after him." He thrust the bird into his mother's hands.

"Edan, don't go..." Asri's voice shook as he embraced her quickly.

"I must. They're coming. I love you." He kissed her on the cheek and stepped away.

"Fortune!" Lodin called.

"And to you!" Edan sped back to the lines. A mighty *thunk*—the mangonel loosed its load and projectiles flew overhead. There were screams and yelling from the enemy. Edan ducked back into line with Alaera just in time. Soldiers were running up the slope towards them.

Edan's heart was banging on his ribcage, but suddenly he was back there on the mountain, hiding with his mother as the Ice Lord's soldiers descended upon his father and sister. Rage filled him, and he raised his sword, his hands suddenly steady. "This time I am not helpless!" he roared, slashing at the face of the man who reached him first.

THE BATTLE

LODIN

As the three worked frantically to complete the walls of snow, the battle raged. Blood flowed and many died. Lodin and Maran did not stop to look and Asri did not ask but cries echoed over the plain, punctuated by the occasional boom as one of the rattling, wind-powered Gai Renese constructions went off.

They filled the space between one monolith and the next, as high as they could reach, and moved round to the next.

"We'll never finish in time." Lodin slammed a fist into the snow block he was working, shattering the corner off. "We will fail and it will all be in vain. What is the use of going on when we cannot finish?"

"We do not know that yet," Maran soothed. "We have still a little time."

"But not enough—nowhere near enough!"

"Do you mean to give up?" Asri interrupted, fierce as a hawk. "After all this? After all that the Ice Lord has done, would you let him win?"

"Of course not, but against so many, what hope is there?"

"That battle is not ours to fight. Those who can are fighting the Ice Lord with spear and axe, we with snow and shovel." She stabbed her shovel into the snow viciously. "Edan is out there fighting for us. I cannot see well enough to fight beside him, but I can see where there is snow, and I can build it into blocks. Do not let us waste these moments. They are dearly bought, and we have walls to build before the enemy come for us."

EDAN

There was no way that Edan could tell how long he had been fighting. His shoulders were weary with the ache of thrust and parry, and of endless impacts on his shield.

When the first wave had passed, he looked about and was appalled. All around him were the dead and dying. There seemed to be equal numbers of the Ice Lord's men and those from his own side. The defenders were fighting with unstinting ferocity, but that had eaten into their numbers badly and the Ice Lord's armies still covered the plain.

That said, there were pockets of uproar well into the enemy ranks. The Gai Renese had set off their contraptions a few at a time. These were great rattling things like skeletons of giant centipedes, multi-legged and with little sails along their backs. As the wind caught them it wound up springs and joints so that they scuttled across the field, flapping and rattling. They were terrifying enough if one bore down on you, but in addition they carried a fire in their belly and every so often would flick out little rags soaked in burning pitch. The enemy fled before them, but in the crowd there was not room enough to get out of reach of the pitch, and so there were screams and flames tracking across the army. After a while the bamboo itself would burn, though it had been soaked in water beforehand. Edan could see two burning in heaps and one afire, soldiers trying to upturn it with pikes as it crept its last steps and then exploded in a shower of sticky flames.

There were another four left tethered behind the defenders, unlit, but shifting in the breeze.

"They make me shiver," Alaera gasped, following his gaze as she leant on her axe. "They scuttle like giant insects."

"Insects taller than horses." Edan shuddered. "I'd probably run if one came towards me."

"That's the idea." Alaera straightened a little. "You look mostly unhurt."

"A scratch or two." Edan raised a hand to his face. Blood trickled from a scratch to his scalp. "You?"

"No wounds. A couple of blows from a stave." She handed him the axe. "I think we have a few moments. Take this."

She slipped a dagger from her belt and while he watched, horrified, she went round the enemy soldiers nearby and made sure they were all dead. Some had been screaming, but stopped with a gurgle as she cut their throats. She wiped the blade on the jerkin of the last, and returned to her place as the drums began again. "How my father would laugh," she said bitterly. "He always said that I was too soft. He would not believe how ruthless we have become in these latter days. What kind of healer kills without attempting to heal? But they would have received no help from their own."

Edan could not help staring. More than the blood on his hands, more than the split guts and death littering the ground about him, this brought home to him that they were fighting beyond hope.

Alaera saw his face. "One of the evils of war is what it turns us into." She wiped her eyes on a sleeve, leaving a smear across her cheek. "But now we are here, and hopelessly outnumbered. Every death wins Lodin and Maran a little more time, and your mother. If it is easier, fight for her."

Edan took a deep breath. *To keep my mother from these beasts, what would I do? Anything.* "I will do what is needful to keep her safe."

Alaera patted his arm. "So will we all." She looked down into the field where another charge was coming together. "A few moments and they will come again. Straighten your jerkin, Edan. The leather is pulled up so there is a gap along your side. If they see that, they will aim for it."

As Edan yanked his jerkin down, the mangonel *thunked*, sending its load into the crowded enemy. Many were killed or maimed, but more took their places. The front rank were taken by crossbow bolts. As they fell, the second ran into a shower of arrows.

The archers fired and knelt so that the row behind had a clear view. Children ran back and forth with bundles of arrows for the archers and bolts for the crossbowmen, who reloaded much more slowly but sent their bolts further into the enemy. For all the hail of deadly projectiles, there were still those who got through to the front line of the defenders and when the arrows and crossbow bolts ran out, Edan knew they would quickly be overrun.

The Gai Renese were heating more pitch for the next of their contraptions, and the oldsters who could not fight were dragging the wounded to the centre to be tended. The air was thick with screams and roars, the clang of weapon on weapon and the rush of arrows. Acrid smoke drifted across, making their eyes water and further away was the dull boom of another of the Gai Renese contraptions exploding.

The next wave of fighters came, and for a time all thought was lost in the fear and exhilaration of fighting. Beside Edan an older man died, nearly cut in half by the curving sword of a giant man. The warrior paused, triumphant, but quick as a snake Edan slid his sword between the man's ribs. Blood pumped out over Edan's fists. He tried to jerk his sword free as the man toppled, but it was stuck firmly. There was someone behind him. Edan turned, helpless. Alaera lunged forward with her axe but she was too far away to help. All Edan could do was watch the blade descending and hope that it would not hurt too much.

LODIN

Lodin paused to warm his hand under his armpit again. They had a wall of snow inside the standing stones nearly all the way round, leaving only a gap between two stones, but he could not see how the three of them could complete the snow roof over the Heart of Wood as he had seen in his dream. He stepped inside the Heart of Wood and looked closely at the interwoven ropes, caked with slabs of snow. There were gaps between them, and areas which they had not been able to reach. *Will it work, incomplete? Against such a powerful entity as the Ice Lord, how can it? It has to be perfect or all the sacrifices of Maran and all the others around him would be in vain. What can I do?* No inspiration came to him, and he sank down disheartened.

"Lodin? Are you all right?" Maran came into the Heart.

Asri sat back on her heels. "What has happened?"

But the moment that all three of them were in the Heart of Wood a great wind arose and a great lashing of hail and sleet. Cowering in the Heart of Wood, they crawled together and sheltered under the beams from the ships. After a short time the wind fell and the sleet stopped. They emerged from the Heart of Wood to find that the sleet and hail had filled the gaps in the roof, flung around by the wind into all the tiny corners and areas which the humans had not been able to cover. The roof was now as complete as the walls, and only the doorway remained. All that had to be done was to lure the Ice Lord into the Heart of Wood.

"It is nearly finished." Maran breathed. "All but the doorway..."

"How do we seal up the last gap? The Ice Lord will not wait there for several hours while we close him in," Asri objected.

"The ships said walls of water, not walls of snow." All of a sudden Lodin saw again that one solitary drop that had fallen from the top of the Heart of Wood into the pool of visions–but this time it shattered on the frozen–"Ice."

"Ice?"

"Yes. There are icicles, Asri." Now Lodin knew how it was to be achieved.

Choosing an area round the side of the circle where there was a space he placed the cloak on the ground, oiled side up. Taking a chisel, he went round the Heart of Wood gathering the long spear-like icicles that hung from the edges. Felling them with one sharp tap, he lay them one by one in the cloak. When they lay top to toe, lengthwise across the whole piece, Lodin laid down his chisel.

"What next?" Asri asked.

"Now we drip on a little more water, and wait for it to freeze."

"Where will we get the water?"

Lodin sprinkled a light covering of snow over the icicles, and then taking a handful, let the warmth of his hand melt it. "Pack between the icicles carefully, and when it is packed we will wet the surface so that it holds together. The snow is already frozen so we just need to make it stay together."

"Can we bind it?" Asri was thinking hard.

"We have no yarn or thread."

"I can help with that." Asri pulled the bone pins out of her bun and her hair slithered down. It was long, down past her waist. "Do you have a knife? If we make braids of a few strands each, we should be able to make something long enough to hold it. Then the snow need only pack the gaps."

"You'll know more about braiding hair than we do." Maran took the knife. "Are your hands warm enough to do the braid-ing? I'll cut the hairs." She grimaced as Maran pulled the hairs tight, then he laid a strand upon her lap and guided her hands to it.

She knotted the ends and held it up to him. "Hold this for me while I braid, please. I shall need a few strands at a time. I will tell you when to pass me another. Lodin, when the braid gets long enough, tell me. I'll knot it off and you can be working on the door while I work on the next."

"If it is bound and just needs packing, how long will it be before it is strong enough to lift?" Maran asked.

"I cannot tell. We will need all the time they can buy us." Lodin fell silent, watching Asri's clever hands as she intertwined the hair into a tiny braid. She braided more and more strands into it until it was the right length, and then she passed it to Lodin, who set about binding each of the wrist-thick icicles to the next. It gripped the ice better than he had expected and, to him, seemed stronger than it had any right to be.

Maran cut another strand and passed it to her. "Asri, this is going to need a lot of your hair."

She snorted. "Yes, and I am sure to be very upset about that for the next few hours while the Ice Lord is hacking us to bits. I have more to worry about than my hair, Maran."

"I know, but I'm sorry it will look so messy, nevertheless."

As he waited for the next braid, Lodin packed snow in the gaps between the icicles until they were tight and solid. "The cloak will support it for now. How it will fare when we bring it upright, I do not know."

"The shipspirits have been with us so far." Maran laid another strand on Asri's lap. "They will not fail us now."

EDAN

Edan awoke with screaming in his ears. A jolt sent pain burning through him like knives, and he realised that it was he himself screaming. There was a shape looming over him. He cringed away.

Alaera's voice gasped. "Don't fight me, Edan. I can hardly keep a grip as it is."

He blinked, but the sun was bright and low behind her, searing the sky with a million colours of bruises. "Alaera?"

She did not reply but tugged at him again. Something lay heavy over him—yes, the big warrior. He started to wriggle free, but almost blacked out again with the pain. After a few moments it ebbed a little, but stayed, burning in his left leg. "How long...?"

"I thought you were dead. It looks bad. I'm sorry." She sounded strained and faint. Edan gritted his teeth as she yanked him free and began to drag him across the field. Little more than crawling, her arm hooked under his shoulder as she pulled him in fits and starts in towards the centre, where the healers were. Edan knew he should be afraid but with Alaera there, he was not.

Around him the battle was shrinking in towards the Circle. Out where they had been there were only bodies. None of those who had stood near him were anywhere to be seen, and the Ice Lord's soldiers were not even pushing at that area any more. As pain stabbed at him, he looked further out. "They are playing with us. They send in one row at a time, and when they have all fallen, they send in the next. There is no end to them. We must fail, as surely as the sun sets."

Alaera paused in her dragging. She gasped for a while. "We knew that. We delay them, that is all."

"Alaera, are you hurt?"

"Yes. But I can get you to the healers before I go." She dragged again and he helped as he could, though every movement sent agony through his leg. They crawled through the sharp grass of the plain, made slippery with blood and viscera. Edan's world narrowed to the next movement of arm or leg, the next breath, the next stab of pain. A corpse lay sprawled in their way. They struggled over it. *The face.* Edan had seen the face before. *It was a Skral,* he thought absently, biting his lip against the agony of his leg. *A Skral. A boy a couple of years younger than me.*

"Ranfrith. That was his name." He gazed at the contorted face as he dragged himself further away. "He was my friend."

"We are near the fighters. Do not call attention to yourself. If they come, play dead."

The battleground was a storm of noise. The drums kept up an insistent beat and the horns yelped, but mostly the air was thick with the stink of sweat and blood and excrement, mixed together with the clutching mud. His ears hurt with the clash of weapons, the screams of the dead and dying and—worst of all—the laughter of the rest of the Ice Lord's men who lolled about on the plain, cheering on their favourites.

The ground was a mass of bodies. Some were dead, others writhing in agony and a few, a very few trying to crawl to their brothers by the Circle. Alaera stopped again, and her breath came in sobs now. She did not let go of Edan and so he could not turn to her, but he hugged her arm.

A wave of men dashed across the field. Edan and Alaera fell limp and stayed still. The Ice Lord's men leaped and stumbled over the corpses, making their way across to where a knot of Gai Renese had become separated from the rest of the defenders. *More screaming and shouts.* Edan was weak with pain and fear, and ashamed to find himself weeping quietly.

Alaera gasped again and her breaths bubbled. "We must go, while we still can."

"Not far now, not far," he crooned, and she seemed to take strength from this.

They began the slow crawl across the field again. They were close now, so close that skirmishers tripped and slid nearby.

A heavily-built Skral slew his foe and turned to find no enemy close.

"Edric?" Alaera called--faintly, but he heard his name.

"Gods, Alaera!" He strode over and knelt.

"Take the boy first."

"I'll take both of you." The Skral tucked his axe in the back of his belt and grabbed Edan by one arm and Alaera by the other. The pain of his leg made Edan dizzy and sick and as he was dragged behind the lines, every jolt made grey spots dance in front of his eyes but he was limp with relief. *Alaera sounds to be badly hurt. At least now she will be safe for the moment.*

The jolting journey ended as the smith dropped them unceremoniously in a space on the ground and called for healers.

With a great effort, Edan turned himself over. *I have to see.* Alaera lay beside him. Her face was smeared with the red muck of the battlefield, and blood was dribbling out of the corner of her mouth. Her breathing rattled and bubbled. He could not tell how much of the blood on her clothes was her own, but there was a bad wound to the side of her torso.

"Alaera?"

Her eyes flickered open. For a moment, there among the shrieks of madness and death, he did not think that she would recognise him but she smiled weakly. "Edan. See, I said I would get you here."

"And you did." Tears ran from his eyes, pain, weakness, sorrow. "But you must not leave me."

"I don't think I have any choice in the matter, but do not be sad, Edan. Remember I am Skral, and this is our chosen manner of dying."

"Lying in the mud, in the middle of this horror?" he demanded bitterly.

"In truth, it is overrated but at least I shall be welcomed into the Hall of our Forefathers. I am glad you are here though, and not lying out there with the enemy. Even if death is the end of everything, that is something to be proud of."

Edan took her in his arms. "You saved my life, Alaera," was all he could manage.

"For a little while, at least. There is a dagger in my belt. Take it. When the Ice Lord gets tired of playing with us..." She gasped for breath again. "... He will overrun us entirely. They do not spare the wounded." Her breath rattled in her chest. "...Take my dagger. The arteries in neck and groin, or the heart will bring you ease quickly..." He could hear the bubbles in her breathing, but she struggled to finish. "Better that... better that than... the fate they bring..."

Edan reached down to take the dagger, and he tucked it in his belt carefully. "I will do it. I promise."

Alaera seemed to relax a little. "My sight... is fading. I am cold."

He brought a fold of her cloak over her, filthy as it was, and tried to warm her with his own body heat. Further off, the smith was coming back with one of the oldsters. Edan willed them to come faster, to somehow save her. "Don't worry, Alaera, help is coming. They're nearly here now." She lay quiet. He rocked her back and forth as his mother had rocked him as a baby, anxiously watching the others hurry across.

It was only a few short moments till they got there, but even so, they were too late.

The smith closed Alaera's eyes with a gentle hand. They composed Alaera's body with what dignity they could, covered her face with her cloak and left her there on the battlefield, with so many of her clan. Edan they moved away to the centre, near the Dragon's Teeth where he lay, one among the many wounded, and wept for the healer who had saved him.

SPRINGING THE TRAP

EDAN

The mangonels were shattered. The Gai Renese contraptions had long since burned. The crossbowmen were on their last bundles of bolts, and many of the archers had been killed by poisoned darts, their bows passed on to the remaining children and wounded. The last wave of the Ice Lord's men had fought and fallen and now there was a brief breathing space while the next company shuffled into place and lined up. The drums were silent, unneeded while the companies were manoeuvring, for which Edan was heartily grateful. The endless drum beat seemed to echo the pulse of the pain in his leg until he could not tell which of them was booming in his head.

Edan was propped up against a boulder, facing outwards and waiting silently. He had a bow, but only a handful of arrows. *It will not be enough.* A child came along the field past him, face streaked with dirt and tears, carrying a bow which he had taken from a dead body further along.

Edan lifted a hand to attract his attention. "Could you bring me another bundle of arrows if there are any, please?"

"Are you fighting still?" the little boy asked.

"I think we all are." Edan replied wearily. "It's better than lying there waiting to die."

"What happened to your leg?"

"I don't know." Alaera had not lived long enough to tell him. "It is shattered but my arms still work enough to use a bow."

The boy regarded him solemnly. "Your hands are shaking."

"Yes, they are." His hands were shaking with pain and fear, but Edan would not give up now. *For my mother, for Alaera, I cannot.* "But there are so many men out there that if I can get an arrow flying, it's bound to hit someone, and that will be one person less to come and fight us here."

The boy nodded. "I will bring arrows."

Edan watched the boy run away to take the spare bow back to Ranulf. The bard, too old to fight, was supervising the wounded. Now there were no bandages left, he was left with the task of providing them all with weapons for the last push.

Edan lifted his hand and looked at it. It was shaking quite badly, but all he had to do was to get the arrows flying. There were so few defenders left now that it could not be long before the end, and when he had need, Alaera's dagger would bring him to a safe rest. *I hope that my mother will find an easy death... Lodin will do what was necessary if he has to, though. The Maker is a good man, and has already suffered at the hands of the Ice Lord. He will not let her be captured by them.*

The boy returned. "These are all that are left." There were maybe a dozen arrows in the bundle he passed over.

Edan glanced at the Ice Lord's men. They were still milling around and the drums were silent for the moment. "There are arrows lying on the ground in places–could you gather some of those for me please? Watch out for the army, and come straight back if the drums start."

LODIN

MARAN, Lodin and Asri stood in the centre of the Skrals, by the Dragon's Teeth. Lodin had been packing thin layers of snow onto the icicles, waiting for it to freeze and then adding more until the long spears had frozen into a great panel of ice. It felt as if he had spent hours constructing this fragile door, ready to shatter at a blow. But he trusted in the spirits and kept at his work doggedly, trying not to think of the battle which raged around him and the friends who were dying to earn him time.

Maran chafed his hands in his gloves to be sure that the fingers were warm and supple enough to play when the time came.

Eventually a child ran over. "The Elders say if anything is to be saved, you are to call on the spirits now."

"How is the door coming?" Asri asked anxiously as the child sped away.

Lodin looked up. "It is as near ready as I can make it."

"Time to bait the hook." Maran took off his gloves and began to uncover his harp.

"With what?" she asked.

"With me."

"What will you do?"

Maran smiled sadly. "I will show him a new kind of magic." He embraced the two of them. "Take care."

Maran took his harp into the Heart of Wood, which was so built that when he played, even the softest note, it was amplified and echoed across the plain. Lodin went on working on the door, Asri beside him, for there was nothing else to be done now.

After a moment's thought, Maran began to play. In the absence of the drums, the notes whispered across the plain, quiet but carrying. As his melody floated across that cold, blood-sodden field, those who heard it stopped in wonder to listen; and the field fell quiet.

"How beautiful," Asri breathed. "There is magic in that music. My mind has been full of blackness and terror for so long that I had forgotten how to be at peace. Now it is filling with memories of my old life. It seemed just everyday then, but compared to this place it was a paradise."

Lodin let the music wash through him. He remembered the wonderful homely smell of the basil that grew in a pot on his workshop windowsill at home, and the soft coolness of water on his hands as he washed them in the little waterfall he had built. He savoured the rich blackberry flavours of Kuhrin's favourite red wine, and smiled at the thought of the fresh wind from the mountains as it swept away all the dust of summer, bringing the gentle autumn rains and a relief from the parched Lyrian sun. Across the field, people stood quiet to hear the lingering strains.

Almost before the last note had faded, Maran began another song, and this one was of poignant loss.

Sitting with his back to the boulder, Edan wept for his sister, for his friends, for Alaera. To Lodin and those who had seen the sack of the cities, it spoke of the burning of fields and the killing of the innocent, and it brought every man there to a just realisation of the horrors he had seen and committed. Many of the Ice Lord's army fell to their knees, and tears ran down their faces.

But then the song began to change. To Lodin, it spoke of redemption, of returning to the old ways and helping to rebuild the life he had known. Into his mind came the exuberance of the first green blade of grass rising from the blackened earth, and of a multitude more to follow. Lodin was vaguely surprised that the entire plain did not erupt with grass, such was the power of its call.

Maran sang of the beauty of growth, of trees covered with flowers and fruit, and of forgiveness and peace, beautiful peace. His words flowed out over the field like balm over a hurt.

Lying among the wounded, the Mother smiled as another

Shantar bent over her, weeping. "Do you see it, Anara? I see our home and family, and a thousand cunning ways of repairing what has been lost. I see how to bring it back to fruitfulness and prosperity." She smiled faintly, despite the pain. A similar smile was on many of the faces around her as the music went on. Then the song stopped.

It did not end, but simply stopped, leaving that note resounding in the air like the warm bronze tones of a bell in summer. Even when there was no sound and the harp was silent, it still echoed in the hearts of those who had heard it at a fundamental level. There was no avoiding it.

The battlefield was silent.

A beat sounded on the drums, and another, but it faltered and stopped.

All was still for a moment. Then Tiris swooped down from nowhere and perched on the hilt of a sword sticking out of the ground in between the two lines. Caught in a stray shaft of the setting sun, he gleamed like all the colour and richness and joy in the world, there in the middle of that sea of carnage.

A man stepped forward from the chaos that was the front line of the Ice Lord. There was something of the look of Lodin about him, as if he was Lyrian.

Certainly the little green bird seemed to spark some kind of memory in him. The Lyrian whistled at Tiris, who chirped but did not move. The man looked down at the sword he held, and wept. He let it fall from his hand, and began to walk away. His comrades watched him. For a long moment no-one moved.

Then another man seemed to come to a decision and stepped out of line too. A third and a fourth followed, and suddenly the plain was awash in ripples of movement, this time heading outward from the Circle, not towards it.

EDAN

Officers shouted and cracked whips. Some picked up bows and shot the deserters, but the Ice Lord's glamour of fear was broken. Each soldier was overwhelmed by horror at what they had done. The urge to find their own place and make amends gripped them, and a need for home as strong as that which guides birds across oceans and continents.

Edan watched in wonder. *The shipspirits' magic is powerful indeed.*

"Is it over?" The young boy was back, with handfuls of arrows.

"I don't know." Edan dared not relax, not yet. "There are so few of us left and so many of them. Thousands could leave and still enough would remain to defeat us. But I am not so sure that they will bother, now."

"We aren't that important, are we?"

"I don't know. I guess we will find out, but perhaps not as quickly as we thought..." Edan took the arrows from the boy. "Thank you."

The plain was in chaos. Here and there amongst the trudging men, officers on horses cut their way through, trampling over people where they had to. Slowly, Edan became aware that the Ice Guard were converging on a point, a richly embroidered tent from which a black pennant flew.

Around Edan, the able-bodied were dashing into the field to bring back their wounded while the Ice Lord's troops were not attacking. A couple of Shantar carried the Mother in, and lay her near Edan. Tusken Seal turned up, blood across his face and part of his ear missing, and shortly after, the Potentate with his arm strapped uselessly to his front.

"Gentlemen." The Mother coughed. "It is good to see you still in the land of the living."

"Madam." The Potentate knelt. "Are you in pain?"

"Not for long, I think. Your bard seems to have done us good service."

"Aye. But also not for long, I think." Tusken Seal was watching the enemy troops. "Enough of them are waiting to finish us off."

"That was never in question."

"At least this will give Lodin the chance to finish whatever he is doing." The Potentate looked out over the field. "Come, they are gathering together those who still wish to fight. We should do the same."

"Without help from me, I fear." The Mother coughed again, and a small trickle of blood made its way from her mouth.

Tusken Seal knelt to wipe it from her face with surprising deftness. "As for that, you go before us to the Hall of our Forefathers. They will have a place set aside for you."

She smiled at that. "Generations of Skrals would be speechless to hear you say so, my friend! Fight well, die cleanly, and who knows? Perhaps you and I shall drink a horn of mead together in the afterlife!"

Tusken Seal saluted her. The Potentate bowed, and they left.

LODIN

The last few defenders gathered about the Dragon's Teeth. There were perhaps fifty who could stand and fight, and twice as many of the injured who had been given crossbows and even slingshots in an effort to arm them. In what seemed like a very short time, they were arrayed so as to defend the Heart of Wood. Lodin's door of ice was as ready as it could be, and the inside of the Circle was dark and cold as the tomb. Asri was stroking Tiris who had returned to her. She put him back under a fold of her shawl where he nestled, crooning quietly to himself as he fell asleep.

"We are ready now," Lodin informed Tusken Seal. "When the Ice Lord comes, retreat here so that he follows. I do not know what deaths can be avoided, but you have bought us the time we needed."

Horns sounded. A growing space had cleared between the fleeing army and the Circle, but now the Ice Lord and his chosen officers strode towards them.

"Just as well that you are finished, I think. There are still too many of them." Tusken Seal rubbed absently at a bloody blister on his palm.

"The Heart is finished but I am not quite done. Let me try once more." Maran took up his harp again and this time he played a song of such joy in life that the Skral laughed as they raised their weapons to meet this new onslaught from the Ice Lord and his men. Once again the Heart took the music and amplified it beyond the skill of any harp, so that it lent wings to their feet. But not to the feet of the Ice Guard. They were so mired in death that to them this exuberant vitality stung and wearied them. It could not make up for the difference in numbers, but it made the fighting harder for the Ice Lord's men and easier for the defenders.

EDAN

Edan, sitting in the centre with the wounded, drew and fired until there were no arrows left. A couple of times the boy ran up with more arrows, until he was hit himself and lay near Edan, sobbing quietly.

"Where are you hurt?" Edan called, unable to reach him.

"My leg. At the top."

Edan glanced over. He had an arrow through the flesh at the top of his thigh, but did not seem to be seriously injured. Nevertheless, he was better where he was. Edan threw over his cloak. "Cover yourself up and lie still. If they think you're dead, they won't pay any attention and someone will help you when it is all over." The boy did as he was told. Edan did not know if it was true, but at least the boy was not so frightened any more.

The Ice Guards massed around the Ice Lord in a wedge and

drove at the circle, always aiming for Maran. They were experienced warriors, and the tired remnant of the defenders could not withstand them, but the wounded unleashed arrow after arrow from where they lay. A party of the enemy broke off and attacked them. Ten or twelve of the remaining twenty Ice Guards charged around to the side of the Circle, and lay about with their scimitars. The wounded could not stand to fight, but neither did the hail of arrows cease.

"Lie still!" Edan hissed to the boy. "Even if they stand on you, lie still!"

One of the Ice Guards was making his way along, peppered with arrows already but staggering on. The wounded were scattered over a small area, but he was taking as many of them with him as he could.

He stabbed at a Skral and went on to a Shantara whose head was swathed in bandages, falling on one knee to finish her. The Ice Guard heaved himself up from the sucking mud and staggered across to take off the head of a slender Gai-Renese boy, though it took a couple of blows. Then he saw Edan and turned. Edan had only one arrow left. He would have to save it till the last possible moment and be sure that he did not miss.

The Ice Guard struggled to take every step, but he was determined and staggered towards Edan. He tripped on the little boy and fell heavily.

The boy cried out, and the Ice Guard twisted round and grabbed the child by his hair. As he raised his scimitar, Edan fired his arrow. It went deep into the Ice Guard's armpit. He dropped his scimitar as his arm fell, useless, but he growled fury, and heaved himself upright again. The child scrabbled away.

The Ice Guard retrieved his scimitar awkwardly, left-handed. It was only a few more steps to Edan, and the man dropped to his knees. Edan beat him uselessly about the face and neck with his bow. The Ice Guard raised his scimitar again. Edan was seized by a thought–Alaera's dagger! He dropped the bow and thrust the dagger into the side of his enemy's neck. The soldier stiffened, but with his last strength brought the scimitar flashing down.

LODIN

Lodin watched the carnage with horror. Fifty refugees and a hundred wounded against a cadre of fresh, able-bodied Ice Guards. They did not stand a chance. And yet the defenders had nothing to lose, so the soldiers fell or retreated, one after another, until Tusken Seal felled the last of the Ice Lord's officers and collapsed on the ground, bleeding from many wounds. Now only four were left standing; the Ice Lord, the bard, the craftsman and the Shantara.

Lodin and Asri retreated before the Ice Lord. Even without his armies and his officers, he was terrible to look at, and they were gripped by fear. They retreated around the standing stones, and the Ice Lord ignored them.

"What are you, man of ice?" called Maran from within the Heart of Wood. "What do you intend for this world?"

"What am I? I am not of this world, man of music," the Ice Lord grated as he stalked ever nearer. "I wish for an end to the world, nothing less." The body he was wearing was that of a Skral whose face was familiar to them, but the eyes marked it as the Ice Lord beyond any shadow of doubt. The body was torn by wounds which did not bleed. The face was contorted and starting to change already, though he had not been wearing that body for long. The cheekbones were sharper than Lodin remembered, and this slow alteration from the face of the gruff Skral he had known–*Bran was his name*, Lodin thought suddenly–made the hairs on the back of his neck stand up with terror.

"The end of the world? Why would you wish for that?" Maran strummed as he spoke.

"So that I am rid of all this burning life around me." It paused outside the Circle now. "So I can go back to the stillness of my own land, and be rid of all this noise and chaos."

"Are the lands of your youth so very beautiful, then?" Maran began to hum, and the tune that he hummed was of being lost, alone and exiled in a harsh and bitter land.

"I see what you are doing, man of music!" The Ice Lord stepped nearer despite himself. "It will not work with me though. You cannot play me into laying down my weapons because I have no need for weapons."

Maran's song took on a terribly sad, weary tone then, and the Ice Lord faltered a step nearer, into the Dragon's Teeth.

Lodin and Asri hoisted to themselves the panel of ice and stood to one side of the gap in the Circle, waiting for Maran to slip past his foe so that they could shut the way, but Maran did not move as the Ice Lord came closer, and closer.

"I see what you would have, man of ice," Maran said softly. "I have you now." And he smiled past the Ice Lord at Lodin and Asri. His song changed from weariness into a song of triumph, a terrible song of war spanning worlds and galaxies, a music that could inspire any creature to do anything, however horrific. At this the Ice Lord smiled, and it was the smile of a deathshead.

"I see you have no need of weapons either, man of music. You *are* a weapon, and one that I mean to have." His body crumbled to dust and from it black tendrils of smoke reached out towards Maran.

"No!" Lodin shouted.

"Yes," Maran smiled, and it was a smile of such beauty that it broke Lodin's heart. "Mine is not a gift of the body but of the soul. He cannot have it. Close the trap, Lodin. I am a dead man already, just one given time to say goodbye. He shall not have *this* though, sinews of my heart—make of it a safeguard lest he ever escape again."

He threw his harp out to land in the snow. As he did so the black ribbons of smoke wrapped around him. Lodin stood in horror as his friend convulsed and then, grotesque in that beautiful young face, Maran's eyes rolled open to reveal the black glare of the Ice Lord. But when the possessed body tried to move forward, it found that Maran had chained himself to the central pillar of the Heart of Wood.

"Lodin, quickly!" Asri shouted, and the urgency in her voice jolted him into action.

THE AFTERMATH

LODIN

L odin grasped the panel of ice with his one hand as Asri took the other side. As the Ice Lord turned his deathly glare upon them, they staggered it into place. The ice touched the standing stones, and a great wind arose. They both cowered on the floor as the ice and snow howled and mourned around them. Sleet was whipped and stung by the roaring winds. The ice crystals cut them like tiny knives as the full wrath of the shipspirits rose to capture and render powerless the being who had killed so many people and burned so many ships.

Cold was the wind, cold and enduring as the endless depths of night. The wind's howl rose to a scream, unbearably loud, and then just as they had abandoned themselves to dying in that fury of sleet, all fell quiet.

Lodin cautiously looked out from under the cloak he had thrown around himself and Asri.

"Lodin...?" Asri's voice trembled a little.

"It is done," he said dully. "The spirits have done as they

promised. The whole Circle of Stones is encased in ice, around and over."

"The Ice Lord is trapped?"

"Yes... and Maran's voice is stilled forever."

They sat for a moment, overwhelmed. Around them the air was heavy with the stink of war. The plain was a sea of bodies. Lodin was glad that Asri could not see it. The sun was sinking towards the horizon. Soon it would be dark, and they were alone, tired and weary in the cold. Lodin hoped that death would come easily, and then he could be rid of this life and all its anguish.

Far off on the plain there was movement. It would be the deserters from the Ice Lord's army, probably looting the Skral clan-halls. He hoped they would not come back to make sure the job was done.

Suddenly there was a muffled chirp, and another.

Asri laughed mirthlessly. "All this time, he lay quiet. I had forgotten he was there. Come out, little one! You were lucky not to get squashed." She unwound a fold of her shawl to let Tiris out. The bird flew to Lodin who ignored him. Then he darted about the plain a little, stopping here to perch on a sword, there on a shield's edge. Finally, he stopped just out of sight behind a hulking corpse. There was a cry–almost a gasp. Lodin ignored it. He was watching the path to the clan-halls. People were getting nearer. *I do not want to die at the hands of the Ice Lord's deserters, not after all we have gone through.*

Tiris fluttered back, but Lodin brushed him aside. *There must be a weapon somewhere. Even a dagger would do, just to open a vein with. This is a battlefield, damn it!*

Tiris flew back to Asri, but did not settle. "What is Tiris doing?" she asked. The bird flew back to where he had been.

"I will go and see." Lodin heaved himself to his feet. He did not want to mention the deserters to Asri in case they were just looting, but this was a good opportunity to go find a dagger. Staggering over the slippery mud, he found himself following the bird the short distance to where the large warrior lay. He was dead–there was a dagger through his neck–but behind him, half-hidden by a rock was –

"Edan! Asri, I've found Edan. He's hurt, but alive."

"Where! Bring me to him, Lodin, quickly!" Asri began to crawl in the direction of his voice, but Lodin was back with her, helping her to come to her son. "He's so cold..."

"Here." Lodin laid his cloak over the boy. "We might be able to get him back to the halls. There might be shelter there."

A movement startled him; a child, whose face was streaked with tears and filth. He crawled painfully out from a bespattered cloak and held it out. "This is his, Edan's. He gave it to me to hide under, but if he's cold he might need it."

Tears started to Lodin's eyes. He had thought that they were the only ones left alive. "Thank you, child. What is your name?"

"Ran," the boy whispered miserably. "Rankar was my brother. But everybody's dead now."

"Not everybody. And we shall need your help. Are you hurt? May I see?" Lodin judged the boy's wound to be more painful than serious. "Can you stand?"

Ran struggled to his feet, grimacing in pain, but stood. "Yes sir."

"Brave boy. We shall need two spears and a cloak. We shall make something to carry Edan back to the halls." What would happen then, Lodin could not tell, and he was beyond planning further than that.

"There are people over there. Do you think they are on our side?"

Lodin looked over. The deserters were definitely coming closer. It looked as if they were making a beeline for him. "Perhaps so. I can't tell from this distance. But we will need to carry Edan in any case."

"I will look for the spears."

Lodin stood. "Asri, there may be trouble." But Asri was rocking her son in her arms and crooning as if he was a baby, and she did not pay him any heed. It was down to him, one-handed and unskilled as he was, to defend them. He picked up a weapon and stood between Asri and the deserters, hoping that it would be quick but too cold and tired to really care.

As they grew close in the failing light, he realised that they were not as huge as he had thought. They wore heavy furs and hefted axes in their hands.

"Ho there! Who stands watch?"

Ran dropped the spear he was dragging and limped over to throw his arms around the burly newcomer, shouting "Uncle Drankar! Uncle Drankar!"

The Skral whisked the boy up in his arms and held him tightly. "I am glad to see you, Ran. Are you injured?"

"I got an arrow. It went right through my leg, and there's blood. It hurts." The boy pointed over to the others. "Edan looked after me but he is hurt. Will you help him?"

"Aye, lad. We're here to help any that are left." Drankar clambered over the treacherous battlefield and took Lodin's forearm in the warrior's greeting. "We were cut off behind the Ice Lord's lot in the mountains and could not get back in time. There is much to tell, but for now we must get the wounded into the halls. It is going to be a cold night."

Two burly warriors carried Asri and Edan back to the halls on a makeshift stretcher, for she would not let go of him. Lodin followed numbly behind. He had resigned himself to death and welcomed it–but he had also promised Edan that he would look after Asri so for this day, at least, he must live.

The path to the halls was long, and seemed longer because every step was a stumble and slip over bodies in the dusk. Tiris flew ahead at first, but soon came to sit on Lodin's shoulder, his feathers fluffed against the rising cold. Step, and step: soon it lost all meaning. Lodin did not know who he was or why he kept taking steps, and he did not remember reaching the halls.

Lodin woke in the dark of the sleeping hall to the sound of quiet sobs, much muffled. "Asri?"

"Edan... He is gone." Her voice broke on the words. "He died in my arms. But he knew me, and he died safe." She stopped for a few moments to regain control of her voice. "He said–he said he had avenged his sister, and was content. And he said that he would hold you to your promise."

Lodin bowed his head in the dark. "His only thought was to look after you, right to the end."

"He asked you to watch over me." Her voice was heavy with tears.

"Yes."

They did not speak more. Asri's sobs were soft and convulsive throughout the night. Lodin felt his way across to her bed, holding her while she grieved. As the light grew grey she finally subsided into sleep, and Lodin returned to his own bed to watch the night fade to bleak morning.

The returning Skrals worked hard. They spent the next two days on the battlefield, bringing back such of the wounded as could be saved and moving the dead into separate pyres for the defenders and the Ice Lord's men. It was a vile job, but they worked without complaint in the stinking mud and cold. On the third day the living assembled to sing the death rites of the Skral, and the pyres were lit. Lodin stood empty of heart and dry of eye. He did not speak Old Skral but had heard the melody of the death rites so often of late that he hummed along with the others who did not know the words to sing.

A young lad stood forward. "Shipspirits and gods, hear our plea. We cannot honour the fallen as they should be honoured.

The names of the dead should be recited by the bards of their clans, singing the names and the deeds of the fallen at the feast in their favour. The bards have died with their clans, however, and with them the wisdom of a thousand years. I am the oldest acolyte to survive, so though I cannot tell the families and deeds of those who were my brothers in arms, I will at least sing their names. We leave it to you, oh gods and shipspirits, to guide them to the Hall of the Forefathers and show them to places of honour, for all have fought like warriors and Skrals." He took out a scroll–the last scroll of the precious parchment had been dedicated to this purpose–and sang the names of the dead. There were many, and more would be added. Many of the wounded were dying slowly, and there was neither the expertise nor the supplies to help them now.

After the ceremony, the few remaining Shantar gathered to one side for their own rites. Many Shantar had fallen defending the Mother. Badly injured, she had seen the battle out and had survived long enough to choose her successor. Normally it went to the daughter most suited to the task, but the Mother had no surviving daughters after the long flight from the Mountains and so she had chosen another; Asri. Lodin approved. She was fierce as a hawk and stubborn as a mule, and she would not let her people despair.

Lodin made his way back to the halls with Tiris. The little bird was a constant companion in the cold and Lodin was grateful. Tiris distracted him from the roaring abyss in his soul caused by the loss of Maran. It coloured everything as if it was he and not the bard who had been devoured by the Ice Lord. Still, here he was, walking over the plain without Maran at his side, returning to the clanhearth where Maran would not join him, listening to the conversations in which Maran was not taking part, and eating the food that Maran could not share.

Tiris came to sit on his shoulder, and Lodin tilted his head to feel the softness of the bird's feathers against his cheek. "The world has gone dark, Tiris, and I have lost my way." But he trudged back to the clan-halls, all the same.

THE SICKROOM WAS a horrible place now, for there was little enough in the way of salves or tonics to help the suffering, and virtually no-one who was versed in the arts of healing. Those who helped did whatever they could, and cursed the Ice Lord and his wars. Amongst the wounded was the Potentate of Gai Ren, his breath rattling and bubbling.

"Maker..." he wheezed. "I am not...long for this world."

"You cannot be sure of that."

"I can barely... breathe. It does not... improve. The winter has... settled... in my lungs."

Lodin drew the blanket a little further over him. "Are you warm enough? Is there anything that would help?"

"I am... cold. Always... cold. But I do not expect... to be warm again."

There was little point in contradicting. The Potentate had always been little and birdlike, but now he was so frail that it seemed the slightest breeze would blow him away. Gai Ren was much warmer than the Skrallands, and a night lying wounded before Drankar's men found him had left the man with pneumonia.

"Bring me... the box." He gestured to a rubble of wood on the floor. It had obviously been a beautifully inlaid box once upon a time, but now it was partly smashed. Lodin set it on the Potentate's lap.

"This is all... that is left... of the treasures of... my people." He gasped for a while. "Use what you can...."

"I will, I promise." The Potentate, too short of breath to speak more, pushed the box at him and Lodin sorted carefully through the remnants. It was a small collection of things salvaged from the looted clan-halls and the battlefield but as he looked, Lodin found ideas springing into his head. "Some short lengths of bamboo... silver wire... a clear crystal..." He went through, telling the dying man what purpose he saw for each, but the Potentate was sinking fast, so he ended quietly, "Potentate, these are treasures indeed."

"I... am glad." The Potentate's eyes were closing now. "Use them... wisely, Lodin, and... Fortune continue to ... guide your hand. You... have been the saving... of us all."

Lodin thought of that long list of the dead, of the carnage of the battlefield and the vision that he could not unsee, of Maran's beautiful face contorting into the deathmask of the Ice Lord. "Not all."

He sat with the Potentate as the rattling breaths became slower and more laboured, the gaps between more pronounced. When finally they stopped there was silence. He closed the Potentate's eyes with a gentle hand. "I will use them wisely, I promise."

Another death, another promise. The air was heavy with vows and tasks and duties. He had made so many promises he was not even sure he could remember them all. *So many have died. All I am left with is promises to keep.* Lodin gathered the Potentate's treasures into the box and left it in the little alcove under his bed.

A boy shouldered his way into the hall. He had one arm in a sling and was carrying something in the other. "Maker." He nodded respectfully.

Lodin racked his brains. "I know you, don't I? You were playing knucklebones with Edan."

"Yes sir. My name is Eldred. My brother and I were good friends with him." The boy's voice caught a little and he looked away, embarrassed.

"Eldred, yes, I remember."

The boy changed the subject. "I found this on the field, by the Circle. They said that you would want to have it." He held out a bundle wrapped in dirty cloth. "Perhaps it can be mended?"

Lodin unwrapped it to reveal Maran's harp. Soaked in the filth of the battlefield, it felt heavy and lifeless, a heart that had stopped beating. "I do not think so, I'm afraid. There is no music left in it."

"I am sorry, Maker. I thought that if anyone could bring it back, perhaps you could."

"Thank you. It was a kind thought but... Some things cannot be fixed."

The boy slipped away solemnly and Lodin clasped it to himself, a tangible reminder of the lost half of his heart. He held it so tight that the wood creaked, and for the first time since the battle he wept like a child, full of loss and hurt at the unfairness of being left behind.

THE FOLLOWING MONTHS WERE HARD, in every way. At first there was no time for sorrow. The little group of survivors found themselves with virtually nothing and winter approaching. They spent most days out foraging for food, and in time reached the far side of the island, where they found one of the Ice Lord's ships, beached and battered but whole. This allowed them to cast nets for fish, which were virtually all that they had to eat over the winter months, but also to collect supplies from all over the island, wherever oddments of food or edible plants could be found. It was exhausting work to get through the days, and by the time the light failed, early as that was, they were usually far too tired for song or storytelling or anything that might have made the long nights easier to get through.

In the evenings Lodin and Asri generally sat together. Sometimes they talked of those they had loved and lost, and sometimes they sat silently, comforted by sharing their grief.

"There are moments where I envy those who fell," Lodin murmured one evening. "As if it were not bad enough to lose them, there has been so much to deal with just to stay alive. No stores of food, and precious little wood once the armies burned everything they passed."

"What a blessing that the sea provided for us," Asri returned. "If it was not for the fish, driftwood and even seaweed, we would have starved."

"Ugh! Seaweed. I used to love the smell of it when it meant visits to the shore, but now... the stench of it drying and burning makes my stomach turn." Lodin sighed. "I suppose I should be thankful for the heat but all the same..."

"Huh," Asri snorted mirthlessly. After a while she asked, "Did you hear about the raid?"

"More of the deserters?" Lodin replied. "Was it the same ones Drankar and his men fought off at midwinter?"

"The ones that killed the men from Tusken Seal clan, yes. Drankar sent scouts out to their camp and they were all dead but one man who was terribly wounded. He said they had found the food cellar in the Halls of Knowledge and though most of the food was spoiled, the spirits weren't. Everyone got drunk and a huge fight broke out. Everyone else had died of their wounds or infections, and he was in his last hours."

Lodin looked away, sickened. "What happened to him?"

"His wounds had gone rotten days since, and the poison was in his blood. He asked for mercy and they gave it him. Drankar thinks that is the last of them, thank the skies," Asri patted her hair back into place as the light breeze made it whip round her face. "Not just that, but they found a couple more goats and some cows when they were out, and one of the cows is pregnant. Between those and the sheep that we found in the hills, we have the start of a herd, though it's a very small one."

Lodin nodded absently. "It may be that the worst of the winter is over, though it is still so dark and cold that it is difficult to remember what summer was like. Sunshine and warmth are a world away, and Lyria seems almost impossible." The fire in front of them had burned low and the turves glowed and smouldered.

"But spring is coming, my dear," Asri said. "The nights are shorter, and the cold does not bite so sharply. The first flower is opened on the plain, and that speaks of hope to me. I hesitate to say it, but I think the worst has passed. We have endured a winter of the soul as well as the body, but we have survived."

After a fashion, Lodin thought. *What is left to us?* He stared at the fire a while longer before Tiris dropped down from the rafters onto his chair, then bobbed up onto his shoulder. He settled down, snugged up against Lodin's neck, and chirped sleepily then fell quiet. The soft warmth of his feathers made Lodin smile, as always.

"Would you go back?" Asri asked. "If you could?"

"Back?"

"To Lyria? In time, when things are easier. We could go back to the mainland. We could use the ship, though the Skral are very sniffy about it."

"There is only one ship. We cannot risk the loss of it for those who remain here." Lodin thought about it. "I don't know. What is there to go back to? All my friends were in the city when it fell, and like enough it has been burned to the ground. Even Laerzinan fell in flames and destruction."

"Not even to go and see what was left?" Asri was oddly persistent.

"We have only just come through this winter. It might not be so cold there but it would be equally hard work trying to scratch a living in the shells of burned buildings."

"Is there nothing of Lyria that might have survived the flames? Surely you can't be the only survivor? If there were others, where would they go?"

Lodin frowned. "I have not heard of others. Some were sent towards Gai Ren, and we know that the Ice Lord swept through there. Some went to Laerzinan, and it fell. But many escaped from the city…" He thought of all the boats that had been swept down to the sea with him. "Where would they go? I don't know. The army was everywhere, but surely all of them cannot have been killed." Antor? Bellara? What if his friends were still alive, and he was not as alone as he felt? Hope squeezed his heart painfully. "But in any case it doesn't matter. The Ice Lord's armies fled in the ships they came in, bar the one we found abandoned. The Skral ships were all sunk or burned. It might just be possible to salvage some of the smaller ones when summer warms the waters..." He sighed. "We should not get our hopes up though. By all accounts most are too deep or too damaged, and in any case there is very little left in the way of wood or trees to mend them with."

Asri nodded but did not reply.

"Just out of interest, why do you ask?"

Her fingers found a loose thread on her shawl and she knotted it carefully before replying. "It may be nothing."

"But?"

"I dreamed that you and I returned to the mainland and I saw us both in what must be Lyria, as well as in the Shantar heartlands. But sometimes a dream is just a dream, and homesickness has gripped my heart for many months now." She patted the threads back into place. "But if we were to leave this place and your home was gone, Lodin, there will always be a place for you with the Shantar. And Eldred too, if he wishes to come."

"Thank you." Lodin sighed. "But I suspect it will be long before we can leave these islands, whether we would like to or not."

They did not speak of it again, but Asri had sown a seed of hope and longing in Lodin's heart. He was too tired and hollow with grief to give it much thought now, but it was a future he had not foreseen. He set it aside to think about later.

For now, he spent what time he could helping Asri or the healers, watchful in case he could make things to make life easier for the struggling group. Before he could start, he had to build a forge and make tools. At least with all the weapons scattered across the plain, he was not short of metal. Every one of the Potentate's treasures was used in one way or another. The one thing he could not mend, though, was Maran's harp.

He spent a long time cradling the harp as if it was a child, stroking the wood and trying to make it sound as it had when Maran was alive. He dried it out carefully and oiled the wood so that it was smooth to the touch, but the strings were spoiled. It squalled like a gull and did not sing again, and so he wrapped it in its cover and set it on the side in his workshop, a task unfinished.

ONE DAY, Lodin was in his workshop when a shadow fell across the doorway. He looked up. "Can I help you, Eldred?"

The boy came in hesitantly. "Maker. You know I broke my arm? It has healed a little crooked and is taking a long time to regain its strength. I am conscious that I cannot do my fair share of the work. I cannot dig or hoe or look after the animals or help with the rebuilding. It is driving me mad. I know it is a lot to ask, but I thought perhaps given that you know what it feels like, you could help me?"

A LOOSENING OF GRIEF

L odin laid down his tools and straightened. "Are you asking for some kind of false arm like mine? I am no healer, lad, but if your arm is healing, no matter how slowly, you probably should not be using a false one. But I know well how frustrating that can be. Is there something you could do that does not involve strength or lifting heavy things?"

Eldred leaned against the wall, dejected. "Not that I can think of."

"Do you mind menial tasks like fetching and carrying?"

"Not if I can be of use." Eldred's face lit up. "Is there anything you need fetching and carrying?"

"Always, lad, always." Lodin gestured to the wooden stool by the workbench. "For a start, why don't you bring in another one of those so we can both sit. Then you can help me mend the runner for this sled. I have yet to design a fitting that will grip a nail as steadily as I'd like, but if you'd care to chance it, I promise you I am extremely careful with a hammer!"

Eldred stood straight again. "Thank you, sir. I'll be back directly."

Lodin watched the boy as he dashed off to the dining hall. It would be nice to have a bit of company when he was working and if the lad was interested, there was a lot he could teach him.

SUMMER WAS over when Asri asked Lodin to take her to the shore. She waited outside the hall in the early morning. The plain was wreathed in autumn mists as he approached, and he saw she held a bundle. "Asri? Is all well?"

"I do not know what the Lyrian customs may be but we Shantar allow ourselves a year and a day to mourn those who have left us. They go to the silver seas, and are freed but we who are left behind, we need a little time to let go of them. A year and a day has passed since my son fell in the battle of the plains. You mourn for Maran as do I for my son. It is time you released him, too."

"I do not know how to do that." Even now, even a year after he had lost Maran, his voice locked on the words.

"I will show you, if you will take me to the shore."

Lodin took her arm and walked down to the deep bay from which the ship of children had sailed. "Where do you think they went, the children? I hope they found somewhere safe to land."

Asri's face was sad. "I do not know. I wanted Edan to go with them, but he was adamant that he was not a child any more, but a man grown. I have asked myself a million times if it would have been better to send him away, shamed that I thought so meanly of him, or to allow him to be the man and to die out there on the field. My heart says that to have him alive would be the better path, that given time he would have got over it... but my head is not so sure. He died bravely, and was content that he had done his part."

"He was with you at the last and he did what he could to protect you. That was what he was determined to do from the start." Lodin felt his eyes fill. "But somehow it doesn't help much. I know Maran did what was necessary, and that otherwise there would be nothing left but dead ashes but even so, sometimes I want to rip the world to shreds with my bare hands because it is still here and he is not."

"We all have those days, but we cannot bring our loved ones back with rage or grief and they would not want us to waste our days in unhappiness. If Maran was with us now, he would tell you to let go and allow time to salve the hurt." She stopped and turned to him. "It is not a betrayal to let go, Lodin. It is the first step towards being able to remember them with happiness instead of sorrow, and this is what they would want above all else."

Lodin blinked, trying to get the tears away before they could trace hot tracks down his cheeks. "I cannot let him go, Asri. I cannot."

"Why not?"

Lodin sobbed. He could not help it. "What if I forget him? Grief is all that I have left. If I let go of it, I have nothing." He sobbed again, and wiped the tears away from his face with his sleeve. "I am afraid, Asri. I cannot bear to be without him. I do not know how to let him go."

Asri felt down his arm to his false hand and pulled it up in front of him. "You had a hand here once. Do you remember it?"

"Yes."

"Do you remember how it looked? How it felt? How easy it was to pick things up?"

"Yes, I remember it."

"Do you still mourn it?"

"Yes..."

"Really? Is it the first thing that comes into your head when you wake up? Or is it more that when you find things difficult you wish that things had happened otherwise?"

Lodin thought about this. "Too much else has happened for it to be as important as I thought it was. It's inconvenient sometimes, but I think more about ways to make things happen without it."

"And if that is true for your hand, do you not think that your heart can also heal? We do not lose our loved ones really, not while we remember them. We miss them, aye, and we never will stop missing them or turning to say something to them or wishing we could share the sunset or the scent of a flower or the taste of food with them; but though it stings now, the sting fades to poignancy. The memories never fade, though, and when the sting has gone the memory remains." Asri sighed. "I would give everything I have to bring Edan back but there is nothing I can do to make that happen. That being the case, the only way I can get something of him back is to let him go."

She took Lodin's arm again. "Take me to the end of the quay, Lodin. I am weary of grief. I want to relive the happy times with a smile on my face, not drown them in tears."

They walked silently to the end of the quay from which the children's ships had left, and Asri opened the bundle. It contained two or three items, personal belongings.

"This is the story of Edan, last of my line," she intoned, taking out a woollen hat. She held it close to her face to squint at it, and then hugged it briefly. "This is his hat, that I made for him when he was a young boy. Young he lived and young he died, and all my heart is gone with him. And yet here is his hat. I give it to the water, that it may be taken to him on the silver seas, and with it my grief."

Lodin cried out as she flung it into the water, where it slowly sank under the surface.

"Salt of my tears, salt of the sea, wash away grief and set me free." She looked out over the water, and Lodin stood silently by. The sun had risen now and the water was sparkling and beautiful. He knew that all Asri could see was the brightness, but the sibilance of the waves seemed to wash through him like breathing.

After a while, she reached once more into the bundle, this time taking out Alaera's dagger. "This is the dagger that a brave woman gave to him so that his death might be easier. It was a gift borne of mercy, not of despair and he used it in the defence of a child. Brave he lived, and brave he died and all my heart is gone with him. And yet here is his dagger. I give it to the water, that it may be taken to him on the silver seas and with it my pride in him." She flung it out over the water. It arced high, and fell point first, disappearing into the sparkling swells with hardly a ripple.

"Salt of my tears, salt of the sea, wash away anger and set me free."

Again, she stood quiet. Lodin suddenly remembered how Edan had been proud and relieved when his mother had allowed him to learn to sword-fight with his friends, the way he had stood a little taller, and the sheer adulthood of his determination to keep his mother safe. As the waves washed at the shore, Lodin realised that though painful, this had absolutely been the right decision for Edan. *I hope Asri has come to this conclusion. It will help to lift the weight of uncertainty and guilt from her mind.*

Finally, she turned back to her bundle, and now she pulled from the shawl in which it had been wrapped a pendant, a simple thing, made from a smoothed stone with a hole in it, through which was threaded a leather thong. She smiled as her fingers found it. "His lucky stone. He found it in the stream near one of the camping grounds when he was a tiny boy, and his father told him it was lucky. He wore it around his neck every day until his sister was born, then insisted that they take turns so that they would both be equally lucky. He was wearing it the day his sister died, and when we got back to safety, he gave it to me and would not allow me to go anywhere without it. Caring he lived, and caring died, and all my heart is gone with him. And yet here is his stone. I give it to the water, that it might be taken to him on the silver seas, and with it my love for him."

Lodin knew what was coming now, and yet he still found himself wanting to protest as she threw the pendant into the water. *How can she make herself part with something so precious?* But as she chanted "Salt of my tears, salt of the sea, take him my love and set him free," he thought that if it would really take a message of love to Edan, then it was absolutely worth it.

Asri fell silent, and the waves sparkled as they washed at the shore in the mild autumn morning. The mist was beginning to burn off the water, the morning becoming less veiled, but the stillness of the shore seeped into Lodin's soul like balm.

Asri held out her hand and Lodin took it. Wordlessly she turned to him and he took her in his arms, each holding onto the other while the sea washed a little of the pain away with the hush of every wave.

After a while, Asri stood away. "The sun is not warm enough to stay here this late in the year. Let us go and sit by a warm hearth, and talk of cheerful things."

Lodin took her arm, and they started along the path back to the halls. "Is that how it works, for the Shantar?" he said at last. "That they go to the sea when they die?"

"The silver seas are the seas at the end of life. They are made of tears, but tears can be for joy as well as sorrow. We believe that we will find our loved ones again. When we return to the silver seas, they will be waiting to embrace us." She walked on a pace or two. "What of your people? What do Lyrians believe?"

"We are not very much inclined to believe anything, though we have our legends. In Lyria they say that the afterlife is like a beautiful garden full of wine, women and so on, which doesn't make it any more likely. As for me, I've never really known what I believe. All these stories of an afterlife seem just stories. But having been to the ships' graveyard it is clear that there is more to it than that. Either there are other ways of being alive than wandering round in a body made of flesh, or it's much more complicated than I can ever hope to understand." He sighed. "I wish I had more concrete answers. It's all so nebulous, but it seems there is something more to us, something indefinable. I'm clinging to that."

Asri nodded. "We give it a shape that we can understand. The stories are only stories, but we tell them because there is something there that we find difficult to grasp, not because we are trying to fool ourselves. I don't really think it will be like a beautiful garden, or a Skral hall, or even a silver sea as our own legends suggest–after all, how would we know? But all legends agree that we will meet up with those we have lost, and if something remains when the body dies, it is just a matter of time before we meet Maran and Edan again."

Lodin's heart wrenched within him. "I want to believe that. Gods, how I want that to be true!"

"It is what I believe. It won't help us to get there any quicker, but there is some measure of comfort in the fact that all we have to do in the meantime is to get through the day as well as we can."

This was a new thought, and one Lodin needed to mull over, but for the first time since the fall of Lyria, he felt the possibility of hope.

"I do not know when," he said suddenly, "but I would like to have a ceremony like yours for Maran. It feels like a way of–not sending him a message, exactly, but--"

"Sending him your love. I believe that it reaches them somehow, though I don't know how or why."

"I will need to think about it." They turned into the main path to the clan halls now.

"When it is time, you will know."

THE IDEA of having some sort of ceremony of his own took root in Lodin's mind. He realised that he too was weary of grief, though his love and longing for Maran were no less. The idea of a world without the bard was not so overwhelming now that this obscure certainty had gripped him. He had no logical reason to think that he could possibly meet his love again, and yet logic had no power in the face of this certainty.

"Am I deluding myself?" he asked Tiris, on one of the bird's passing visits. "Is it just that I want to believe in something that cannot possibly happen?" Tiris jumped onto the table and started sorting through the food on Lodin's plate in case there were some dried berries somewhere. There were none, but the little bird simply eyed Lodin accusingly and gave another chirp.

Lodin laughed and reached up to the shelf behind him, taking down a little wooden box in which were a few dried berries. Tiris was such a favourite that people saved them and passed them onto Lodin, and the bird was no fool. "You might not see the berries but you know they are there, don't you?" He took out two or three of the treats, and placed them one at a time on the table. Tiris gobbled them up greedily. "I should learn from you, perhaps. And where is the disadvantage? If I live my life in hope and there is nothing after death, when I die I shan't know I'm wrong!"

Tiris checked the plate again in case more berries had magically appeared and then flew up onto Lodin's shoulder for a moment before swooping away into the rafters again.

Lodin watched the emerald bird flash out of sight and smiled fondly. "You are a happy soul, Tiris, and one whose company I treasure."

He began to sort through his belongings and those few items that had been Maran's. He had the beginnings of an idea, and though his own ceremony would not be the same as the Shantar one, he hoped that it would serve the same purpose. The details though... The details were hidden from him.

And then that night he had a dream.

THE NEXT MORNING, he went to seek out Asri. "Asri, your people know about dreams, don't they?"

Asri was sitting outside the hall. It was chilly, but in this sheltered spot the sun was warm. "We know a little, certainly. Why do you ask?"

"I had a dream, and I'm not sure whether it was simply a dream or..."

"Guidance?" She patted the bench beside her. "Sit down and tell me about it."

"It started out as the same dream I have had a thousand times, the dream about the Dragon's Teeth." Lodin took a seat beside her. "I first had it when I was a child. The landscape was so alien I thought no such place could possibly exist. It was a long way from the sand and heat of Lyria. I dreamed that I stood on the plain, and in the distance was a circle of standing stones, the Dragon's Teeth as they were when we first got here. I walked round, marvelling at the roughness of the stone, but when I had done a full circuit, I saw the Heart of Wood building itself inside and Maran standing in it. At first I was afraid lest it was the Ice Lord wearing Maran's body, but as he smiled I knew that it was Maran. He beckoned me in, and all was as it was when the Heart of Wood was in the ships' graveyard. There was the pool in the centre, and the drop that fell and shattered the reflections into pictures."

"What did the visions show?"

"They showed time passing, a long time. Cities rose and fell, until the world was new and totally different. And then the Circle began to crumble," he took a deep breath, "--and Asri, it fell, and the Ice Lord was released into the world again."

"No!" Asri gasped. "Then all of this was in vain?"

"That was what I thought, and I looked up to Maran. His face was sad. "I could not stop him, but we can delay him while the world recovers, and in that time those will come who can take him back to his place.""

"But so many have died!" I shouted.

Maran looked at me sadly. "I of all people know that, my dear. They died to give us time to trap him, and we trapped him to give the world time to bring together the forces it needs. You cannot kill what is already dead, but that does not mean that he cannot be sent out of this place. We cannot do that, but we can contain him until the right time comes. Nothing is wasted. Because of us, millions will live their lives before the Ice Lord returns. Thousands of years will pass. Much will be lost, but more will be achieved. Cultures will rise, knowledge increase, lives be bettered. All this we have bought, and it was worth the price."

"But he will come back?"

"Yes, and when he does, others will be there to fight him. We must not leave them defenceless though."

"What do you mean?"

"My harp. There is no music left in it, but it is not lifeless wood. Use it. Make of it that which can be used against the Ice Lord when the time comes."

"But what should I make?" I asked.

"He is made of the darker emotions. Despair, fear, resentment--all these add to his power. He cannot abide life, love, happiness, unselfishness. Remember, emotions are our tools, you and I..." But Maran began to fade, and I understood that it was a dream.

"I would have given anything to spare you what happened," I said quickly. "That I lived and you died. My life is filled with the emptiness where you should be."

"What makes you think I am not there?" Maran laughed. "You cannot see me, that is all."

"You are there? I miss you. I miss you with every breath I take."

He was fading into the mist now. "I am with you always, my brother. Take comfort. This shall not be our last meeting."

"Will I dream of you again?" I whispered, but he had gone. There was only the sun through the mist, and I was alone again." Lodin sat back, and looked out over the plain. "I awoke, still alone but comforted. And I think I know what my ceremony will be. I will make the harp into three things. Love, happiness and unselfishness, he said. I must think about these."

Asri smiled. Her smile was always surprisingly beautiful, in a plain face. "And what is it you wish to know?"

"Was it a real dream? Was it one of your type of dreams? Or was it just born of my fears and longing, and because I miss him so much?"

She sat back against the wall, thinking. "Lodin, when the ship-spirits told you how to trap the ice Lord, did they give you detailed instructions?"

"No. They showed me what must be achieved by using their timbers. I worked out how to put it together. I knew what the end result should be, and what the qualities of the materials I was using were, so it was like building any of my other inventions-- just a matter of finding the simplest way from the start to the end of it."

"But no-one else could have done it."

"Anyone else could have put together the materials in the same way."

"But they did not think of doing it. I suspect the same is true for many of your inventions."

Lodin shrugged. "Often they seem perfectly obvious to me, certainly, so I never really understand why it takes me to invent them."

"It takes you to invent them because you are the tool that is made for the job." Asri turned to him. "To the awl it must seem obvious that the way to make a hole through leather is to be pushed against it with great force, but the hammer will not be able to achieve the same end, even if it was pushed against the same piece of leather with the same amount of force."

"But what does that have to do with the dream?"

Asri laughed. "It means that if there needs to be a hole in the leather, the question of who put the force behind the tool is irrelevant. The important bit is that the tool is capable of making a hole in the leather, and that the hole is made."

Lodin looked at her with some irritation. "Do Shantar leaders always talk in such obscure terms?"

"Always."

"But if the dream is true, I must take the harp and do as the spirits have shown me. And if the dream is just a dream..."

"What then? You will keep a harp that doesn't work? From the way you speak, you have already decided to do this, Lodin. If you are asking me whether you are a fool or not, I have no answer for you except--does it matter if you are? If this is all nonsense, does it matter? What do you lose by doing it?"

Lodin had not considered this.

"You enjoy making things, so that's hardly a task. You are using something that is no longer able to do what it was designed to, so there is no waste. And if all of this is nonsense, you will have had some hours' enjoyment making something useful from something useless. What's the disadvantage?" She nudged him in the ribs. "Go do your job, Maker!"

"As the Mother of the Shantar commands!"

LODIN TOOK Maran's harp and walked down to the bay. For a while he sat on the beach and remembered Maran, the good days and the horror of his ending. He wept regretfully, cradling the harp in his arms.

Finally he sighed. "It does not feel any easier. I see now that it is not that our grip loosens, but that we that must decide to make ourselves let go." He left the beach and went to his little workroom behind the smithy, where he set the harp on the worktop in the sunlight and considered it from all angles. After some thought, he took it to bits and laid out the pieces gently on the worktop.

"Maker?" Eldred was by now a regular at the workroom, and learning fast. Lodin found him an intelligent boy with a thoughtful approach. "Is there anything I can help with?"

"Perhaps so." Lodin gestured at the harp. "I have to make three things of this, things that represent love, happiness and unselfishness. At the moment I don't know quite what they will be though." Eldred took a seat on his stool and did not interrupt as Lodin continued, almost talking to himself. "What is Love? Love is the soul's union. Perhaps a token to symbolise the union of two souls..."

He considered the pieces in front of him, and then picked out the various keys which were used to tune the harp. "Can you fire up the crucible, please, Eldred? We will melt these down."

SAILS ON THE HORIZON

E ldred set the crucible to warm as Lodin cleaned the keys as much as he could. Going to the back of the workroom, the boy selected a small wooden frame and set it on a stone slab, adding sand and tamping it down, wetting it and adding more until the frame was a solid, dense block of sand.

Lodin left him to watch over the melting keys, and took out a sharp knife. In Lyria the smiths had shown him the art of making moulds for casting metal. Now, he wet the sand and compressed it once more, to be sure it was as solid as possible. When it was compacted into a solid block, he carved into it the shapes he would need. "How are the keys coming on?"

"Starting to lose their shape. Shall I get the tongs?"

"Yes. Are you happy to pour?"

"Yes." Eldred's arm was much improved, and he was getting more confident. A few moments more, and he gripped the crucible firmly in the tongs. "Watch out."

Lodin moved out of the way. "Try to get as much of it in the mould as possible. The neater the pouring, the easier it will be to smooth it off later." He watched as the boy poured the fiery liquid into the moulds, where it hissed and steamed. "Good. We'll leave that to set now, and while we're waiting we'll make the decorative bits."

They melted down other metals, and Lodin moulded little inlays in gold as red as sunset. Then he took from his pocket one last item.

"What is it?" Eldred asked.

Lodin showed him. "This little piece of metal has come a long way."

"Is it the silver pin? The one you brought all the way from Lyria, that Tiris had brought back?"

"Stained with the blood of my King. It is that same pin."

"And you are going to put it in with the rest?"

For a moment Lodin clutched it in his hand, thinking of his old life. "It is a piece of my past. It comforts me to think that a piece of my past will be part of what we make of Maran's harp. Even when we are long gone and our names have been forgotten, he and I will be intertwined in this piece." He held the pin out to Eldred who dropped it into the crucible, and melted the silver ready to take its new form.

When all the pieces were set, Eldred knocked the metal out of the sand. Lodin picked it up with a pair of tongs and scrutinised it, and then with his help and guidance Eldred ground and polished each piece to silky smoothness, and the pair of them fitted the pieces together carefully. Eventually they were finished. Eldred held up the amulet they had made in the light of the setting sun.

"Are you happy with it, Maker?"

Lodin bent close to examine it, nodding to himself as he did so. "It is as I had hoped." He straightened and patted the boy on the back. "Now all we have to do is to design the other two artefacts."

THE FOLLOWING DAY they began to work on the second.

"Happiness." Lodin mused. "What is happiness?"

"Happiness is something you share with your loved ones." Eldred scratched his ear.

"Yes: but you can also be happy alone. It is... being able to do something for those that need help, and being able to accept help from those that offer it with no question of payment. It is the calm of the soul, the openness of the heart, the fulfilment of being a part of this world. It is a communion, it is as vital to us as bread or water..." He stopped.

"It is difficult to think of one thing that captures happiness."

"Yes, it is. Perhaps there is something else we could do. We share food with our loved ones and eat it alone, make meals for those that cannot feed themselves or accept food from others. It brings us comfort and contentment when it is good. It can be complex and creative in the making. Eating together is an act of sharing that encompasses all who partake. What do you think?"

Eldred paused to consider this. "Yes. Yes, I think it fits. But in what form?"

Lodin picked up a piece of the wood of the harp and turned it over in his hands. "In Skral tradition every man should have his own knife."

"An eating set. Of course." Eldred melted down metal to make a blade, and while he was working on it, Lodin took the wood and shaped it into a handle for the eating knife. He bound long thin pieces together with metal bands like a cooper's barrel to make a mug, and polished the wood until it was smooth. Then they made a spoon to match the knife, and a metal box into which all of them fit snugly, and the set was done.

"Good work, lad."

Eldred set down the box, giving it one last polish. "There is not much of the harp left, other than a few scraps."

"We will use these for the final and most difficult part." Lodin began to pick up the remaining pieces carefully, setting them aside so that nothing was lost. "Start thinking, Eldred. Tomorrow we will need to make something representative of unselfishness."

THE NEXT MORNING Lodin entered the workroom to find the morning sun arched through the dooring, dancing on the metal coils of the strings. They shone so brightly he could barely look at them. He placed them in a little crucible until the heat melted the silver of the harp strings into a glimmering liquid. Lodin carved another mould from wet sand, and Eldred poured the silver in. When the pieces were cool, they knocked the hardened metal free of the mould, and Eldred filed it and ground it until it shone like captured moonlight. The pieces were cunningly fashioned and Lodin showed him how they fit together to make a pendant, a beautiful thing with a tiny compass in it. The compass needle took a deal more skill, and for this Lodin relied strongly on what the shipspirits had shown him in the dreams that continued to guide his hand as he worked.

"Can you see a little box on that shelf?"

Eldred reached down the box and opened it cautiously.

"Look carefully. In there you will find one glittering splinter, dark as obsidian."

"Yes, I have it." Eldred picked it out with his fingernails. "It is sharp! What is it?"

"The very last shred of the keels. This is a splinter chipped from the oldest figurehead's eye."

It was fiddly work, but between the two of them they eventually got it mounted it on a tiny pivot. This needle did not point North, but that was not its purpose. Eldred made a hardy case, and from the Potentate's treasures Lodin took a small clear crystal. He took a chisel and tapped it just so, chipping off a tiny slice which he polished into a solid lens to protect the compass needle. When all was polished to a gleam, they wrapped it carefully in silk and leather and placed it in the Potentate's box, now solidly mended, with the other two treasures. In the corner of the box there was something wrapped carefully in cloth; the last of the Potentate's clear crystals.

Lodin weighed it in his hand for a moment. "Stir up the fire under the crucible again, Eldred. We still need to make one last thing."

"WHAT BECAME OF THE KING?" Ran asked, all agog.

"Nobody ever spoke to him again. He had to stay in the kitchen and wash out the cauldrons after every meal, and the only thing they ever gave him to eat was cabbage."

"Why didn't they kill him? I would have done."

Asri laughed. "Because they were not bloodthirsty Skraelings, but cultured Gai Renese, you little barbarian!"

Ran thought about it. "That makes sense. They don't seem to kill people very much at all. Oh, hello Lodin!"

Lodin returned the boy's wave as he approached. "Hello, Ran. Who are you killing today?"

"A bad king, that's all. Asri was telling me a story."

"And what brings you out on the plain today, Maker?" Asri asked.

"I was looking for you, and for Tiris."

"Tiris was in the meal hall this morning," Ran offered. "He was begging for berries again."

Lodin laughed. "The greedy little thing! He's incorrigible. Come on, let's go and see if he's still there." He took Asri's arm while the boy dashed on ahead. "There's something I want to try today and it could be useful if Tiris was around."

They chattered idly as they walked. By the time they arrived, Tiris was perched on the edge of the roof nearby. Lodin reached into his pocket for the last of the dried berries. He placed one in

Asri's palm and Tiris swooped down delicately onto her hand to get it. Perched on her thumb, he eyed the berry with his head on one side and then the other, and took it very deliberately.

"What can you see of Tiris, Asri?"

The Shantara squinted at the little bird. "A flare of emerald happiness, no more. He is a little spark of hope through dark times but I cannot see his shape, only a blur of colour in the sunshine."

"Stay still just a moment." Lodin reached into his pocket to pull out the little frame he had made, and held it in front of Asri's eyes. "Now?"

Asri froze for a moment. Slowly she brought her free hand up and moved the frame with the crystal lenses closer to her eyes, and further away again. Then she inhaled sharply, looking at the little bird. "He is so beautiful. The iridescence on his wings... I cannot see every detail but I see a bird, Lodin, a bird rather than a blur!" She looked up at him, still holding the lenses in front of her eyes. "And you! I have never seen your face before, but I see the shape of it now. Lodin, you have given me my sight back! How have you done this?"

"This time I can claim no credit. The Potentate's scribe had something of the sort, and we had a long discussion about it. I do not have his skill, but I understand the principles, and it may be that we can improve these further with a bit of work. The only thing is, they will not help forever. He told me that if your vision is worsening, these cannot slow that; but at the very least you will get a little more time."

"I do not know how to thank you..." Asri's smile faded a little.

"Asri?"

She looked up again, her eyes magnified greatly by the lenses he had given her. "Edan... I wish that I could have seen my boy before he died. I would have liked to know what sort of a man he had grown into."

Lodin held out a slip of parchment. "Drankar has a daughter, a pretty girl in her early teens. She took something of a shine to Edan, I suspect because he spoke to her respectfully instead of dismissing her as the Skral tend to do. She is a rather exceptional artist. I had one last scrap of parchment..."

Asri took the parchment with trembling hands. On it was a picture, carefully inked, of Edan. A lot of work had gone into it and the girl had captured his likeness very well, from the determined tilt of his chin to the mischievous glint in his eyes. Asri moved it near to her face, and then further away, and gasped as it came into focus.

"Is he as you imagined?"

"He is the image of his father. It is as if both of them have been returned to me." She clutched the parchment to her chest for a moment. "Such gifts you bring me, Maker. I can never repay you."

"To give to my friend is a gift to myself." Lodin was a little bit startled to find himself using a Lyrian courtesy, but it had never been as apt as it was then. "Now, tell me where you can see most clearly, and I will see if I can refine the lenses to suit your eyes."

IT WAS a couple of weeks more before Lodin was satisfied with his work. By then he had brought the lenses as near to sharpening Asri's vision as he could. It would never be perfect, but she could now see people and places, and spent several confusing days taking her usual walks and discovering what they looked like.

One morning the drowsy warmth of the halls was shattered when the doors banged open and Ran dashed in. "Uncle Drankar! Uncle Drankar! Sail on the horizon, a square one!"

The hall stilled suddenly.

"A square one? Are you sure, boy?" Drankar surged to his feet.

"Yes, definitely."

There was a sudden uproar, as people dropped everything and ran.

Lodin looked at Eldred. "A square sail?"

"One of ours…"

"The children?"

"Yes."

Lodin sheathed his knife and set down the piece of wood he was shaping. "Go. I'll bring Asri."

He found Asri making her way to the door—even with her spectacles she did not see well in the dimness of the hall—and together they followed the general rush towards the quay.

Eldred met them halfway there. "Two! There are two sails!"

"Which ships, do you know?"

"The first is the *Aelfrith*. We think the second might be the *Dreda*. There's no sign of the *Gundal* so far."

When they arrived on the quayside, the various parents were clustered at the edge, each straining to see their children in the faces that lined the guard rail.

Suddenly Drankar rumbled, "Enough with this waiting!" Regardless of the snow and ice around them, he threw off his cloak and tunic, and dived into the frigid water.

A cheer came from the *Aelfrith*, and splashes abounded as others followed. They surfaced, spluttering with the cold, and swam strongly to the ships, where ropes were flung down. The last few to ascend had to be pulled in, as the cold had numbed their hands, but the sounds of joy from the ships came across the waves. Lodin smiled at Asri, who had taken off her spectacles so that the tears spilling from her eyes did not mist them.

"That's better. They were a little off-course," Eldred murmured as the ship corrected its course and slowly drew alongside. The gangplank had barely hit the quay when a stream of children charged down it, and the air was filled with screams of delight and calls from parents and relatives. Lodin felt tears come to his eyes as he watched one joyful reunion after another. The children were thin and dirty, but most seemed to be unhurt and reasonably healthy.

However, as the reunited children and their families begin to drift back to the clanhalls, a little group remained, clustered together, their glad faces gone sombre. One little girl wept quietly. Drankar, huddled in his cloak, stood nearby, talking to a gaunt young man of a similar age to Eldred.

"Come on." Lodin began to make his way towards them, and the others followed.

"What of those whose parents were killed?" Asri asked softly.

"The clans will take them in." Eldred watched the second ship start to turn towards them. "No-one is lost who has a clan around them."

"And the *unSkral*?" They glanced at Lodin in surprise. It was a while since anyone had used that word.

Drankar overheard the question. "No-one here is *unSkral* any more. We are all brothers in arms now." Asri cleared her throat pointedly. "Er, and sisters. Sorry."

The remaining Shantar and Gai Renese families came forward and one by one the children went with them.

One Shantar girl of about eight years of age came over timidly. "Asri?"

At the sound of her voice, Asri beamed. "Ysal?" She held out her arms to the child who threw herself forward into the hug.

"My mama and papa…"

"I know, my dear. I'm so sorry."

The girl sobbed. "We so looked forward to getting back."

"Ysal, would you like to keep me company for a while? I… I lost Edan, and it would be good to have someone to look after again."

"I'd like that." She shivered as Asri stood again. Eldred blinked away tears.

Of course, Lodin realised. *He lost all his family too. And he and his brother should have been on the ships.*

Eldred unpinned his cloak. "Here." He wrapped it round the girl. "You look cold."

Ysal cast a dubious glance at Asri, who smiled. "Eldred is one of the family now too."

Drankar finished his conversation, and the gaunt young man turned. "I need to make sure my crew is safe and fed."

Eldred stared. "Alar?"

"Eldred! You made it? It's good to see you. Ranfrith?"

Eldred shook his head. "Only me."

"I'm sorry." The boy looked down. "Are you coming back for some food, Ysal?"

"Yes Captain." The girl nodded, and Drankar flushed with pride at the term.

Alar nodded to Asri and Lodin. "You're her parents?"

Ysal sniffed, and Asri hugged her. "Ysal has agreed to home with me for a while."

Drankar intervened. "Alar, why don't you and Eldred go on ahead with Ysal and warm up? We'll be just behind."

"Yes, father." Alar held out a hand to the girl, and he and Eldred followed the others to the halls.

Lodin cocked an eyebrow at Drankar, who waited till the others were out of earshot before following in their footsteps. "There was a storm and the ships were separated. Afterwards, these two came back to the point where the storm hit, and stayed for as long as they could, but there was no sign of the *Gundal*. They made landfall but the oldsters who were there to guide them were taken ill, along with several of the children. In the end, with no options left, they decided to come back to see if anyone was left alive here who could help."

"Your son took charge?" Asri asked. "He did remarkably well for his age."

"He did. I am proud of him. But not just that. He took all sorts of measurements during the storm, which they used to find the *Dreda* again. We may be able to use that to work out where the *Gundal* would have ended up, and now that we have two ocean-going ships, one can be at sea while the other is being made ready."

Lodin exhaled. "That would be a mighty undertaking, and yet one well worth the attempt."

"Indeed. It will not be easy though. We will need all the help we can get. Start thinking, Maker. If you can find ways to keep the food fresh for longer, to make the water last on the voyage, things such as that would allow the searchers to stay out for longer. If you can help our farms to be more fruitful, our woodlands to grow faster, anything of that sort, it will allow us to provide for the journey, perhaps even to build more ships in the fullness of time. Will you help us?"

"Of course I will." Lodin paused in thought. "We should think about ways to salvage your other ships if we can. With the coastal ship and whichever of the *Aelfrith* or *Dreda* is not searching, we may be able to refloat some of the others."

"They are too deep," Drankar replied.

"May I interrupt?" The newly-elected Potentate came up behind them, his son clasped tightly to his side. He was a young man, slight as all the Gai Renese, but his eyes were full of lively intelligence. "My countrymen delight in pearls, which we harvest from clams in the deep waters around our southern islands. Amongst those who fled with me are two of our more accomplished divers. The waters here are colder than we are used to, but in the summer, we can at least see how deep the ships are, and whether we can get to them."

Asri nodded. "Your pearl divers are born with gills, according to legend."

The Potentate laughed. "Not quite that. But we dive deeper than many. And in the fullness of time, when life is flourishing here, there will come a point where the island cannot support us all any more. These are your ancestral homelands, Drankar, and we are beyond grateful that you allowed us to take refuge here, but nevertheless our hearts yearn for the familiar. We will help you raise your ships if we can and when the time is ripe, if life has returned elsewhere as it has here, my people will return to Gai Ren and send back whatever may be useful to the clans from there."

Drankar nodded. "We will discuss this further, but if you can help us restore our ships that will be a great service indeed."

They followed the road to the clanhalls, Drankar and the Potentate striding ahead and talking excitedly while Lodin paced along with Asri, lost in thought.

THERE WERE great celebrations at the children's return, as far as that was possible, and it was a few weeks before things settled down again. The clanhalls were once again noisy with the sound of children playing, and though they all had their moments of grief and heaviness, their laughter lifted the spirits of the adults too. Lodin found the days passed more quickly for their presence, but he was also very conscious of the autumn drawing on. He needed to get back to the ships' graveyard before winter made the journey too difficult.

Asri had not forgotten that he had asked about the grieving ceremony though. Once Ysal was settled, one of her first requests was to see what he had made from the remains of Maran's harp.

Lodin took her to the workshop.

"Love, happiness and unselfishness..." she mused. "A difficult task, to make things that represent these."

"Let us see whether you can tell which is which." Lodin laid the amulet, the eating set and the compass on the worktop before here.

She examined them all closely, exclaiming at the cleverness of the fashioning, and then considered them all for a long moment. She picked the amulet up and twisted it. It became a figure of eight, cleverly jointed, and as she twisted it back the loops swung together. "Two that are one, just like you and Maran. This must be love."

She ran a finger over the smoothed wood of the beaker. "If the amulet is for love, I would hazard that these are for happiness. Certainly some of my happiest times have been the sharing of meals with my family, before the Ice Lord came. And these are a pleasure to hold in the hand." She laid down the beaker and cutlery. "So this is for unselfishness?" She picked up the compass and looked at it closely.

"It is a guide. The needle is a shard of one of the keels. The shipspirits guided Maran, and his acceptance of that sacrifice was the only thing that stood between the Ice Lord and his domination of the world. The keels are locked in the Dragon's Teeth and thousands of years from now, how can we be sure that anyone will know about the shipspirits still? There are temples in my country that are older than the hills, but we do not know whose they were or who worshipped there. All I can do is put a little part of the keels into something that provides guidance. The compass does not point North. It points to where the shipspirits want you to go. It is my hope that they will find someone willing to follow the path they are led upon, even when it is not in their interests to do so. I do not know if it is likely or even possible, but that is my hope."

"And where should we be now?" Asri laid the compass flat on her palm and it pointed across the plain to the interior of the island. She looked up at him. "The ships' graveyard..."

THEIR PREPARATIONS TOOK SOME TIME, even with Asri's newfound sight, and Eldred and Drankar insisted on coming with them as guides.

"Must I go?" Ysal whispered as they were sitting by the hearth one night. "To the graveyard? I have only just got back here."

"Wouldn't you like to see the ships?" Asri asked

Ysal shivered. "I just want to stay here. Please, I don't want to go."

"But what would you do instead?"

"Just stay here. I could be helpful. I want to learn to be a healer, and Maskal has promised to show me how to grind the herbs."

Asri frowned.

"Is there a way she could stay?" Lodin asked. "It will be a hard journey and Ysal is not yet fully recovered. Staying to get her strength back seems like a sensible option." Ysal sent him a grateful glance.

"I don't want to leave you alone, though, Ysal," Asri replied at last.

"I won't be alone. I have my crew here, and my Captain. Alar will make sure I'm all right."

Asri smiled wearily. "I don't think we can impose on Alar, my dear. He has just got home too and will want to spend some time with his family."

Ysal looked mutinous but did not reply. She was a child of few words still, though Lodin suspected that that would change. She was not lacking in character; only in confidence.

"Did I hear my name?"

Ysal's face brightened as Alar leaned over the back of the bench. "Yes! Alar, if I wanted to stay here while Asri and Lodin travel-"

"You would be more than welcome at my hearth. I have been telling my father how helpful you were with the navigation and he is very interested in the measurements you took." Alar came to sit on the bench with them. "Does that help?"

Ysal directed beseeching eyes at Asri, who shook her head, laughing. "Your father is intending to come with us, Alar. It would be just you and your mother. And it might take us a couple of weeks. Are you really prepared for that?"

"Honestly? Yes. Ysal is a valued member of my crew. I know

my mother would enjoy her company, and she is genuinely good at helping me work out the calculations. We want to refine them to help us track the *Gundal*. It would be a good opportunity to work on it."

Asri nodded. "Well then, I will speak to your mother. There are a few of my people who will be happy to look after her for a while if needed, but if your mother agrees, that seems to be the best outcome for all of us."

Ysal threw herself at Asri and hugged her tightly. "Thank you. For listening." Her gaze took in Lodin as well. "I just want to be safe for a bit. I don't want any more adventures."

"I totally understand, child. We're hoping it won't be one either." Asri picked up her stick and stood. "Now, let's go and talk to your mother, Alar. Why don't you go ahead and warn her so she has time to think about it? Ysal and I will follow on." And with Ysal clutching her hand and skipping with delight, Asri made her way through the hall to the hearth where Drankar and his wife sat.

FROM THEN, it was a matter of days until they departed. Lodin packed his things but the three artefacts he had made caused him some bafflement.

"They must be kept safe," he told Asri. "Maran said that they must last while the Ice Lord remains here, and it is a very long time for such to remain intact. When the time comes, they must be ready."

"Wrap them in oiled silk, and in leather," she suggested. "That will not preserve it forever, but it might help." They oiled the wooden parts and waxed the metal, and then they put them in little boxes, well-oiled and sewn into greased bladders so as to stay as waterproof as possible.

It was a gruelling journey. Asri did her best but she could not focus for long with her new lenses before her eyes started to hurt. The sleds they used ran on wheels over the first part of the plain and when they got to the snowline, there were the runners to fit. However, Drankar was used to this kind of travelling and Eldred did much to keep their spirits high. Finally, the irregular hill of the ships' graveyard hove in sight, and the great scar of the road where all the keels had been removed. They set up camp and settled down for the night, wearied to their bones.

Outside the embers of the fire burnt low, glimmering red. Lodin lay awake in his bedding for long hours, listening to the hiss of wind-swept snow on the tent walls, and thinking about Maran. He missed him more than he missed his arm. Maker or no, there was nothing he could build that would take the bard's place in his heart. But Maran was gone, and Lodin was left behind. The ceremony the following morning was the last gift he could give to his soul-twin.

MORNING CAME RELUCTANTLY BUT LODIN, though tired, was far from bleary-eyed. He rose quietly so as not to wake Asri, who was sharing a tent with him. By the time the others woke, he had swept the fire pit clear of snow, fed the embers of the fire into a blaze and had water heating. They ate a good breakfast of porridge sweetened with honey from the bees that had returned to the hives near the clan hall.

Once fed, Lodin stood.

"Is it time?" Asri had her spectacles in a leather pouch in an inside pocket; now that they were up and doing, she put them on.

"Yes it is." Lodin gathered up the three precious gifts he had made. "Shall we go?"

The cleft into the great horseshoe hill was thick with snow. It was a beautiful morning, the sky a deep blue. The still silence was as calm as water, and the snow sparkled in the sunshine.

Eldred slowed to a halt, cautious not to slip. "Is this the graveyard?"

Asri peered through her spectacles. "These shapes..."

"The ships." Drankar gazed around in awe.

"This is where the Heart of Wood lay." Lodin came to a halt in the middle of the basin. "The keels were intertwined in the same way we put them in the Dragon's Teeth. This little pool was right inside, in the middle. I'm going to leave the three gifts here for the shipspirits to guard over."

He waited. He felt approval from the ships surrounding them. It was probably as clear an answer as he was going to get. "Will you help me with your ceremony, Asri?"

"I will do what I can to help you, and to honour him."

There was a fallen beam to one side of the pool. Lodin laid his three treasures on it, taking each out of their bag.

Asri joined him and when he was ready she began. "You are weary of grief, my friend. Let go of your sorrow and relive your memories with happiness. Tears help neither us nor those we have lost. " Asri turned to address the amphitheatre of ships around them. "This is the story of Maran, last of his line. Well do you know his story, for he is of your people. We bring you these treasures, that you may carry them to him with our love and respect."

Lodin took up the amulet. "This amulet is made of the keys of his harp. It is both two and one, as were we. Young he lived and young he died, and all my heart is gone with him. But here are the keys of his harp, made into an amulet for those whose souls are intertwined. I give it to you who guarded his clan and his people for so long, that you may take it to him and with it my loss."

Lodin wrapped it in box and bag and took it across to one of the ships nearby, setting it on the ledge under the figurehead. "Salt of my tears, salt of the sea, wash away loss and set me free." It seemed to Lodin that the figurehead had nodded to him, but his eyes were wet and the sun was bright and he could not tell whether he had imagined it.

Lodin took the cup, spoon and knife now. "This eating set is made from the wood of his harp. Many a time we sat together, eating and laughing, and there was much joy in the sharing. Hopeful he lived and hopeful died, and all my heart is gone with him. But here is the set, made from the wood of his harp. I give it to you who carried his forebears over the seas, that you may take it to him and with it my joy in him." He took the set to another of the ships and set it in its wrappings on the ledge under the figure-head. "Salt of my tears, salt of the sea, take him my joy and set us free."

Finally he took out the compass, and there was a feeling of increased focus from around them. "This compass is made from the strings of his harp. His music and your guidance allowed us to achieve that which seemed impossible. Maran's gift to us was time to find another way. Though it took his life, it was a gift he was ready to make and with the passing of the seasons I have come to see that his unselfishness and your guidance allowed what is left of this world to be saved. I have made this compass against the day the Ice Lord is freed from his prison, that there is a way to guide those who do not know of you. Keep it safe until it is needed, and when the world is threatened again, bring each of these gifts to someone who can use it. Use this compass to guide their steps, and bring an end to the Ice Lord as we have not been able to."

He began to wrap up the compass in its little box, trying to remember the words that came next.

Asri was there before him. "Edan, Maran and all who died did so to prevent worse happening. Hopeful they lived -"

"And hopeful died, and all my heart is gone with them." Lodin joined in, and was a little startled when Drankar and Eldred did so as well.

"But here are the gifts he bid me make," Lodin continued

alone. "I give them to you that you may safeguard them over the years as you once safeguarded the clans of the Skral. Take them to Maran with my love, that he may know I have done as he asked and will remember him with every breath that I take." He set the compass on the ledge below the third figurehead that made the lowest circle of ships in the graveyard. "Salt of my tears, salt of the sea, take them to him and set us free."

He backed away slowly, and went to stand with Asri who grasped his arm tightly. They stood in silence for a moment, while the sun glinted crystal tears on the frosted hulls of the ships.

"The ships are happy, aren't they?" Eldred said suddenly. "Did we get it right?"

"Yes, I think we did." Drankar looked around him as the wind picked up, and snow began to blow across the clearing. It was beautiful but cold, and their faces stung in the blast, but Lodin showed no signs of moving. "We'll wait for you outside."

Lodin did not reply. He was staring at the puddle in what had been the Heart of Wood. Reflections danced and whirled, pictures and futures that might be, a kaleidoscope of faces. A girl; a girl with long hair. A tall man, and a strange figure which could have been male or female. Indistinct behind them all stood a figure that was both dark and light. The shipspirits would guide them to where they had to be. Lodin felt Maran there looking over his shoulder and turned, but with the movement, he was back in the bright snow of the ships' graveyard, grinning like a fool.

"Are you all right?" Asri asked again.

"Sorry, I was miles away." If he was going to tell anyone about the visions he had been granted, it would be Asri, but the visions were too new, too precious to discuss yet. The time would come, but it was not now. Instead, he linked her arm though his. "I am all right. Yes, I truly am."

They followed Drankar and Eldred's footprints along the road to the open plain. Suddenly Tiris was darting about, agitated, before them.

"What is it, Tiris?" Lodin stared. Behind the bird a tree was moving. For a moment he simply goggled at it, and then he took a firmer grip on Asri's arm. "Landslide!" They ran the last few paces to safety. There was a thunderous roar. A great chunk of the hill slid in on itself, bare seconds after they had reached Drankar and Eldred on the plain.

When the mist of snow died down, Drankar brushed the powder from his beard. "Now no-one shall have your treasures. They are buried under the hill."

"I do not think they are lost." Asri peered through her lenses at the great slope of earth where the path had been. "When the time comes, they will be there. I think this is merely to safeguard them."

As Lodin looked back, it seemed to him that there were black shapes circling in the air, but when he blinked there was nothing to be seen but the brightness of snow. All settled back into stillness. "Then I have finished the task that I was set." A weight he had not realised he was carrying fell from his shoulders.

THEY MADE good time back to the halls, the wind behind them carrying the sandships, hissing, across the snow. The changing of the wheels went without hitch, and the ships set off again, speeding back towards their destination. For much of the journey Lodin and Asri sat quietly in the prow of the ship, while Drankar and Eldred manned the helm and adjusted the sails.

At last they coasted around an escarpment and found themselves on the final run down to the halls. Lodin watched the smoke rising blue in the sunshine from the chimneys of the clanhalls, promising warmth and food and good cheer. It seemed at last he would be able to set his mind to helping the Skral, and it pleased him to think that Drankar had come to him for aid in their efforts to raise the ships from the bay.

Maran would have shared his pleasure at being able to help in such an important endeavour. *Not so useless now, eh, Maker?* He could hear the bard saying it so clearly that it was as if he stood right there at his side. Suddenly Lodin knew that Maran was not gone, not while he had such sharp-cut memories of sunlight on those blonde curls, and that laugh ringing out across the plain, carefree as summertime.

It felt as if his soul had suddenly been freed from the shackles that weighed him down. He took a deep breath of the cold, crisp air.

Asri sent him a questioning look.

Lodin smiled. "When we get back to the halls, I must look into the making of the Gai Renese sandships, perhaps with willow. We'll be able to get supplies and people across to raise the ships in the bay so much faster if we have more of these." He twinkled at her. "Besides, they are fascinating little craft."

BEFORE YOU GO...

Thank you so much for coming with Lodin on his journey. Whether you loved or hated it, it would be really helpful if you'd leave a review to help inform other people with your tastes.

Reviews sell books and help spread the word, but they also tell me whether you want to read more about Lodin and Asri and their friends, or whether I should be writing something else.

Do you want to know what happened next? If so, let me know! Take care:

JAC

ACKNOWLEDGMENTS

Huge thanks to:

My lovely husband who is remarkably tolerant in the face of the latest plot twists.

The insane lurcher who keeps me on my toes and going out for walks every day.

The friends and helpers from 20Books and SPF who keep me informed and very well entertained. And all my lovely readers who keep me writing .

And one last word to those of you who have lost someone you love and are in a dark place right now: it does get easier.

Be kind to yourselves, yeah?

OTHER BOOKS BY WEASEL GREEN PRESS

J.A. Clement

Before Holly

A Sprig of Holly

The Holly & The Ivy

Holly:

Holly, Forgotten

Holly, Awakened

Holly, Ablaze (due winter 2020)

On Dark Shores:

The Locket

The Lady & The Other Nereia

Parallels:

The *Black-Eyed Susan*

The Scarred Artisan

Dulcie Feenan

Christmas Comes to Oddleton

ABOUT THE AUTHOR

J.A. Clement lives with her husband and a lordly lurcher in the South of England. She absolutely loves having the opportunity to share her stories and hopes you love her storyfriends as much as she does.

However if you have questions or comments, she'd love to hear from you - email is probably best but she lurks in cyberspace as below.

You can connect with JAC via:
jaclement.wordpress.com
jaclement.ondarkshores@gmail.com

www.ingramcontent.com/pod-product-compliance
Lightning Source LLC
Chambersburg PA
CBHW021223250626
47155CB00008B/2906